To: Ryan
Thanks for
+ motivation

ArkDar

The Two That Are One

By Geoffrey M. Metcalf

Best,

Dedication

To My Bride, Linda, My Heart

And

To My Son, Chandler, My Soul

Acknowledgements

No story is the product of one person. This work is a collection of both imaginings and life experiences. It has been enabled by a vast collection of both good and not so good people.

Rather that replicate and/or edit past acknowledgements from past books, this time, I want to specifically mention just five (of the many) who have contributed in this work finally being available.

Despite the import of their impact, two people who helped make this happen in ways they may not realize. They are at best casual acquaintances (although I have been a long time reader and fan of their works).

Barry Eisler enjoyed worldwide success with his John Rain series before reclaiming his destiny for more control (and profit margins). Robin Burcell is another successful crime author who in addition to her own series has been tapped to co-write Clive Cussler's Fargo series. Burcell also will be continuing the late Carolyn Weston's series about homicide detectives Al Krug and Casey Kellog. Weston's novel *Poor, Poor Ophelia* was adapted into the 1972 pilot film for ABC's *The Streets of San Francisco*, which starred Michael Douglas and Karl Malden.

Both authors have been gracious and generous with their time and input when they didn't have to do so.

My brother, Captain Greg Metcalf suffered the heavy lifting for both our parent's illnesses. He is a good man, and better son and brother.

My wife, Linda, and my son, Chandler, are both the foundation and the mortar of our family. We are quite literally 'The Three-That-Are-One'…

January 2016 Sacramento, California

Forward

Several years of relative peace had passed since the Stoellean Wars. With the exception of occasional Xighian conflicts and transport raids by Belt pirates, the Federation eventually relaxed back into comfortable, peaceful prosperity.

The Mandate had been suspended and the Directorate had been restored to power. As if following some ancient law of Archimedes, things sought their natural level and life proceeded apace.

Arkell and Dar remained under direct control of the SOG, which General Ferr still commanded. They had been used most successfully against Xighian adventurism and as a surgical tool against Belt piracy. However, in the wake of the newfound *peace*, they had been reduced to occasional reconnaissance missions and to a role as instructor assets at the Academy.

With marital concerns more or less behind the Federation, attention reverted to commerce. Increased focus was directed at expanding mining operations on the outskirts of the Federation, and convoluted, complex banking practices became the rule rather than the exception.

One day Arkell and Dar were ordered to a remote barbaric planet called Dolfin—so named for its current ironhanded ruler. What transpired was *interesting*.

Chapter One

Four men on horned mounts entered the clearing. Arkell stood alone, sensing the increased heartbeat of Dar, who was some two hundred yards away. They both knew these four were the point element of another twenty men hidden over the rise. Their attitude as they approached with their weapons at the ready left little doubt as to their intentions.

"Ho! Stranger, you trespass on Lord Dolfin's land. State your business or meet your death," announced the big man on the lead mount.

"A big one like that will feed a village for a week." A smaller bearded man laughed behind the leader.

"I don't speak to lackeys or cannibals," Arkell responded evenly, never moving for his weapons.

"Then you die to fill the company's stewpot." The leader then lowered his lance and charged.

Arkell stood his ground, noting that the other three remained back but fanned out in a wide semicircle. His feet were about shoulder width apart and his arms hung loosely at his sides.

The horned animal with the armed man raced forward in a cloud of dust as Arkell braced himself for the action. His heightened senses seemed to slow everything down as his attacker came forward in what appeared slow motion. He noted that the lance was about eight feet long, three inches around, and tipped with a broad steel point head. The lance was aimed at his chest, and yet he still did not move.

What happened next happened incredibly fast. Too fast for those watching to comprehend. He grabbed the advancing lance tightly behind the broad point with his left hand; his right hand lashed forward and broke the lance on the downstroke and seemed to bounce back as he leaned his back fist blow into the right shoulder of the animal, breaking its shoulder and driving a rib into its heart. Before the two bodies (animal and rider) had hit the ground, Arkell drew his laser pistol and fired three rapid shots, hitting each man in the center of the

1

forehead. All four men were dead before the dust had risen to his shoulder from the fall of the dead animal.

His attacker was trying to rise, but a broken collarbone and twisted knee hindered him. When he saw Arkell standing over him, he fumbled for his short sword and held it out in front of him to ward off this devil.

Arkell looked down at the fallen and laughed out loud. "What in the Nebula do you think you are going to do with *that*?"

"You … you … keep back … My men will cut you down."

"Your three companions are already dead." Arkell smiled. "Now you can either join them or talk to me."

A look of confused comprehension crossed the dark face as he beheld his three comrades fallen beside their grazing mounts.

"What kind of a man *are* you?" he mumbled.

"A very big one." Arkell grinned.

"I have many men over the rise," the wounded assailant sputtered. "They'll be here soon. If you kill me, they'll cut you down like wheat."

"The twenty men you have hidden over the rise are just now meeting my partner. If any survive, they are moving rapidly in the other direction. Now let me tend to that knee and shoulder … then we can talk." Arkell leaned down, and ignoring the short sword in the hand of the injured man, he proceeded to tend to his injuries.

They had landed before dawn on a quiet plane less than one hundred meters from a dense wood. They concealed their four-man shuttle craft and smelled the cool night air. Their mission was supposed to be reconnaissance, but they both knew better. Arkell was collecting his gear while Dar sniffed the ground and relieved himself against a rock.

The Directorate did not send their most uniquely skilled killing machines on mere reconnaissance missions. Although, of late, the political atmosphere in that learned body was at best "unstable."

Arkell was an imposing enough figure in and of himself. He was six foot ten, a hard-muscled three hundred pounds sculptured through generations of genetic manipulation and a lifetime of physical conditioning. That extraordinary physique had been given the most complete martial training history provided: ten thousand earth years of martial arts expertise, which made him a *master* without peer before he was twenty-six standard years; weapons skills with all blades known to man and every weapon of destruction from a hand laser to the placement of nuclear artillery and particle beam weapons. Hyperbole aside, he actually had the eyesight of an eagle, the strength of a bear, and the speed of a panther—all the product of genetics, mutations, and cloning. He had won the Federation's highest honor when he was still in his teen years by singlehandedly destroying over a battalion of Xighian storm troopers, reportedly the best in the quadrant. And that was before he even bonded with Dar.

The bonding had been a curiosity at first ... then an almost unbelievable asset to be exploited. And exploited it was.

Arkell had been sent to the jungles of Merrill-7 by accident while seeking medical help for his wounded combat mentor, General Ferr. He eventually eliminated a tribe of nasty quadruped natives who had been harassing the medical detachment sent to receive General Ferr and a mining detail, collecting various bodily parts as trophies. As he was cleaning up the slaughter he had wrought on the village, Dar just walked in. Apparently, he also had been some sort of genetic experiment, but one abandoned by his creators.

Dar appeared to be part *bear* and part *cat*. When standing on his hind paws, he was just a tad over nine feet in height. He weighed over seven hundred pounds and seemed front heavy with massive shoulders and chest. His hind feet were very catlike, except that he had fourteen claws on each paw. His front legs were heavier and covered in long fur. The front paws were like those of a grizzly bear with long talons. He had seven on each paw, one of which was positioned, and functioned, similar to a man's thumb. In profile, he looked much like a male lion, except for the thickness of his front legs and the long snout that stuck out from the mane, which was more bearlike. Despite the ferocity of his visage, his lips could be as gentle and nimble as to be able to button a tiny pearl button on a gossamer blouse.

When Arkell and Dar first met, there was no tension or danger, which in, and of, itself was strange, given two such dangerous beings. Rather, an instant bonding that defied all scientific analysis for the ten years they have been partners took place. They communicated both telepathically and empathically. Regardless of distance, they *felt* what the other felt. Words like loyalty, trust, understanding, and even love were inadequate to express the strength and depth of that symbiotic bonding.

From the day Arkell first saw Dar, they *became* one. And for the past ten years, they had become a legend in the Federation—the penultimate fighting machine. They had never failed in a mission. Eventually, the mere threat to dispatch the *Two-That-Are-One* became sufficient negative incentive to precipitate immediate discussions and to end conflict.

It was partly a result of their awesome reputation and incredible successes that virtually put them out of business. And who said deterrents don't work? They couldn't be retired to teach. What they did, and were, couldn't be taught. And despite efforts to duplicate it, they remained unique in all the known sentient worlds. Therefore, they had found themselves relegated to clandestine missions of subversion or *reconnaissance*.

Arkell sensed Dar's approach before he actually saw him. He had just finished the splint on his attacker's knee when Dar melted out of the woods into the clearing.

"Kill it! Quick! Kill it!" shouted the wounded attacker as he shook Arkell's massive shoulder.

Arkell smiled and said, "Don't be silly, fool. I could no sooner kill sweet Dar than rip out my own heart."

Excitable little human, isn't he? was Dar's thought about his fellow.

"Yeah, he is that." Arkell grinned. "Not much of a challenge either."

"Who ... who are you talking to? Is this beast dangerous?"

"This *beast* is my partner and soul mate. And *yes* ... he is dangerous ... *very* dangerous."

Dar sat down on his haunches and proceeded to groom his face and paws. There was little question as to what the dried reddish brown crusty patches were that clung to his mane and paws.

I let two of them escape as we agreed, although I'm afraid if they don't slow down, one of them will bleed to death.

"Will the other one survive?" Arkell asked.

If he doesn't bury himself in his own dung. He stayed in the back and mostly blubbering orders to those who died. He acted like he was a leader.

"As long as you made your presence known, and Lord Dolfin hears of it …."

"Y-y-y-you talk with the beast?" The wounded man was terrified and more than a little confused. "How does it talk back?"

Tell him eloquently.

"Eloquently." Arkell smiled.

I found us a suitable camp. I go now to make it ready. Run west toward that saddle in the mountains. When you have gone about five miles, call out and I will come to lead you.

Dar stood on all fours and shook the dust from his mane. Then he turned away and stopped to look over his shoulder at the two men in the dust.

I still think you should kill him … but if he can't die like a warrior, at least he can sing like a songbird. Be careful, Ark. Dar leaped off into the wood and was gone as quickly and silently as he had appeared.

The wounded man sat like a little child living through his worst nightmare. He was a big man by this planet's standards, almost five nine in height and over one hundred seventy pounds. His long black hair and beard were braided and strung with tiny bells. He had a long diagonal scar across his nose. Saliva and blood mingled on his trembling lips. A warrior used to being in control, he was now obviously out of his element.

Arkell sighed and breathed deeply as he felt the exhilaration of Dar's gallop. He looked down on his prisoner and smiled a cruel smile.

"Now we talk," he said. "You live only to share information with me and to deliver a message to your lord, Dolfin."

"It matters little. Whatever I tell you, you take to your grave when Lord Dolfin crushes you like an arrogant spider." He sighed and through split bloodied lips muttered, "My name is Phen of the clan Stru, and my life is forfeit anyway."

"Oh, little man, this is a large galaxy we inhabit. Your lord Dolfin is as significant as a sand flea on my partner's ass ... and less threatening. Within thirty of your sunsets, a delegation from the United Federation of Sentient Planets will arrive to negotiate mining rights to this planet. If he puts aside his cannibalism and accepts our largess, he will be permitted to continue as planet, Governor. If he resists our generous offer, he will be flayed and made into boots for a mining foreman."

"Lord Dolfin bows to no man ... *or* beast. His armies have unified this world for the first time in history. His rule is absolute. He commands ... he does not negotiate. Whatever you offer, he can take should he choose."

"I will not debate fact and fantasy with you, Phen of the clan Stru. You will answer my questions and deliver my message ... or I will peel off your skin like a Kobo fruit and salt your raw meat for the carrion birds."

Phen cringed visibly at the image. "What would you know, giant?"

"The large city behind the mountains ... what is it called?"

"It is called for its ruler—Dolfin."

"How large is the army and what are its defenses?"

Phen smiled weakly. "The army is the world. All men over sixteen cycles bear arms for the greater glory of our lord. Our navy controls all ports. All landholders must bear four sons—two to work the land and livestock and two to serve. Every cycle the brothers change roles."

"What of a merchant class?"

"Women all. Men who bear no sons do service labor."

"Are blade and lance your prime weapons?"

"Those and the heart of our lord."

"Who opposes Dolfin?" Arkell asked.

"Fools and those who wish to die impaled on the lance."

"Are there no enemies?"

"Only the wild beasts..." He paused a moment and looked into the dirt before he added, "...and off-worlders like you."

Arkell smiled. He was an expert in politics as well as war. He well knew the lessons ignored from history. There had never been an absolute monarch ruling with an iron fist who wasn't pestered with insurgents in some form. The only exception was the Stoellean Empire, and that was because they strictly controlled all births and created a drug dependency in the entire population. The only source of the drug was the empire. It had been a virtual zombie empire in which there were no dissenters. But that was the only exception Arkell could think of or was aware of ever happening. Lord Dolfin had enemies and always would have as long as he lived.

"When was your last revolt, Phen?"

"Three cycles past, a mountain tribe led by Steward Thain refused to pay homage to our lord." Phen paused and looked up into the steel gray eyes of his interrogator. "His body rotted on the silver lance for a week before the carrion birds picked his bones clean. His skull now serves as a footstool for our lord."

"Phen, listen to me well. Tell your lord I would parlay with him four sunrises hence. I will await him at the base of the two mountains over there." He pointed in the direction of the city. "I claim privilege as an ambassador of the Federation. Tell him to come to me with an open mind and hand. I can offer him new found wealth … or death."

"I will tell him, giant. But he will eat your heart at banquet," Phen sighed.

"I will pluck his teeth and gift them as necklace"—Ark smiled— "to his least concubine."

"You are a skilled warrior, big man. It is sad to think the man who finally defeated Phen would be stew meat for lesser men and boots for some court dancer."

Arkell smiled and said, "Greater beasts than your lord have tried and failed."

"What *is* that beast you talk to in silence?" Phen asked, genuinely curious.

"That beast is me, and I am that beast." Arkell smiled as he mused over his absent other half. "I will build you a fire and leave you with food and water. Do not yet die, Phen of the clan Stru. Your message will enrich your lord."

"I hope you have lived a full life, warrior," Phen replied looking at the ground. Then he lifted his face to look at Arkell and said, "It will end in four sunrises."

7

Chapter Two

Lord Dolfin sat on a cushion made from the hide of his predecessor and stuffed with bird feathers. His large head was shaved bald and adorned with a tattoo of a large predator bird in flight. The wings covered each side of his head to the ears. His forehead held the open mouthed art of the great bird and talons flanked his face to end at his jawline. His neck was massive corded muscle. Although he stood less than six feet, his floor-length black robe made him appear taller. His waist was girdled with a wide belt made from his father's hide. His boots were finely made from the skin of an admired enemy. One foot rested on the skull of his last dissenter. He chewed a sig leaf for its mild narcotic effect. Blank faced, he listened to his magician and advisor, Vanjar.

"My lord, my prophecy of the spring snows is come. A man who is not man and a beast which is not beast have entered your domain. Even now two messengers bear news for you. One limps into the city as I speak. Phen of the clan Stru sits defeated in a clearing over the mountains, singing the death chant of his comrades and holds words for you."

"My sons will feast on Phen to gain his strength. He was a good soldier. When does my trial begin, old man?"

"Three sunrises from now," Vanjar muttered as he struggled to keep his hands still in the folds of his robe. "The voices of your ancestors advise parlay, sire."

Dolfin plopped another leaf in his mouth and asked the old man, "When do I kill these two … this man and his beast?"

"The spirits are mute, my lord." Vanjar shuffled his feet and avoided eye contact with his ruler. "You should speak to this self-proclaimed ambassador, Lord."

"How many men were with Phen?" Dolfin casually asked.

"Twenty-four of the clan Stru, sire. All warriors of experience and robes of scalps."

"And how many survived?"

"Three ... no ... two, my lord." Vanjar closed his eyes and concentrated. "Nam enters the city now. Phen is wounded and awaits help."

"How many enemy killed twenty-two from the clan Stru?" Dolfin asked.

"One man ... one beast," Vanjar said as he looked at his feet.

Dolfin raised an eyebrow, causing the beak of the tattooed bird to rise. "I will speak with this man." He spit onto the rug and grinned an evil grin as he added, "*Then* I will cleave his skull and suck his brains ..."

****

Dar was resting on a cliff face some fifty feet up from the floor of the valley. He had killed a deer and had eaten. He saved portions of the carcass for later and for Arkell. He had saved one of the loins knowing his partner preferred the sweet meat to bone and marrow.

He was licking the marrow from a large femur he had just cracked with his teeth when he sensed Arkell running like a gazelle less than a mile from him. It troubled him slightly that he had not noticed his partner until so late, but he had been concentrating on his meal. He stood up, stretched, and smelled the air. This slightly lesser gravity made running a joy, although, on his full belly, he would walk down to meet his companion.

Arkell had run the five miles in about fifteen minutes and paused now at a stream to drink. He was sweating and the gentle breeze cooled him. It was spring time here, and the smells of erupting nature filled his nostrils. Then he noticed the smell of Dar mixed with wild dill weed. Without turning around he laughed.

"Ho, hairy one, I sense your belly is full."

Fear not, little one, I saved you a loin.

Dar ambled down to the stream to join Arkell and drink from the cool waters of the stream.

"These people will be hard, comrade," Arkell said as he patted the flank of his partner.

The oak breaks in the wind while the willow survives.

"And what of us, brother? Are we not hard?"

We have yet to meet the wind that can break us, Ark.

"How far to camp?"

About a mile. I found a cave once used by a small bear.

"It must smell wonderful."

It is good. Deep enough even for you to have a fire.

"I need no fire in this climate. Your warmth will suffice me this night."

Let's get you fed, little one. I feel a nap coming on.

"A short one perhaps. No twenty-hour naps for you this mission, Dar." Arkell smiled as he tugged Dar's tail.

It is your *rest I think on,* Dar responded. *I can still outdistance you on my worst day.*

"And I can still beat you at chess on my worst."

Ah-h-h ... hubris in two such as we is unnecessary. Come eat. You can have deer loin, berries, and a sweet nut or two.

"You spoil me, Dar."

Yes, I know. Dar responded as he nuzzled his great snout into Arkell's side. *And it gives me great joy.*

****

Vanjar lay on fur throws with his young concubine, Petal. She was curled in the nook of his arm with one leg draped over his. He played her hair through his fingers and stared at the ceiling, thinking deep thoughts. She ran one finger up and down the inside of his thigh.

"What troubles you, oh wise one?" she asked.

"There is trouble amongst us, my precious," he answered, still staring at the ceiling.

"Lord Dolfin crushes trouble like a beetle under his boot."

"Ah, this time, little one, I feel the trouble is greater than our lord's capacity to appreciate it," Vanjar sighed.

"What has ever stood before his sword that didn't end up in the stewpot?" she asked as she turned on her side and looked down into the old bearded face of her lover.

"This is different, child," he said as he turned to look into her sparkling blue eyes and admire the soft, creamy texture of her skin. "Things greater than our world threaten the Dol. He will need skills he does not have or even understand."

"Isn't that why he has you, wise one?" She smiled and then nibbled at his shoulder.

"Yes, my love, but how can I counsel compromise to Lord Dolfin? He who has never compromised and knows not how? The fish cannot be taught to fly, and birds cannot be taught to live underwater."

She snuggled closer to the thin wrinkled body next to her and rested her head on Vanjar's shoulder. "If it is necessary, you will find a way."

"I *must* find a way," he said with such force as to startle his prize. "But I must also be careful … oh *so* careful. For over twenty years, since before you were even born, I have told him he need never give in to any man. He should *take* what he wants, for it has been his right." He paused and resumed his staring at the ceiling. "But *now* … he must be made to see the reason in this ambassador's proposal."

"Perhaps I can tickle his short sword, my lord." Petal giggled.

"You'd like that, wouldn't you, little one?" he said as he tweaked her nose between a finger and thumb. "No, he must be made to reason with his mind, not with his loins or his heart."

"Will he lose this final battle?" she asked diffidently.

"I do not know … and *that* is what terrifies me. Never has my vision been so clouded. Never have the spirits been so confusing. I must see this man and his beast before Lord Dolfin."

Petal looked startled again as she quietly asked, "Is that wise?"

"No it is not. But I fear it is most necessary."

"May we not share bliss one more time before you go?"

"You have blunted my short sword once too often, little one." Vanjar smiled.

"Oh, but I can make it a lance again if you let me," Petal responded as she slid down his body.

"I will let you."

****

12

Chapter Three

The Directorate of the United Federation of Sentient Planets was convened on Merrill-2, awaiting the delegation from Earth Prime to arrive. The Archbishop of the American West New Catholic Diocese was filling his pipe as the chairman of the First Galactic Banking Commission was pushed into the room on his antigravity sled that looked like a cross between a bobsled and a computer. Governor Gospatrick of Merrill-2 rose to greet the bank chairman.

"Isaac, how was the jump?" Gospatrick asked with his cosmetic smile. "Did you rest well?"

The chairman was an obese, foul-tempered man. Confined to an antigravity sled for twenty years since having been crippled in food riot on Fortes, he was a powerful and feared man, partly because he controlled with autocratic privilege the economy of over half a galaxy and partly because he was as volatile and unpredictable as a black hole.

"Damn, drugs make me hungry as a Vanovian hedgehog. Is everyone else here?" he asked as he moved to the buffet table and grabbed a thick drink containing carbohydrates and ground veal.

"Everyone except the Earth Prime group. They are expected shortly."

"Is the mining detachment prepared to depart?" he asked as he reached for a large fruit with a thick stubby hand tipped in three-inch-long nails filed to points. It was a poorly kept secret that one nail on each hand was coated in a lethal poison. That fact largely accounted for a natural reticence in anyone to shake his hand. Not that he ever offered such a familiarity.

"They will be by the time we vote." Gospatrick smiled while struggling to hide his revulsion and fear of this man. "General Charles-Henry Ferr wants to wait for word from the Two-That-Are-One," he whispered to the bank officer.

"Why by Omega's left ball did he have to send *them*?" Isaac snapped. "We want information and a trade agreement, not another bonking Armageddon."

The governor inclined his head and avoided eye contact as he answered, "The last three emissaries were never heard from. The planet is listed as hostile and … backward. The general wanted results this time before we dispatch the survey team."

"That freak sends a particle beam destroyer after an ant? The satellite reports have already confirmed the geological analysis. We *need* those crystals and that ore within one full rotation. Kybritz-17 has played out, and if we don't replace that production soon, the bug-infested Andromeda Cartel will have us by the balls."

"General Ferr's disfigurement was earned in defense of the Federation, Mr. Chairman," Gospatrick responded stiffly. As much as he feared Isaac, he feared General Charles-Henry Ferr in kind. Ferr was a warrior hero, and despite the myopia of many in that room, he was also a consummate politician—not a man to be trifled with or provoked. "Our schedule will be met, Mr. Chairman."

****

General Charles-Henry Ferr stood behind his huge desk pouring over maps of the planet to which he had dispatched Arkell and Dar. He had already plotted the landing sites, base camps, and warehouse locations. Weather was of little concern, but he hoped to win the locals' hearts and minds without having to level their cities. He had protested the Directorate's timetable. There was too little reliable information on the population and the planet itself. His decision to send Arkell and Dar was met with some resistance, which he quickly crushed. He would have gotten less flak had he suggested genocide rather than sending the Two-That-Are-One. Although the power brokers respected success, they were still frightened by the awesome legend of Arkell and Dar. They *never* failed no matter how absurd the odds against their return. He now knew for a fact that on at least two occasions, they were given certain suicide missions that the computers projected they had virtually no chance to return from. They returned unscathed from each, except for Dar's singed pelt and Arkell's bad temper. When Ark had threatened to peel the skin (without benefit of blade) from the entire family of the next bureaucrat who sent them off without complete and up-to-date intelligence data, the general had to intercede to prevent an indictment. Nevertheless, subsequent missions included more data than four Series 111 computers could process.

There was no question that the Federation would establish a mining city on that little planet. The only question was their ability to do so without creating more revolution and dissent. Fifty years ago, during the Carbon Jihad, they (the Federation) were the good guys. Lately, since the end of the Stoellean War, and the bankers moved into control of the Directorate, he was feeling less confident with more and more remorse. The only good that came out of that particular debacle on Merrill-7 ten years ago was the bonding of Arkell and Dar. But then he was a soldier. He took orders and he gave orders. Others made policy decisions—for now.

Ferr knew that he should have died ten years ago when they raided the palaces on Stoellus. The laser blast that burned off half his face could have killed him. It was remarkable luck that Arkell was able to rescue him from an impossible situation and get him to a med team. His private nightmares were still haunted with the vision of Arkell gone berserk, like some ancient Viking dodging lasers and dealing death. Over a full company of Stoelleans had died around him that day. He became a freak with half a face. The thought of Ark dancing death through the Stoellean ranks and the smell of sweat and slaughter sobered him. Never again.

"Ark, don't fail me now, friend," Ferr said to himself in a soft whisper. "Perhaps when you sit in this office, you will be able to better control events. God knows I don't."

****

Arkell was sleeping on his back between a moss-covered wall and the warm body of Dar. As he awoke, his mind touched Dar's, and he spoke.

"Did you sleep well, my hairy friend?"

I slept some ... your snoring woke me twice. I thought Stoellean tanks were storming our position.

"I slept like a babe."

Your dreams were most unbabe-like. I've shared your erection for hours.

Arkell swung his legs up over his head and pushed himself up into a handstand from which he proceeded to do upside-down push-ups. "Remember that little dancer from Sogra?"

I vaguely remember she drained you like a sponge under the tread of a tank, Dar responded with his approximation of a smile.

"Dar, do you ever think of finding one with whom you could mate?" Ark asked as he continued to do push-ups from his handstand.

Little need ... the slight sexual needs which were not bred out of me are more than sated by your many conquests and the blessing and curse of our bonding, which allows me to share your feelings. He reached out one massive paw and knocked out one of Ark's hands. Rather than fall, Arkell shifted his weight and continued to do the handstand push-ups on one hand.

At times I think you must carry the genes of a mink or a rabbit.

"I wonder what flavor this planet's courtesans are," Arkell mused.

If their menfolk are any indication—bitter.

"You have no romance in your dark soul, Dar."

Not true. If you live to hear my death haiku, you will cry rivers.

"If I live to your death, I will commit suicide so that our ashes might mingle for eternity."

Then let us not die. Dar came up to all fours and stretched as he looked at his partner pumping like a piston. *You look like a hairless gibbon. What have you planned for us today?*

Arkell flipped over to his feet and took a drink from a canteen as he answered, "I want to force *march* to the rendezvous point, so we can prepare a day in advance for the arrival of Lord Dolfin."

You truly think he will come?

"Of course, if only to try to kill me. He will come."

You can explain your plan while we eat, Dar answered as he moved over to collect the food.

Arkell erupted into a rapid-fire thirty-second kata of incredible speed and complexity, and then slowly settled into a sitting lotus. Dar brought over some food, and Arkell outlined his plan for their meeting with Lord Dolfin.

****

Petal was naked as she braided Vanjar's beard and hair. He was reading his notes and deep in thought.

"You didn't wake me for the dawn service, wise one," she said as her fingers twisted and braided the long thin hair of the magician.

"I needed to be alone to conjure the spirits," he answered. "I swear they intentionally taunt me, yet I know not why."

"In what way, my lord?" She tied off the end of each thin braid with a black strip of fabric that contrasted starkly with the white of his hair.

"Those that will speak, speak more than ever in riddles. They refer to these two off-worlders as the Two-That-Are-One and claim they are invincible."

"Certainly, two cannot be one nor defeat a whole world," she said, "especially the realm of Lord Dolfin."

"Apparently, these two are some sort of a scouting party for a much larger enemy with fierce magic and thousands of worlds' worth of soldiers."

"Impossible!" Petal shouted in disbelief. "They seek to frighten you for envy of your majesty."

"Petal, the spirits are not like men, though men and women they once were. They cannot lie. They can only tell what was, what is, and what is to come."

"Cast a spell on them to *make* them tell you what you want." She smiled.

"Petal, my sweet, innocent young fool, one cannot cast a spell on a spell—it defies the order. The voices are the result of a spell. I cannot command the voices."

"You should not try to meet this Two-That-Are-One, sire. I am fearful it will kill you." She paused in her braiding and looked deep into his liquid eyes. "Or Lord Dolfin will kill you himself."

"I *must* … the spirits have told me the only hope we have for survival is in my meeting them and helping our lord Dolfin to see and act on reason," Vanjar sighed.

"What of Lord Dolfin?" she asked. "Will he not miss you today?"

"No," said the old man, "he hunts today with the clan T'sui for the wild pig."

"Who goes with you?"

"I will take three apprentices and Captain Cron."

"Be careful, wise one. If anything ever happened to you, what would become of poor Petal?"

"I will be careful, my sweet, although I have no doubts about your abilities to prosper in life ... with or without me."

****

Dar flared his nostrils and breathed deeply. *It is a good plan as plans go, but the unexpected is always the key to any plan. I don't like being separated from you for this.*

"Dar, we will never be separated, just apart for a while. I need you on the outside to collect data. And I need you to come when I call."

Like a tornado on an old Kansas plain. That's right, isn't it? Kansas? Like in The Wizard of Oz?

"Yes, that is right." Ark smiled. "This Lord Dolfin is a competent warrior, but he lacks much. His pride will force him to confront me himself."

Then he is a fool and no competent warrior to underestimate my Ark.

"Oh, he will come with a show of force, but not to overwhelm me with numbers."

Why then?

"For an audience. He will want a large contingent of loyal warriors to sing his praise at his great victory."

They will only sing his funeral dirge.

"I intend to spare him ... and go with him into the city."

As a prisoner? Dar asked as his lips raised over his fangs.

"Probably."

I am beginning to think I will enjoy this. You intend to do battle with this prideful monarch, not kill him ... not let him kill you, and still go into his city?

"You got it."

I think you must have been eating Lec weed. Dar stopped and turned his head and sniffed the air. *A wagon approaches. With one outrider.*

Arkell jumped up to his feet and moved toward the opening. "You circle them. I'll confront them out front."

Dar leaped out of the cave and was gone. Arkell donned his sword, knives, and laser pistol. He left his pack against the wall of the cave.

Vanjar and his apprentices were in the wagon being pulled by four-horned beasts of burden. Captain Cron rode separate on a similar beast, scanning the tree line.

"Good day, traveler," said Arkell as he stepped into their path. Cron immediately drew his sword with instinctive practice.

Although startled by his sudden appearance, Vanjar collected himself and proudly announced, "I am Vanjar, magician to Lord Dolfin, whose lands you trespass. I seek the Two-That-Are-One. Are you part of that couplet?"

"I am called Arkell, and I know of whom you speak, although how you ever learned of that appellation is a mystery worth noting."

"I am a magician. I speak to spirits. They tell me much. Although they did not tell me what a huge man you are. May we parlay?"

Arkell looked over at Captain Cron and then back to Vanjar. "Tell your man-at-arms to sheath his weapon or die.

Cron bristled at the threat, but Vanjar quieted him with a wave of a hand as the magician stepped down from the wagon.

"You would meet with my lord in three days hence?"

"Yes. I have a proposition he needs to consider," Arkell replied.

"He intends to have your hide for boots and eat your brains in feast."

"His intentions exceed his grasp." Arkell smiled.

"He is a powerful and skilled warrior. None have ever even come close to defeating him."

Arkell shook his head slowly from side to side. "He should talk rather than fight."

"I agree." Vanjar nodded and looked up into Arkell's eyes. What he saw there confirmed his worst fears. "But my lord is a prideful man and as such has never had to learn the art of compromise."

"Am I to take it that you, on the other hand, *have* learned this valuable art?" Arkell smiled.

Vanjar barked a laugh. "My *life* is a compromise. But I only want what is best for my lord and his realm."

"What if what is best for your land is not best for your lord?" Arkell asked as he stared hard at the old man.

"Impossible," Vanjar responded without sufficient strength, "they are one and the same."

Arkell sat on a stump so he could look Vanjar face-to-face at his own level. "Look, magician, I bring greetings from a very great and powerful Federation of many planets…"

"…thousands of worlds of warriors?"

"Yes. And merchants, and scientists, and miners…"

Vanjar shook his head slowly from side to side. "Lord Dolfin recognizes no equal."

"Your lord is in for a most rude awakening." Arkell grinned and stood up to his full height. "Why did you come to me?"

"I came seeking two," Vanjar responded quietly. "You are but one."

"I am one that is two … and two million million …."

Vanjar put his hands up in front of his face and complained, "Please speak not to me in riddles. I tire of riddles. I would help if I can, and if you allow me."

"How many men will your lord use to try to kill me?"

"He rides with two companies: one cavalry; one pike men. However, he has already announced he will kill the humiliator of Phen himself man-to-man or man-to-beast."

"Your lord has more courage than good sense. Does he intend to hear my proposal before we battle?"

"Oh yes, although, were you to attempt to buy your safety with a city full of jewels, he would still kill you. He eats Phen's heart tonight so that Phen may share in your defeat."

"Vanjar, your master cannot kill me—not alone and not with a mere two companies of his finest troops."

Vanjar laughed as he said, "Ah, Gods save all warriors. And *now* who speaks more courage than common sense?"

"Magician, I do not boast when I tell you I have killed more than *twice* that number in a single battle, and they were armed with far more formidable weapons than mere blade and pike."

"Impossible! Your lies and braggadocio will not save your life."

"Ask your spirits of Arkell. Then ask them of Dar. Finally, ask them of the Two-That-Are-One. You will hear in their truth that I speak no lies."

"Are you a demon?" Vanjar asked, suddenly frightened.

Picking up on the thought, Arkell grinned and nodded. "*Yes* ... I am a demon. A demon with a ferocious familiar. Surely, your master, the Lord Dolfin, could slay any *man* as you say. But I am *not* a man but a *demon*. Tell him I do not wish to kill him, but that if he needs proof, he should send one hundred of his finest soldiers against me. When they are dead, *then* perhaps he will grant me an audience to negotiate an arrangement mutually agreeable to all parties."

"One hundred?" Vanjar asked with fear, confusion, and doubt. "Why not just kill them all, demon? If indeed you can."

"Oh, have no doubt but that *I can,* mage. You tell your lord Dolfin that as an act of mercy and good faith, I will kill no more than he sends against me. *He* may be the one to choose how many of his loyal soldiers must die."

"I will tell him," Vanjar said as he started to climb back up into the wagon. "By the way, demon Arkell, what is it you would propose to my lord?"

"That, magician, is for your lord's ears only if he chooses to live past our meeting."

Cron had been listening with a disbelieving face. When Arkell turned to leave, Cron whispered to Vanjar, "He *is* a big man, but he lies—he is no demon, sire."

Arkell's extra sensitive hearing heard the exchange, and he turned back to respond.

"Ho, soldier, this big man/demon does not have to lie to mere mortals." He stood with his balled fists on his hips. "Run me through if you be fool enough to dare."

Before Vanjar could stop him, Cron wheeled his mount and charged at a gallop. Arkell met the charge and, grabbing the lance,

21

lifted Cron from his saddle and hammered him into the dirt as he would a sledge. He then took the lance and threw it at a large tree, sending it half its length through the trunk. Then there was a loud roar and Dar leaped to the ground next to Arkell and stood on his hind paws, his wide arms with talons exposed.

Vanjar lost all pretense of calm and was visibly shocked and terrified. "Gods, protect us," prayed Vanjar.

"Pick up your fallen soldier and tell all this to Lord Dolfin. I will await him on the plain spoken of in my first message. I send no more."

Arkell and Dar sprinted into the woods as the dumbfounded party stared after them.

I thought that was a rather nice touch. Dar chuckled.

"Perfect."

I take it there is a change in your plan.

"Yes. Do we still have that old plastique?"

You have not used any, and I have not chosen to eat it.

"This is going to be fun." Arkell laughed as he roughed his companion's mane.

I like fun. Let's eat.

Chapter Four

The delegation from Earth Prime had just arrived, and the president and prime minister were just leaving the medical lab where they had undergone routine post-jump testing.

President Patrick Henry Jobikan was a fit man of eighty years. He was just over six foot tall, and Elvas-12 clone bred for classic Greek beauty and Andromeda political insight. He had served eight years in the office and was destined for a long career. His white hair was closely cropped and melded perfectly with his white beard. His skin had been dyed to a rich cinnamon color to contrast with this white hair and accent his clear, light blue eyes. He looked as much like a Vid star as a politician (not that there was much difference these days). Actually, if the truth be known, that was precisely what he was, the handsome front piece for policy created by less attractive power brokers and manipulators of destiny.

The prime minister, Kor-Zem, was shorter, just under six foot, immensely fat, and with rolling jowls and dark blue circles under his small, beady, dung-colored eyes. The package was far less pretty than his president, but the mind was keen and computer swift. He could claim perfect recall, a photographic memory equal only to the larger DfES computers. He had been responsible for both eliminating the galactic debt and establishing the ways and means of profit-oriented policy. His ruthlessness was a well-kept secret legend. His few detractors lived short lives or found themselves employed in far-off mining posts with few sentient constituents and no hope for fermenting rebellion.

"General Ferr wishes a private meeting prior to the full Directorate gathering," said the president as he poured two stimulant drinks.

"I suppose we should see him, although the chairman has already warned me of Ferr's desire to postpone," the prime minister responded.

"Ferr is seldom wrong, comrade."

"Right or wrong are immaterial. That planet's resources are *crucial* to Isaac and to us. If the Cartel gets to set prices without an alternative, the Merrill group will be put out of business, and you'll have to tap dance for a decade."

"I've done it before," Jobikan answered nonplussed.

"Why expend the energy when we have alternatives more attractive.

"I don't find another war attractive, friend."

"It would hardly be a war, Pat. A minor surgical exercise. Colonel Arkell could handle it alone with off-world fire support."

"Damn it, K-Z, I will not have you spend those two so lightly. You have already tried twice to get them killed. Don't piss them off. I'd sooner battle the Cartel than have Ferr, Arkell, and Dar against us openly."

"Pat, my lad, they are merely *tools* … and obsolete tools at that. Your concerns are hyperbole personified."

"I don't deny the need to speed, but I *will not* permit you to turn those three into open adversaries."

"Do you have an alternative, my dear Mr. President?"

"Possibly. First, I want to hear what Ferr has to say. I believe we may still be able to compromise on your timetable and yet meet our objectives."

"We can't afford to bone up on this one, my pretty," Kor-Zem muttered."

"I have no intention of bonking up. I also have no intention of handing the opposition leadership a wedge to drive into the Directorate. We were lucky no one ever learned of our last little genocide. If that guild navigator had been able to report what he found, you and I would have traveled from taxidermist to the mantle of some Kenova lord to collect dust."

"But he *didn't*, and we are not. His ship was vaporized before he even left the quadrant."

"And the guild inquiry still goes on. No, a less heavy hand is called for this time. You can prepare for the messy solution, but we hear our General Ferr, and we *don't* piss off the colonel and his bonded griffin."

"My patience has limits, Mr. President."

"As does mine, Mr. Prime Minister."

****

Petal meditated on a fur rug. She lay on her back supine, with her eyes open but rolled back in her head. Her Doutrin trance permitted her astral self to travel out of the castle and to the hills of her ancestral people. High atop a rocky peak, she met the astral self of her half-brother, Lacracken, leader of the rebels.

Greetings, brother.

Greetings, little sister. What news do you bring?

A demon comes to make offerings to Lord Dolfin, she said.

Her brother asked, *What kind of offerings?*

Tomorrow holds the answers.

Would Dolfin of the Dung deal with this demon?

Dolfin would kill the demon, she replied, *but Vanjar thinks he cannot.*

Will the demon do my work and kill the oppressor *of our people?*

Unknown. The magician worries more so than I have ever seen before. He claims the spirits speak in riddles. He wishes to counsel caution to his lord, but Lord Dolfin is ... well, Lord Dolfin.

It would be good if this demon kills him. I would rather deal with a demon lord than Dolfin.

They meet at sunrise on the Plain of Despair.

That is good. We will raid his granaries to the west and salt his fields south of that.

Beware, my brother, I fear. Never have the spirits not spoken to Vanjar clearly.

Does he lose his power?

No, I think not. But I see he fears his ability to give counsel to his lord.

That is good.

No, that is bad. The only hope we have had thus far is Vanjar's ability to instill reason in the heart of the lord who knows none.

I will come to you tomorrow night after the moon sets. Tell me of this demon, and I would hear of Dolfin's reaction to the granary raid and the bespoiling of his fields.

It takes no seer to predict his reaction. I shall look forward to your visit.

****

Dolfin rode into the city at the lead of his hunting party. It had been a good hunt. The party killed six wild pigs, four boars, and two large sows. Lord Dolfin had himself killed three with the heavy lance favored by his cavalry. Two dogs had been killed when the largest of the boars charged the pack. Their meat would be added to the feast this evening, along with the carcass of Phen and Nam, who had delivered the first message from Arkell. The lord was in a good mood, and his blood lust whetted, looking forward to killing this tall ambassador and his pet.

Magician Vanjar stood on the stairs to the palace, awaiting his lord with that pretty young concubine that followed him like a shadow. Perhaps if she put on some weight, Dolfin would honor her with the fight of his short sword some night.

"How went the hunt, my lord?" Vanjar asked.

"Well, magician. I killed three big boars and Captain Pel another. Clan T'sui took two large females. How do spent you your day?" He glanced at Petal and then back to Vanjar with a grin. "Do the spirits have news?"

"We must talk, sire," Vanjar responded nervously. "I have urgent and confidential news."

Dolfin raised an eyebrow and lifted the beak of his tattoo. "Let me wash the dust down with a tankard, and then you can tell me your urgent news, wise one."

Dolfin dismounted and left his mount to a livery boy. As the boy passed Dolfin with head bowed, Dolfin slapped him between the shoulders, knocking him to the ground with a red handprint on his thin bare back.

"Don't overwater him this time, lad, and rub him down good!" Dolfin barked. Before he had reached the first step, a large tankard was handed to him by a young woman with large naked breasts. He drank the entire liter in one swallow, belched loudly, and turned to Vanjar. "Speak," he commanded.

"My lord, my words are not for the rabble." Vanjar shifted from one foot to the other under his long robe. "Perhaps we could retire inside?"

"Very well. Your little concubine can remove my boots for me if she had the strength."

****

They sat in a large parlor and Petal pulled off Dolfin's boots of man-hide as the lord bit into a large sweet fruit. Vanjar stood as soon as his lord sat and started to pace.

"My lord, I was seeking herbs and magic roots today, and I encountered the one you meet with on the morrow."

"And he let you live?"

"To your best interest, my lord." Vanjar bowed his head and silently prayed he would not be asked how far he had roamed in search of his roots.

"What was he like? Is he as big as Phen claimed?"

"He is indeed bigger than any man, sire, but then that is why I sought this privacy." He paused and looked directly at his fierce ruler. "You see, sire, he be not man himself."

"What?" Dolfin threw the remains of his fruit at a wall. "Speak not in riddles, Vanjar, or forfeit your nose."

"My lord, he is a *demon*. He told me so himself. He is the Two-That-Are-One the spirits spoke to me of. His manlike half is this tall, muscled giant calling himself Arkell, and he offers a proposal."

Dolfin brooded quietly a moment and stared at a shield on a wall. He asked his next question, still looking at the shield. "Be he truly a demon?"

"Most certainly, my lord. His familiar is a large catlike bear more fierce than any six wild pigs."

"We killed six wild pig today, old man." Dolfin grinned.

"My lord…." He was obviously agitated and struggled to retain his little composure. "Oh, how may I speak his words without earning your wrath?"

"Vanjar, we have been together many years. No one hears your words but your shadow and me. I grant you pardon for any offense his words might spark."

"My lord, this Arkell said he would prefer not to kill you." He paused and swallowed. "He needs discuss merchant business."

"Then let him talk to women," Dolfin said through clenched teeth.

"My lord, he said he *knows* you could surely kill any man."

"A wise demon." Dolfin nodded.

"But he is no *man* and will surely kill you if you push battle." This phrase earned him a stare that could curdle milk. He silently backed up two steps, awaiting the outburst he fully expected.

"If we do not battle, how may he prove himself worthy to speak to me?" Dolfin quietly asked.

"He suggests that you send one hundred of your best warriors against him. He said after he kills them, he would speak to you in counsel."

"One hundred?" Dolfin rose to his bare feet and glared at Vanjar. "What manner of fool is this demon/man to challenge one hundred?"

"My advice, my lord, is to do as he asks. He cannot possibly survive an attack from one hundred. If he dies, as I am sure he will, we shall eat his heart." Vanjar moved his eyes from his ruler to the floor in front of his bare feet. "If he lives, he would make a worthy ally."

"I seek no allies!" Dolfin barked. Then he calmed himself and smiled an evil smile. "Although to watch one fight one hundred would be a fine morning's sport."

"He is not one but two, Lord."

"I agree. He will fight one hundred of my finest. Then we will either eat him or sing his song at banquet. What say your spirits of the outcome?"

Vanjar nervously looked at his ruler and answered, "That a song master should be present with your company."

****

As much as I love running with you, six hours to get to a rendezvous is excessive, even for you, Dar complained.

"If my pace was too fast for you, you could have said something."

You hairless blemish, it is your lagging pace that bored me. Now that we're here, can we eat? I smell a pig nearby.

"You set the charges. It is my turn to hunt for you, Dar." Arkell smiled as he slapped his companion on the rump.

As you wish. Your quarry is about a half mile to the northwest amongst some oak-like trees, Dar responded as he proceeded to extract the pyrotechnics.

"Try not to blow yourself up please."

And you try not to slip in pig dung.

Dar fumbled in the pack as Arkell ran off to the northwest. He had to alter his course to be downwind from the hogs. Normally, he would have attacked with blade alone, but this was a meat hunt, and time was a concern. He approached to within fifty yards of three large pigs rooting at the base of a stand of trees. He drew his laser and shot the largest in its left eye, burning its brain before the big body hit the dirt. The other two hogs turned and ran off into the brush.

Arkell walked cautiously up to the fallen pig, and, drawing his long antique Randall knife that had been a gift from General Ferr, gutted and field dressed the animal. He saved the heart and liver and wrapped them in a plastic bag, which he put in his hip pack. Then he hoisted the two-hundred-pound animal up onto his shoulder and started the jog back to Dar.

Very sporting of you, Dar teased.

"Very quick and efficient," Arkell answered as he dropped the carcass and started to skin it.

No matter really, let's eat. Did you save the insides?

"Of course, love, the heart is for you. We'll share the liver."

Ark, you are too good to me.

"Impossible."

True.

****

Lord Dolfin was a successful, though unsophisticated, ruler. He had achieved his position of absolute despot by a simple synthesis of two basic elements: his own brutal physical superiority, which sparked loyalty through fear, and the superior advice and counsel of Vanjar, who enjoyed the counsel of omniscient spirits.

The Dolfin rule had been the result of perfect intelligence coupled with ruthless execution. This new situation with the demon and uncooperative spirits rankled him. He was not really bright enough to be worried or concerned, but he did suffer, as a beast does from an itch it cannot reach.

Vanjar suffered a symbiotic itch. Never in all the years since his grandmother had instructed him in converse with the spirits had he ever received anything but clear, simple guidance and instruction. Now, when he needed it most, the advice he received was in riddles. Metaphor and allegory replaced the simple who, what, when, where, and (yes) how. He was being forced to be a translator/interpreter, and it was a role he was frustrated by.

Petal, however, shared the knowledge of her master's messages, but *she* held a skill and insight into interpreting those messages that she neither revealed nor shared with anyone. She knew what the spirits meant and struggled how best to use that information. Her goals, unlike Vanjar's or Dolfin's, were loftier. She sought the greater good for the greater number. But she lacked the tool to mold her plans, until Arkell and Dar arrived.

Her plans were both complex and simple. She intended Lord Dolfin to die. At whose hands it mattered little. That he was the disease her world suffered from was no question. Her brother, Lacracken, would be the one to split Dolfin's tattooed dome and burn his black heart. Although she would never say such to him, she knew he had no chance of defeating Lord Dolfin in individual combat. Vanjar had the needed skills and ample opportunity, yet despite his depth of knowledge of things unknown, he was in essence a two-dimensional pawn bred to be loyal to his ruler. Originally, she had thought to take the oaf to bed and kill him after letting her body be used. Now, however, there was a powerful man/demon amongst them. Apparently, with needs of his own which needed filling, *and* more importantly, the strength and skill to crush Dolfin. If this man/beast was as much man as beast, she would take *him* to bed and win his favor. She would discover his needs and reveal ways to achieve them. Whatever ways those were she was certain of one thing—it would include the killing of the tyrant.

****

Chapter Five

The formal meeting of the Directorate had regressed into an unruly shouting match. General Ferr sat back quietly and watched with awed fascination at the yelling and pointing going on around him. *These* were the men who controlled an entire galaxy. The money, the power, the science, and the very well-being of trillions of sentient life-forms were ultimately impacted by the decisions of these braying myopic adolescents. Petulance, greed, envy, and stupidity reigned in equal portions around the table. There were more hidden agendas lurking amongst that loud rhetoric than facets on the eyes of a Gandymedean dung fly.

Ferr grew weary of the charade and rose to leave the table. As he collected his small computer notebook, he was noticed by the chairman of the First Galactic Banking Commission. Isaac signaled across the table to Kor-Zem, the prime minister, to draw his attention to the departing general.

"General Ferr, the rest period has not yet been called!" Isaac growled. "Where do you think you are going?" he asked in his most patronizing manner.

"This entire proceeding is an exercise in rhetorical defecation. I have survived hundreds of battlefields and the stench they always result in. But the fragrance of the words bouncing around this room have made me ill," Ferr responded.

"Now *see here,*" Kor-Zem snapped. "You will keep a civil tongue in your head and apologize to the chairman."

"Mr. Prime Minister," Ferr responded stiffly, "I most certainly will *not* apologize to that power-hungry little turd any more than I will tolerate *you* attempting to browbeat me. In *this* Directorate, we *all* have one vote. Your vote carries no more weight than mine, whereas my back carries the entire weight of this cabal. I have *real* work to do right now that will probably permit this gaggle of idiots to live to harangue another day. Once you have decided who sits where and what wine is served at Vespers, call me and I will offer my vote...."

President Jobikan stood up before Ferr reached the door and said to those gathered, "The governor general is right *again,* gentlemen. We have weighty business to resolve, and the Cartel still probes our outer defenses." He turned to look at Ferr, paused at the door, and smiled and waved him off.

Ferr turned and thought to himself as he departed, *Omega's left ball ... does that manikin really think I'm that gullible? Aw, bonk it! This is one general with his own hidden agenda this time....*

As Ferr walked back to the Tactical Operations Control Center, he stopped briefly in the Tactical Intelligence Center. That wing of the station had inherited the name *The Clock* because the two elements filling that wing held the acronyms TIC and TOCC.

Inside, the TIC looked like any other modern situation room: computers; vidscreens, comlinks, the usual hardware. The difference with *this* particular TIC was the scope of the data that flooded in every nanosecond. If waterfalls could carry bytes, it would take seven hundred Niagara Falls to hold the volume that flowed into this TIC. The data was immediately routed to two *filtering* computers that edited data and routed it by means of a complex optimizer to an appropriate disk storage facility. Transient data (like wind speed and direction on Remus-21) was held in a loop for 23.6 hours, and then purged into oblivion (unless it was needed and transferred onto a permanent data storage).

General Ferr was admitted into the TIC by voice print authentication at the entry pocket. The OMEGA 8700 computer responded verbally to the name *Arthur*.

"Hell-o, Arthur. Charles-Henry here."

"Clear. You have been authenticated, General Good day," answered the computer's synthesized voice.

The general entered the small holding closet as he issued his orders and waited for the second door to open.

"Arthur, give me the most recent SITREP (situation report) from Colonel Arkell on the planet Dolfin. Put it up on screen 115 and let me have a window lower right classified CRYPTO-88. Link it to my private disk and program direction to my terminal. Manual override only. Black mask." He sat down at terminal 115.

"Shall I make a transcript of your work, sir?" the computer asked.

"Negative! Total black mask ... 00001/HC." He had ordered absolute privacy. The nearly omniscient computer would provide data as requested but was forbidden to collate, synopsize, repeat, or copy ANY of the data flow during a total *black mask* status. Should anyone attempt to compromise such an invocation, they would be immediately jettisoned into deep space sans the benefit of suit or helmet. If the computer were to attempt to override the order, it had been programmed centuries ago with an indelible directive that would spark a crash and scramble, the results of which no one would be able to unravel for a millennium.

Ferr reviewed the data from Dolfin and smiled. So Arkell had somehow positioned himself as a demon. Not too much of an exaggeration really. However, he didn't like the thought of Arkell standing up to one hundred armed warriors. Not that he feared for Arkell, but that the loss of life on that scale could potentially be more of a negative than necessary. He reviewed the balance of the report and was confident that nothing was happening yet that Arkell and Dar could not handle alone. He did note that there was an Andromeda cruise ship on an azimuth that might intersect Dolfin, but that was days off and of no immediate concern. He turned his attention to the details of his little covert operation code-named Cabaret Dancer.

****

Arkell and Dar were ready and waiting on the Plain of Despair when Lord Dolfin and his contingent of cavalry and pike men arrived. Arkell stood alone on the plain, feet spread and arms folded. Lord Dolfin rode to the front of his company and spoke from about fifty yards away. He stood up in his stirrups and shouted as the sun bounced rays of distorted light up through the clouds of dust the approaching army created.

"Ho, demon, my magician says you would do battle with one hundred of my finest!"

"I would parley with Lord Dolfin," Arkell responded, "if the price of that parley be the lives of his warriors, I am prepared to pay that price."

"You interest me, demon. I would enjoy killing you myself, but first, I must judge you worthy of my sword."

"I have no desire to kill you, lord, but I do hold the means and the ability." Arkell had not moved since the beginning of the exchange.

"Talk is empty!" Dolfin shouted. "Here in my realm, men and demons are judged by deeds!"

Arkell uncrossed his arms and spread them wide. On that signal, Dar depressed a detonator and a small explosion erupted in a curtain of flame and dust around Arkell, where strands of discord had been buried in a circle around him. Dolfin was startled and his cavalry balked and fought to hold their mounts in check.

"Then let me be judged by my deeds!" Arkell shouted. "If blood is the currency for buying an audience, send your sacrifice!"

Dolfin smiled and rose back up in his stirrups. He scanned the horizon and then sat back down. He looked at the apprehension on the faces of his soldiers and spoke to Arkell.

"It is said that you are the Two-That-Are-One, yet I see only one. Where is your beast half, demon?"

Arkell grinned and answered, "He is in me and with me. If you wish to see him before I battle, you must pay."

Incensed, Dolfin shook and shouted, "I am lord on this world! I pay not for what is my privilege!"

"The privilege of seeing my other half is not yours but mine to give." Arkell paused and then said, "Hold back fifty of your men from their death, and I will reveal my other half."

Dolfin laughed and rocked in his saddle. "Fifty of my men can kill you as quickly as one hundred." He paused and smiled. "I agree … you shall face only fifty. Now, show me your beast."

Arkell folded his arms again and Dar detonated a smaller semicircle of explosives in front of the rocks he was hidden behind. When the fire and dust settled, he stood on his hind feet with his arms extended and claws exposed.

I trust I look sufficiently horrible, Ark. Dar chuckled.

There was again a shying of mounts and grumbles from the soldiers. Even Dolfin was taken aback by the sight of Dar emerging from the cloud of dust.

"What is that, demon?" asked a shaken Dolfin.

"That is the essence of me. Enough show and tell," Arkell scoffed. "Send me your sacrifice that we might get it over and talk." He paused and smiled. "Fear not my beast; he will not interfere in my sport."

Beast am I? You with the morals of a mink dare besmirch me so? You will pay for your little entertainment, you hairless gibbon.

Dolfin turned to his soldiers and pointed his lance to Captain Pel of the clan T'sui.

"Pel, bring me his head!" shouted Dolfin.

Captain Pel charged with twenty men; thirty others split into flankers of fifteen each. Pel charged head on toward Arkell as Dar sat in the sand taking a small detonator from his harness. Pel paced his charge so that the flankers were to Arkell's left and right. At the moment Dar depressed the detonator, Pel and twenty were twelve o'clock in front of Arkell. The flankers were at three o'clock and nine o'clock respectively. The three charges exploded simultaneously. Arkell drew his laser and killed the entire squad to his right before the dust had settled. He killed half of Pel's rear element and nine of those to his left. There were eighteen men still alive and mounted when the dust had settled. Men fought to control their mounts as Arkell holstered his laser. He drew his long sword in his right hand and his Randall in his left. Pel was stunned but did not yet know his casualties. He lowered his lance and charged Arkell as Lord Dolfin stood in his stirrups to see well.

Arkell parried the lance with is forearm and cut off Pel's right arm at the shoulder with his long sword. He danced behind Pel's mount and cut the legs out from under the mount of the second man, decapitating him as he fell to the ground. The dance of death he weaved through the confusion, and dust was almost too swift to follow, but he slowed it down enough intentionally so that Dolfin could witness what was happening. Dar sat on his haunches and licked his paws as he watched.

Within thirty seconds, all the attackers—except the leader, Pel—were dead. Arkell walked over to the fallen Pel and cauterized his wound with his laser to stop him from bleeding to death.

Arkell then looked up at the ashen Lord Dolfin and announced, "I would have a tankard of ale, and then we talk."

Dolfin fought to regain his composure. Hubris aside, he realized that this demon could easily have killed him. It was a realization he had never had before. He suffered a moment's concern before he steadied himself and relaxed in the realization that this warrior/demon WANTED something of him and sought him as an ally. With an ally such as this, he could crush the rebels in the north and not even have to break a sweat or lose another man. Yes, the price of this parlay was cheap.

"Tork, bring ale and a rug!" Dolfin shouted. "The demon Arkell and your lord will drink and talk together."

As the rug was laid on the plain and ale brought, Arkell brushed dust from his tunic.

Well done, love, although you were pitifully slow, Dar chided.

"Exertion should not exceed the need, furball," Arkell responded.

And what if that pompous tattooed lord had charged you with the remaining hundred fifty soldiers?

"Then I would have had to move faster, and you would have gotten off your flea infested duff."

The day you can't handle a couple of hundred of this sort, I'll divorce you and bond with a dung beetle.

The rug was laid. A small tent was erected around it and the sides rolled up.

"Come and drink with me," Dolfin ordered. "I think we can help each other, demon," Dolfin spoke as he dismounted and headed for the tent.

****

Meanwhile, several hundred miles away, Lacracken and a company of mountain rebels attacked. They raided the granary and took all they could carry. What they could not carry they put to the torch, along with the fields. When the fields were charred, the rebels rode through and spilled black rock salt juice bespoiling the land. Then they impaled Lord Dolfin's steward on lances and rode off into the hills.

****

Vanjar sat on a fur rug in his room and, in a trance, communicated with the spirit of his long-dead grandmother.

"Grandmother, how goes it on the Plain of Despair?" he asked.

Your lord now parlays with Arkell.

"The demon survived?" he asked astonished.

He is no demon, but a remarkable superior man. And yes, he lives, replied the spirit voice. *Forty-nine of clan T'sui do not. Captain Pel shall henceforth be one-arm weaker.*

"Is this Arkell friend or foe, Grandmother?" Vanjar asked nervously.

Yessss.

"*Please,* reverend one, do not talk to me in riddles this day. I *need* answers," he pleaded.

We all seek answers, little one. Arkell is both friend and foe. He will help and he will destroy. But he is not your immediate concern, although concern he should be.

"What mean you reverend, Grandmother?"

As Arkell speaks with Dolfin, Lacracken and a company of his mountain rebels have emptied your granaries in the northwest. They have stolen or burned all the winter grain and poisoned the fields of Asha.

"Ahhh … what shall I do, Grandmother?"

What must be done is, the spirit answered, *you can do no more and must not do any less.*

"And what is that?" he asked in desperation.

Calm yourself, little one, and I will tell you. But you must *do as I tell you, or you are destined to join me in the dark abyss.*

****

Chapter Six

General Ferr had just completed his campaign plan and was reviewing his secondary contingencies when the communicator on his wrist beeped twice. He touched the "receive" button and acknowledged the call.

"General Ferr," he replied.

"General, the Directorate is about to vote on an issue, and they request your presence soonest," said the message center.

"Tell them I will be there in ten minutes. Ferr out." He hit the "off" button on the communicator as he returned to his computer work.

Ten minutes to put the wheels in motion to prevent those greedily vain idiots who controlled things from creating galactic disaster.

He punched a series of commands into the computer and ended with a voice authenticated command.

"Ferr, General Charles-Henry acknowledges. Execute Operation Cabaret Dancer. Classified: Most Top Secret. Execute, execute, execute … O.R. CHF-2679-4987-T.P./008 … OUT." *Well, that does it, Chucky.* He smiled to himself. *The scramble order should reach you just about the time those assholes get ready to call their foolish vote. Omega's left ball! At least you won't be around to see the end of it.*

Those were his thoughts as he picked up his small computer pad and left the TIC.

Eight minutes later, he walked into the big paneled conference room to the same din he had left over two hours before.

"Well, it's about time you got here," snapped Kor-Zem.

Ferr ignored the prime minister and took his seat.

"Now that the good governor general is finally here, can we vote?" asked the chairman of the First Galactic Banking Commission. "Scribe, read the motion in full."

The thin pasty scribe stood up and picked his handheld computer screen and punched in the file on the motion before the Directorate. However, before he could start reading, klaxons started to go off and red lights started blinking. A computer synthesized voice announced over the loud speakers, "Alert … alert … alert … scramble … This is

41

not a drill … scramble … scramble … scramble … Battle stations all. Combat conditions … combat conditions … combat conditions … All personnel report to battle stations. We say again … this is **not** a drill."

An explosion shook the room and the lights blinked off and on twice. Everyone in the room was suddenly less pompous and confident, except for General Ferr, who rose and spoke to the room.

"Gentlemen, will you excuse me? I am needed elsewhere. Please report to your assigned positions and await further orders. This meeting is adjourned by *my* order, and this station is now under martial law."

The members of the Directorate exchanged curious glances. The president seemed thoroughly frightened. Prime Minister Kor-Zem was angry and confused. The Archbishop made the sign of the cross, and the rest quickly made for the exits.

General Ferr marched from the room, holding back his private grin until he had cleared the door.

"Here we go," he whispered to himself.

Arkell sat on the rug in Dolfin's tent and drank deeply from his third tankard of ale. Dar sat on his haunches next to him like a pagan temple icon with his senses alert and his eyes constantly panning those about them. He communicated a telepathic monologue to Arkell as Lord Dolfin spoke.

"We have little contact with off-worlders here in my realm," Dolfin began as he drank from his mug. "About two years back, a strange sky wagon deposited four large bug-like creatures. They talked to our minds without words, sending their confused thoughts into us. They also sought to bargain for the resources of our land. I had them impaled and left in the sun to dry. I will show you their dried bodies. I keep them in my trophy room. Lord Dolfin does not traffic with insects or other vermin." Dolfin delivered his speech while cracking nuts in his hand and picking out the meat with his thick fingers.

Arkell realized that those *insects* had probably been sent to recon strengths and weaknesses and not really to negotiate for any rights. Their arrogance and overconfidence in dealing with *inferior* races had resulted in such losses before. It was of constant amazement to Arkell that despite their wealth and communal intelligence, they apparently lacked the ability to learn from past mistakes. Such were the primary race from the Andromeda Cartel. It was one very real strength (their chronic weakness) they yielded to the Federation.

"The Federation I represent, Lord Dolfin, is comprised of *men*, not insects. Thousands of worlds with more men in total than you have grains of sand on this world," Arkell said.

This tattooed barbarian is not to be trusted, Ark, Dar inserted.

"Demon, I think you exaggerate in an attempt to impress us." Dolfin smiled.

"I do not exaggerate, sir, any more than I make boasts I cannot meet," he said as he gestured with his hand to the bodies being loaded outside. "I am but a simple soldier sent by a far more powerful Federation. My superiors seek resources of your world that you not only do not use but have not realized exist. In return for the rights to mine for those resources, we offer the friendship and support of resources far greater than we ask." Arkell filled a fourth tankard and grabbed a handful of nuts, which he crushed in his hand.

"I won't say no to your request." Dolfin grinned. "Yet I choose not to yet agree. You and your beast shall accompany me to my capital, and we shall feast on the bodies of those you have slain this day. The song master will sing of your battle kills, and we will have women and a nights rest on which to think," Dolfin said as he cast a curious glance at Dar. "Do demons such as you couple with human females?" he asked Arkell.

Lock up your mothers' and your daughters' man who would be king ... and any other sacred holes. Arkell, the mink is randy always. Given leave, he would knock up your entire female population and dramatically improve your gene pool.

Arkell cast a reproachful glance at Dar and answered Dolfin, "Yes, sire. My body is that of a man, and I *do* occasionally indulge in the pleasures of the flesh."

Ha! And you do also occasionally *indulge in breathing,* scoffed Dar.

"What of your beast half? Shall I bring in a *lion* or a *bear* for it to copulate with?" Dolfin asked, thinking that it might be a show worth watching.

He treads dangerously close to the cliff, Ark. Perhaps I shall bugger him.

"His short staff, although it be mighty, is used best for putting out fires and showering politicians and priests." Arkell smiled.

Hey, I like that. Maybe you and the general will let me give the Directorate a golden shower?

"Then let us be off. It is a long ride to the capital," Dolfin said as he rose. "Shall I fetch you mounts?"

Arkell again glanced at Dar with reproach. "No thank you, lord. We will meet you there. How long a ride is it?"

"Thirty miles to the gates. We should be there in eight hours. I will leave orders at the gate to admit you when you arrive." Dolfin smiled.

"We will meet you there in eight hours. Leave us here in this tent. We would meditate on how best to reward you when you choose to grant us our boon." Arkell smiled.

Another long run? May I at least set the pace this time? We can do it in much less than half that time.

Dolfin and his aides rose up as did Arkell. Dar remained in his gargoyle pose and watched the departing host.

I smell treachery in that man's blood, Ark. Trust him not were he to give you ten thousand ten thousand virgins.

"I sense the same treachery you do, dear one. But we will play out his game. I'll get the general his treaty with mining rights if I have to have it written in Dolfin's blood on a parchment made of his hide." Arkell smiled.

I love it when you talk like that. It belies your human frailties, Dar responded as he nuzzled Arkell's leg with his broad snout.

"But I *will* rut with his wenches first."

Of that I have no doubt. You would reject food and water, fire and shelter ... but never in our decade of being bonded have I ever known you to reject the opportunity to stab a young (or old for that matter) lovely with your bludgeon.

"Dar, how can one so dear to me so cruel?" Arkell feigned hurt.

I had best rest to prepare for the sensations you are about to force upon me. Wake me in an hour.

Dar curled about himself and quickly was snoring deeply. Arkell reached in his pack and extracted his communicator. The red light was blinking, indicating a message was waiting. He turned it on and acknowledged the call and waited for relays to result in a response. After about thirty seconds, a voice came on. It was General Ferr.

"Griffin One to the Two. Cabaret Dancer executed. Martial law in effect. Directorate adjourned. You have five days. Rendezvous at Proton-Uranus-14. The Two have been designated my second in chain of command. Luck and speed. Note: Be advised. Enemy cruise ship on course to your location. ETA 36 hours. Report status in 24. Acknowledge receipt. Ferr out."

Arkell keyed the communicator and responded, "Two to Griffin One. Acknowledged last. Best wishes. Two out." He put the communicator back in his pack and walked out of the tent to watch the dust of Dolfin's party move toward the horizon. So the old fox had played his finesse and executed Cabaret Dancer. The political arena must indeed be heating up. Well, he has blunted their fangs for a while. After the twenty-four-hour isolation required by the alert, the Directorate would have to be briefed on status. They would shit green apples after learning that he and Dar had been named Ferr's second. They had always been cautious of that old fox, but they were openly frightened of Arkell and Dar. At least he had slowed any plans they may have had for killing the governor and general and replacing him with a lackey. Martial law gave that right to the commander in chief, and for now at least that *was* Ferr. If they tried to poison the old fox, they would be stuck with the Two-That-Are-One as official boss. And they would sooner pray for a supernova enema than that.

****

Arkell and Dar were in a large room with ceilings twice the height of Dar. It was located on the top floor of what apparently was a main building. It contained a large bed, several chairs, a bar-like area for taking refreshment, and a personal hygiene alcove of ancient design. They noted and confirmed that there were four guards at the door. The balcony looked over the merchant sector of the city, which resembled a Kalan Bazaar, except for the excess of women and lack of men. There was another building about ten paces across a dirt street that was one story lower than the building they were in.

"Are you hungry Dar?" Arkell asked.

You need ask? The beast grinned. *I am* always *hungry.*

"I'll ask one of the guards to bring us some raw meat. In the meantime, I will take some of that sweet nuts and fruits. I suppose if you can't wait, you could always eat one or two of the guards."

I may be a beast *to these barbarians, but I am a gourmet beast. I will eat none of their sour man flesh.*

"While I dally with Lord Dolfin's concubines, we need for you to leave this building and recon the area and find at least two exit routes."

That will be easy. While you are plowing the fields of our host's harem, see if you can detect the presence of our astral visitors; that incident is of interest to me.

"And to me. I will do what I can do," Arkell responded. "You just be careful to hide that big furry ass of yours. I have total confidence in our stealth and concealment abilities in the boonies, but you *are* a tad conspicuous in a city."

I will attempt to keep my movements covert and nocturnal. The sooner we are out of this walled city, the better. Ho! I sense someone approaches. He sniffed the air and grinned his strange grin. *It is a woman. I'll just disappear for a while.*

Dar turned and made two leaps. The first landed him on the balcony. The second propelled him across the gap of the street and down onto the roof of the building across the way.

The door opened and in walked Petal, followed by two armed guards. She stood for a moment and just stared at Arkell. He was bigger than she remembered. He stood almost two feet taller than she. His muscles were sharply cut like a chiseled statue. His eyes shone like blue fire, and his short yellow hair was something she had never before seen on man or woman. She turned to the guards and dismissed them.

"I am Petal, concubine to Magician Vanjar. I have been ordered by my master and our lord Dolfin to see to your needs."

Arkell looked at the short woman. Hardly more than a girl despite the bud of her breasts and swell of her hips. He focused on her and *sensed* her essence. Then after a moment he smiled. His smile disturbed Petal greatly.

"I have selected four of the finest and most skilled of Lord Dolfin's harem to service you," she said without looking at him. Her eyes were focused on a patch of floor just in front of his large booted feet. "If you wish, they will see to your bath and tend your needs."

"Petal"—Arkell smiled—"am I permitted to taste the bliss of *your* flesh, or are you reserved for magicians?"

She was momentarily taken aback and her pulse quickened. Although her plan was to try to bed him eventually herself, she anticipated a less direct seduction.

"You may have *any* woman you so choose, lord. I was told you had a beast half with you. Where is he? I'd like to see him if I may," she said as she looked around the room.

"He is with me always—if not in body, always in *spirit*." Arkell grinned.

"I don't see him anywhere," she responded, trying to cover her discomfiture. "How can you hide such a large part of yourself?"

"We all hide large parts of ourselves despite our stature … on this plane as on others." He looked hard at her round eyes and saw a glint of fear mingled with confusion.

"I know not of what you speak, sire. I am but a simple girl trained to give sexual service to those more powerful than I." Her hand moved to her shoulder and she loosed the clasp that held her robe. It fell to the floor leaving her naked.

"You are a most comely lass, Petal. Take me into your loins and show me how you have been trained." Arkell grinned as he moved toward her.

She made very slow and deliberate love to Arkell. They worked their way from the pillows on the floor to the furs by the fire, and eventually to the bed. She was indeed skilled (as was Arkell). He tasted five ecstasies; she many more. When they finally rested beneath the single sheet of the large bed, they were both covered in a thin coat of sweat. She was coiled against his hard left side with her leg over his. Her tongue danced lazy circles on his shoulder; her fingers traced flowered patterns on the scars that crisscrossed his large frame.

"Arkell," she whispered, "you are the most extraordinary man I have ever touched, or ever been touched by. You have driven me to heights never before even dreamed of."

"And you are indeed a most skilled courtesan ... and obviously skilled also in both dreams and great heights." He grinned. "Yet you hide your other skills so well."

"What do you mean?" she started. To cover her nervousness, she started to snake down his body, covering his chest and then his rippled stomach with soft kisses and twirling licks. She grasped his sex in both her tiny hands and prepared for an intimate kiss when he spoke.

"Do *they* know you ride the astral plane in search of information?" he asked. "Or that you have a companion?"

She stopped her sexual play and popped up to her knees, sitting on her heels. Fear raced to her heart and terrified her.

"You *know*!" she exclaimed. "*How?* When you and the beast looked at us, I *thought* it an accident ... but your gaze was so direct."

"Yes, I know," he responded. "I knew when I felt your presence on the Plane, and I knew when you walked in that door. Yet I now feel that this secret may *not* be known to others in this building." He paused and stared at her face. "Am I right?"

Petal buried her head in her hands and started to weep. She feared only two things in the entire world: one was loss of control, and the other was that she might someday be overwhelmed by a man. Now she found herself in a position that presented both fears in one extraordinary man. She was most fearful.

"Oh, my lord Arkell, Two-That-Are-One, I am in your power. *Please* do not tell my master Vanjar or Lord Dolfin of my secret. They will use me even more sorely than they already do ... and beat me for not revealing my secret knowledge. I shall be impaled. *Please* do not tell"—she wept heavily—"or I shall have to kill myself." She threw her body on his and wept hot tears, which mixed with the sweat already on his massive chest.

Arkell put his arms gently around her and smoothed her hair with one hand.

"Calm yourself, my little Petal. No one will ever learn of your wanderings from me. But we have things to talk about, and I believe that you are more than just some small, albeit skilled, pleasure slave."

She looked up into Arkell's stern, calm face—the face of the fearsome warrior that was hard yet strangely gentle at this moment. What did he want?

"Y-y-you m-mean it?" she stammered. "You won't tell? Why?"

"I will tell you my reasons, and you will believe them." He turned his face to look directly into her round clear eyes. "I trust no living creature save my other half, Dar. I believe half of what I see and less of what I hear. I have survived this long because of that, not because of any physical strength or warrior skills. Your lord Dolfin means me harm. I am a threat to him like he has never seen before. He rules because no one has yet been able to challenge him in battle. He knows I can easily defeat him, and that frightens him. It may well be a new feeling he has yet to come to grasps with. But he means me no good. He will search a way to postpone granting my requests until he feels he has discovered a way to control or kill me."

"But you just said he could not kill you," she said.

"True. But he has not yet come fully to that realization. He will no doubt offer me great challenges in the hope that I will die in the failing. Your master Vanjar is a tool for him, like a shovel or a spear. He will do what he can to aid his lord, for despite his magic, he too fears Dolfin."

"*All* fear Lord Dolfin," Petal sighed.

"Almost all. I don't fear him any more than I trust him. You fear him only slightly, and your astral traveling companion does not fear him at all, though he would be wiser if he did." Arkell sat up in bed and poured them each a glass of wine.

"What do you want of me for your silence?" Petal asked.

"Ah, beauty, skill, *and* intelligence." Arkell smiled and patted her head. "You are a rarer flower than even you know, Petal. First, I want information, then perhaps some small assistance. Later, an encore of your performance on the sheets."

Petal smiled and bowed her head once. A slight blush came to her pale cheeks. Her fear was swiftly melting into hope. Oh, if only he could really help.

"Ask and I shall answer. Order and I shall obey. Smile at me and I shall strive to wear your staff into a nub." She smiled.

"How quickly you recover from your terror. That is good. It is a skill you may need often methinks. First, information. Three basic questions to start, love: How long have you known how to travel the astral plane; who is your companion; and what have you learned that can help me?"

"The first two questions are simple, although they are secrets most dear and private. I learned how to go into a Doutrin trance and travel in my astral body before puberty. My mother taught me as her mother had taught her. She was *wonderful*. She could travel not only this world but also strange distant worlds. She could also travel into the past with ease, and sometimes even into the future, although her future travels were less accurate. She instructed my older brother and me until Lord Dolfin came and destroyed our village. He killed all the men and old women and took all the girls and handsome women into his city." She paused and sighed deeply. "He found my mother lying in her bed and at first thought her asleep. Though she had seen almost forty winters, my mother was a handsome and shapely woman with long black hair gently streaked in gray and large firm breasts. Dolfin raped her still body, both front and back. And after he spilled his seed in her, he was angered at her lack of response. H-h-he, he then chopped off her head and hacked her body to pieces. He did all that while two of his men held me and made me watch.

"So he killed your mother and your brother?" Arkell asked.

"No ... not really. He destroyed my mother's earthen vessel, but she had escaped in a Doutrin trance onto the astral plane. My brother and several others were on a hunting party when the raid came to our village. He survived and he has sworn a blood oath to rid our world of Dolfin." She paused and looked hard at Arkell. "It was he you sensed me with on the Plane."

"Your mother is trapped in limbo?"

"Yes … somewhere. But we have been unable to contact her. Perhaps she has flown to one of her strange distant worlds."

"I know of cases in which souls were thus trapped. Perhaps in time, I can find her for you. Where is your brother now?"

Petal paused for a moment and then answered, "He commands a group of rebels in the northern mountains. While you fought the fifty on the Plane this morning, he and his men raided Lord Dolfin's granaries and despoiled his fields. Lord Dolfin will be livid when he learns of it."

"How many men does he have?" Arkell asked.

Petal looked at Arkell with a sudden concern and suspicion.

"Petal, I intend to help you *and* your brother. You are the only two potential allies I have found on this cruel planet. But I need to know what we have to work with."

"He has over a hundred men in his camp. Perhaps another hundred spread out between two other camps."

"That's not very much to do battle with all of Dolfin's armies. Still, it is a start. What is he called, your brother?"

"His name is Lacracken. Lord Dolfin calls him 'the mountain louse.' What will you do, sire?"

"Soon, I will feast with Dolfin. Then (to keep up appearances, you understand) I will sample his harem. Then before I do whatever impossible task Lord Dolfin puts to me, you and I will visit your brother."

"But how?"

"From a Doutrin trance to the astral plane." Arkell smiled.

"Can *you* do that?"

"Child, I was skilled to the third level before you were a bud in your mother's womb. Later, I will not only try to find your mother, but I will teach you how to search for her yourself. But first, you must meet Dar."

"Where is he?" she asked.

Dar landed on the balcony, bounded into the room, and sat at the foot of the bed looking at the pair of recent lovers.

"Oh!" exclaimed Petal. She stared at Dar and clung to Arkell's chest like ivy to a wall. "Is he dangerous?"

"Of course ... *very*." Arkell extended his arm and made the introductions. "Dar, meet Lady Petal, our new ally. Petal, this is Dar."

So, this is the cause of my spilling semen like an overwatered race horse. Tell her it indeed has been a pleasure.

"He says to tell you it is a pleasure."

"He speaks to you?"

"In a fashion. We are what is called telepathic. It means he hears my thoughts and I hear his."

"*All* your thoughts?" she asked.

Tell her that after ten years, I have finally ceased to be shocked.

"He says to tell you that after ten years, he has finally ceased to be shocked."

They all three laughed loudly until Dar interrupted them and sniffed the air. *People approach.*

"Dar, guard the door. Petal, put on your gown and join me at the table for wine," Arkell said.

The door was thrust open by a captain of the guard. He stopped abruptly as he confronted the standing sight of Dar, who roared with his head thrown back. The guards all retreated with arms tentatively at the ready, prepared to die. Arkell and Petal were sitting at the table drinking wine as Arkell waved his arm toward Dar and said, "Do not kill any of them Dar. I believe they may be our escort to the feast."

The captain regained some of his official composure and diffidently announced, "Lord Dolfin the Conqueror commands your attendance at court to honor the men you have killed."

Arkell sipped his wine casually and responded, "Tell your lord I will piss first. Then I will permit this young courtesan to escort us to the feast. You are not needed."

"But I am *ordered* to take you there *now*," complained the captain, suddenly very unsure of himself.

"Soldier, I am bored with killing today. You have watched me dispatch fifty of your so-called finest this morning before breakfast. If I am required to kill you and your squad before I am permitted to have my dinner, I will do so with considerable annoyance." He paused and sipped more wine. Dar looked up and curled his lips over his fangs in a low, muted growl. "Do you prefer to die now or deliver my message to

Dolfin?" Arkell delivered this entire little speech casually sipping wine. Dar sat next to the door licking his paws and grooming his muzzle, occasionally sending a low growl in the direction of the captain.

Rage and confusion mingled with fear to fight a brief battle inside the captain of the guard. Instinct told him to attack this arrogant speaker of those words. Common sense and a deeper sense of foreboding guided him to bow and withdraw backwards out of the room. After he had left and closed the doors behind him, Petal put down her glass and said, "You should not have done that, Arkell.

"Petal, Dolfin and I are playing a little game right now. He strives to gain face with his subordinates by commanding me. I instruct him that I may not be commanded by him. It is a foolish little game, but one which we will play. The captain will no doubt be made to suffer some, and my first task will increase in difficulty. But the end is already determined."

"And what is that, sire?" Petal asked.

"Dolfin has no intention of ever giving me what I need of him. Therefore, I will kill him." He paused and smiled directly into her eyes. "That I also believe is what you have planned for me since you first saw me on the Plane."

Petal bowed her head and blushed.

You can be a cruel bastard sometimes, Ark.

"A quality I seem to have acquired sometime since our bonding, Dar," Arkell responded.

Wipe the dew from your stem then and let's go fart at bird head's banquet.

"Petal, you and I shall retire to the alcove to wash before attending the feast. Dar, my friend, will amuse himself by licking his balls and eating his fleas as an appetizer."

Chapter Seven

General Slar stood at an awkward position of attention in front of the desk of his commander in chief, General Ferr. The two men represented the classic dichotomy.

Ferr was a battle-hardened leader of troops, scarred physically in combat to the point that some called him a freak. He had won virtually every medal the Federation awarded. He was skilled, experienced, and widely respected and feared.

Slar, on the other hand, was what the military derisively called a *chair-borne* officer. All his service had been in staff positions, where he commanded paper and vidscreen data. Ferr was a leader. Slar was a collator. Slar was a handsome man some fifteen years younger than Ferr. He stood an even six feet tall. He had prematurely grayed at a young age, so that his white hair seemed a natural part of him. He had clear blue eyes and an olive complexion. His only commendations had been for *meritorious service* and assorted *longevity* awards. He was much more the politician than the soldier. He was also aware of the details of Kor-Zem's plans to have him replace General Ferr in some politically inspired coup. His repressed insecurities were flooding into the forefront now that he realized fully that he could never possibly replace the man opposite him in any real crisis. And this now apparently was a *real* crisis. He had seen the orders for a task force to attack the advancing aggressor forces.

Naturally, he assumed Ferr would lead that force and crush the attackers. He wondered what role his would play in the developing game. He was quietly thankful that Colonel Arkell and his other half were off on some mission far away. He fully realized that if Arkell and Dar had been available, he would be outmatched three millionfold instead of only a millionfold.

His one hope was for Ferr to choose to lead the battle group himself and leave Slar to command the TOCC. Once Charles-Henry Ferr was off habitat, he would then have the power and authority, as well as the opportunity, to do what Kor-Zem wanted him to do. What was it behind that half-human face of Ferr's that could give him some hint of an opportunity to be exploited?

"General Slar reporting as ordered, sir," he said as he snapped a crisp sharp salute and waited for Ferr to return it.

"At ease, General." Ferr returned the salute casually. "Be seated." Ferr turned his attention to the computer vidscreen on his desk and ignored Slar for several awkward moments. "General, as you know, I have organized a task force to establish an interdiction of the aggressor battle group."

"Yes, sir," Slar responded. *Stay calm, Slar, patience will be rewarded. Speak when spoken to and offer no advice to this man.*

"We have yet to develop a detailed estimate of the situation. Although we suspect the Andromeda Cartel, it is possible that this attack was launched from outside the galaxy. Or even by a consortium of pirates from the asteroid belt off Sirius." Ferr made a random entry in his computer and returned his attention to Slar. "We have two primary missions until we can develop more intelligence: one, we need to contain the probes, and two, we need to take some prisoners." Ferr turned off his vidscreen and now looked up at the apprehensive face of General Slar.

"I assume *you* will take command of the task force, General Ferr," Slar asked.

"No. I will remain here and command the TOCC," Ferr said. It obviously startled Slar, who struggled to remain clam. Ferr continued, "I would have sent Arkell to lead the interdiction, but he is otherwise detained on urgent Directorate business and unavailable for recall. Therefore, I am using this unfortunate set of circumstances to do you a great professional favor, Slar." Ferr looked directly into the blue eyes of his would-be successor and smiled a thin half smile that ended in a sea of scar tissue. "I am giving command of the task force to *you.*"

Slar felt a heavy weight land in the pit of his stomach. Sweat started to roll down the small of his back and his hands turned clammy. A thin veil of beaded sweat erupted on his bare upper lip.

"Me!" he squeaked. "General, with all due respect, although I genuinely appreciate the opportunity, there *must* be better qualified men to assume command of the task force." As soon as he said it, he realized how bad it sounded.

"Indeed there are," Ferr agreed almost too quickly. "Thousands in fact. But none with your rank or conspicuous lack of combat command experience. You have advanced very rapidly, General. You are a skilled politician and administrator. You are a superb briefing officer, but through no fault of your own, you have never had the chance to command troops in combat." Ferr paused and looked hard at his subordinate. "I now offer you that gift." Ferr kept a steady gaze on the now obviously disturbed face of Slar.

"I am flattered with our confidence in me, General. This is a great honor, but *so* much is at risk. Would it not be better to send an officer with greater combat experience than I?"

"Perhaps. We both know fully well that *any* officer over the rank of colonel has more combat experience than *you*," Ferr responded with a casual wave of his hand. "However, I have made my decision. *You* will command the task force." And that was that.

"What if I fail, General?" Slar asked.

"I do not expect this mission to fail, General. Otherwise, I would not send you. If you do fail … you will die and take to your death the responsibility of the lives that will share your fate. I have every confidence in your ability to rise to the challenge and perform as I expect you will." He paused and leaned slightly forward. "If you ever expect to sit in *this* chair, General, you will have to experience the adrenaline rush of combat and the responsibilities for lives and hardware. Here is your Warning Order"—he handed Slar a small computer disk—"you have one hour to brief your subordinate commanders before takeoff. Success to you, General. Medals and honors await your safe return." Ferr turned back to his computer and proceeded to ignore Slar. Almost as an afterthought but with terminal finality, he added, "Dismissed."

Slar stood numbly to his feet and saluted, this time with considerably less crispness. Then he turned on his heel and only stumbled once as he walked out of the office like a sleepwalker walking into a bad dream. *Combat? Me?* His mind rattled off statistics he had watched on vidscreens over the years. Average defensive interdiction casualties: 32 percent; average command casualties: 22 percent; average fatalities: 19 percent. Federation Battle Doctrine dictated that the Task Force Command Post be located along the forward edge of the battle area, with an alternate CP to be established with the reserve in the rear. He could probably arrange to visit the alternate CP just prior to the estimated time of interdiction, but that would be too transparent. He would be censured, certainly reprimanded, probably disgraced—no, he would have to see this through. However, he would do everything he could to stack the deck in his favor. He would select a handpicked staff of the very best combat veterans available, senior NCOs with Stoellean experience, and a dedicated Nova class scout vehicle in case he needed to escape into hyperspace.

****

Command Sergeant Major Burn was the most senior NCO in the quadrant. He had been pleasantly surprised when General Charles-Henry Ferr had ordered him off Training Command to join him for what he was told was a top secret "special assignment." Burn was an old soldier heavily decorated and scarred by over thirty years of service. The last time the general had summoned him for such an assignment, he found himself providing fire support for the *Odd Couple*. Unlike many, he rather liked the Two-That-Are-One. Colonel Arkell was tactically and technically proficient and physically extraordinary. Dar was to many a terrifying beast. Burn rather liked the hairy monster. He reminded Burn of a pet Rottweiler clone he had had as a child—ferocious, loveable, and totally loyal to just one master.

As he came to the door at the end of the corridor labeled General Ferr, he pushed the com box on the wall and announced himself.

"Command Sergeant Major Burn, Lee X, reporting, sir." He did a final quick check of his uniform by habit, already knowing that every pin, decoration, and seam was exactly where regulation prescribed.

"Enter," said the familiar voice of General Ferr.

Burn marched up to the desk, snapped a perfect sharp salute, and barked the old Earth Marine motto: "Semper fi, sir!"

Ferr stood up to return the salute (an added courtesy he did not extend to General Slar) and replied: "Veritas!"

"Have a seat, Sergeant Major," he said as he walked out from behind his desk and pulled up a companion chair to sit next to Burn.

"It's been too long, Lee," Ferr began. "But mere time and parsecs cannot take away what we old war horses have shared. How about a cigar?" he asked as he reached into an old antique oak humidor and took out two long dark panatelas. "Direct from Honduras, Earth Prime, by way of a Xighian smuggler and a Tariff Control Officer on Jupiter."

"A great honor, sir," Burn replied as he accepted the stogie. "It has been over a decade since I tasted an actual Earth weed. Such a decadent gift must mean I am about to do something truly terrible for someone." He bit the end of the cigar and put the end between his lip and gum. Then he lighted the cigar with an ancient pocket Zippo.

"Where in the nebula did you ever get that archeological relic?" Ferr asked.

"A gift from Colonel Arkell, sir." He snapped it open and set the flame under his cigar as he puffed it to life. "The colonel *acquired* it from some museum on Stoellus. Dar gave me a gift too—fleas."

"I wish they were available right now, but since they are not, I turn to you, old friend." Ferr leaned back in his chair and exhaled smoke.

"I consider it no small flattery, sir, to be listed as second best to the *Odd Couple*, sir."

"You had better not let them hear you call them that, or you'll get more than fleas from Dar." The general smiled.

"General, I am crazy, dangerous, and mean, but with all due respect, sir, I ain't bonking stupid." He set the cigar in the side of his mouth held firmly in his teeth. "So, what's the drill, sir? For the cigar alone, I figure you want me to blow up an entire world, or kill someone or many someone's of some import." He flicked an ash into his cupped hand and held it.

"Sergeant Major, we've gone through a lot together, you and me. I count you among the very, very few men in the galaxy I can really trust ..."

Burn held up the hand that wasn't serving as an ashtray to halt the speech. "General, forgive me for interrupting. Between you and I, certain words need not be spoken. We have taken turns saving each other's hides for over twenty years. You just tell me who or what, where and when, and the only question I have to ask you is 'what else,' sir? If you were to ask me to cut off my right hand, I would do it with your antique brass letter opener and thank you for the privilege to serve."

Ferr felt a flush of pride rush through his battered body. Gods, where have all the men like Burn gone? It was true that they had literally saved each other's lives countless times in many different battles on many different worlds. Burn had been offered battlefield commissions on four separate occasions. He refused each one, claiming he could be better used on a field than on a chair in front of some boring vidscreen. There were times when Ferr envied him that luxury of choice. What would become of the Federation after the Charles-Henry Ferrs and Lee X. Burns were gone? Arkell could be a temporary saving grace, but he was an anomaly, and despite all else, grossly outnumbered. *At ease Chuck, this is not the time for introspection. You have already loaded the laser. Now point it and pull the bonking trigger.*

"Okay, Lee, here's the drill. You and I are the only two in the entire Federation who know this plan. Colonel Arkell will be briefed before he needs to be added to the scenario."

General Ferr went on to detail his plan to Burn as they both smoked their cigars. Burn sat erect and blank faced as he listened. The only break in his demeanor was the occasional flick of an ash into his upturned cupped hand. After about twenty minutes and a handful of ash, General Ferr concluded with his standard closing line.

"What are your questions, Sergeant Major?"

"Just one, General," Burn replied.

"Yes, Sergeant Major?" Ferr asked.

"Would the general please be so kind as to tell me what the bonk I can do with these ashes?" He asked with a calm blank face.

"Drop them on the floor, Lee," Ferr smiled.

And Burn did.

Chapter Eight

Petal was supine on her furs and entering her trance. As she entered Doutrin, she could look down on her flesh and blood body. She drifted up on an astral plane and flew to her rendezvous with her brother, Lacracken. When she felt his presence, she called out to him.

Brother, I am here. What news?

Greetings, little sister, he responded as his spirit drifted over to be closer to her. *The news is good. We captured enough grain to more than see us through the cold time. The rest we burned rather than leave it for that roach's army. The fields we also burned and seeded with salt and black rock blood. We killed many and lost few. Any word on the demon and your tyrant?*

Vanjar is in a tizzy like I have never seen before, Petal replied. *Apparently, the demon killed all sent against him, although for some reason it was only fifty.*

Only *fifty!* Lacracken exclaimed. *One man kills fifty and you say* only*? Surely, this demon could kill Dolfin of the Dung.*

He wants *something of us, brother. I don't know yet what it is. But I would go to bed with the Devil himself if we can get this demon to aide us.*

Be careful, little one, our conspiracies grow in scope and depth. Where is this demon now?

He remained on the Plain of Despair but said he would meet Dolfin at the gates to the capital. I don't trust Dolfin in this, brother. I fear he will try to use this demon warrior against us, especially when he learns of your raid on the granaries.

Come, let us fly over the Plain to see this demon ourselves. We must *find a way to turn him against Dolfin and join with us. If not, perhaps we can at least get him to kill Dolfin for us.*

I agree. Let us off.

The two astral spirits of Petal and Lacracken zoomed through the heights and over the Plain of Despair until they sighted a single lone tent. A tall heavily muscled man stood in front of the tent as Petal dipped down for a closer look. He was huge, rippled with corded muscles, and not ungainly to the eye. Behind him in the open tent lay a strange beast of some sort. Part bear, part lion—all terrifying. It was even larger than the demon lord. As the pair hung in the air observing the two, the beast suddenly awoke and seemed to look directly at them. He tilted his heavily maned head to one side and stared curiously at the place their astral bodies occupied. The man then turned and also appeared to look at them. He smiled a full white smile and said one word to them: "Shiva."

This so unsettled the two that they quickly blinked out and returned to their bodies in trance.

When Petal sat up on her furs, she felt cold and exposed. But it was *impossible*. They couldn't have known she and her brother were there. Yet despite all reason, she *felt* as if both the man and the beast had known they were there. She curled up on the furs, pulling one over her and rocked herself to sleep.

****

You frightened them away. Dar observed.

"More likely *you* frightened them away." Arkell smiled.

Strange, this dirt bowl is the last place in the galaxy I would have expected to sense astral spirits spying.

"Interesting to be sure. They did feel curious. One thing for certain: from the brief taste of their essence, they are not allies with Dolfin."

Perhaps then they can become allies with us?

"Time will tell. The female at least I will know if I encounter her in the city."

And since you plan to rut with every female between eight and eighty, the chances are good.

"Ah, but what if she is seven? or eighty-one?"

Ark, I take back what I have said. You don't have the morals of a mink ... you have the libido of a mink. The few morals you have are of a slug.

"And you have the morals of a Dalai Lama but the nature of a shark."

If we are through complimenting each other, perhaps we had best get some exercise. And if you can't keep up, I'll carry you.

"Carry your balls, fleabag. They are a greater burden to you."

Arkell and Dar sprinted off toward the horizon at a blistering pace. Dar's gallop was a series of lunges in which he pushed himself forward with both massive hind legs only to land lightly on his two front paws. His hind legs coiled forward to land just in front of his front paws for another rocketing lunge. Arkell, by contrast, looked like a cross between a sprinter and a long-distance runner. He stretched out his long legs to their full extension and pistoled his arms in rapid movements. They had covered twenty miles in less than an hour when Arkell reached out and grabbed Dar's tail.

"All right already. You made your point." He huffed. "Can we stop for a minute so I can piss?"

If you must. But not too long. I don't want you cramping up on me like you did on Xeric, or I

will *have to carry you ... and my balls as well.*

When they started up again after Arkell had relieved himself, it was at more of a lope than a mad dash. They took another hour to cover the last ten miles before they slowed to a trot in the woods just outside the capital. Arkell walked over to a stream and immersed his head, and then drank slowly. Dar joined him and started lapping up the cool water.

"And just what by Omega's left ball did that accomplish, furball?"

We are here three hours ahead of the fool's small army. We can eat, rest, and get pretty to meet them at the gate, Dar purred. *Besides, you said you wanted to* force march.*"*

"Is that why you rushed us so? So you can fill your bottomless belly and preen your fur?"

Seemed like a good idea to me.

Arkell barked a laugh. "Yes, I guess it is a good idea. If I am to provide stud service for Dolfin's harem, I should take nourishment and wash the stink from my flesh."

What a pair we make. I think of storing energy, and you think of expending it.

Arkell had stripped his clothes off and was stepping into a shallow pool just downstream of where they drank. "Come join me, Dar. Drown some of those vermin you grant housing to."

You should not speak so of our friends. They are at times better company than you, hairless one. And they taste as sweet as any candy.

Arkell grabbed Dar's tail and dragged him into the pool where they frolicked like two young pups.

Chapter Nine

The Directorate was sequestered in isolation watching the progress of the battle they had no say displayed on the vidscreens.

Kor-Zem and Isaac were whispering to each other in one corner of the room.

"We should have had that deformed freak killed before we called this meeting," muttered the prime minister.

"There is still time to deflate our arrogant hero," answered the banking chairman.

"Not now. *He* has control. By our own laws, we cannot interfere until the crisis is averted. I tell you, Isaac, this *emergency* is all too convenient. Do you think he knew?" Kor-Zem asked.

"Possible, but unlikely. We will know more tomorrow when he is forced by the conventions to provide us with the courtesy briefing. Who could it be? Certainly not the Cartel. Those chitin we mutants have never been this precipitous. An attack on a mining operation I could buy, but not an administrative habitat. And *certainly* not *this* habitat. Do you trust Jobikan or the Archbishop?" Isaac asked as he pondered while looking at his filed fingernails.

"Omega's left ball, man. I don't trust *you*," snarled Kor-Zem.

"Which is why I deem to conspire with you K-Z." Isaac smiled. "No, you have Jobikan more or less under control. He is as frightened of Ferr as any. The Archbishop may not totally agree with us, but he could never compromise a confidence. And his concerns about Ferr rival the president's." He moved his sled back and forth like a rocker. "Shit, piss, and corruption. *Could* this be a Ferr plot? Or is it simply coincidence?"

"Neither one of us believe in coincidences. Something is afoot. And if we can't defuse it, we may find ourselves buggered by a particle beam," Kor-Zem snapped.

Isaac drifted closer to the prime minister and whispered in his ear, "Probe the Archbishop. I'll work on Jobikan for you. In the meantime, we might as well eat and drink. We're hobbled until tomorrow."

"And maybe beyond," Kor-Zem muttered.

Indeed, their hobbles would restrain them beyond the morrow. Despite their great wealth, resources, and power, both men had forgotten several elements key to any successful conspiracy, especially one grounded on greed, power, and arrogance:

1. Power corrupts.
2. Absolute power corrupts absolutely.
3. In any battle, *the* crucial element is intelligence. Oh, not the intelligence of the mind, but the intelligence of knowledge and data—the details of weather, terrain, and the enemies' movements and plans. The fatal flaw to their plan for dominating the galaxy was their own overconfidence in their abilities compounded with underestimating General Charles-Henry Ferr, who, despite his physical deformity and loss of various body parts, retained his fifty years of battle experience *and* the most sophisticated, complex, and covert intelligence gathering network in the galaxy. For over two and half decades, he had had every member of the Directorate under six different forms of surveillance. He knew what and when they ate, who they slept with, when, and what they did. He knew their heartbeats, blood pressure, and specific gravity of their urine on Earth Prime. He also had had microscopic transmitters installed into their dental work. The result was that a taped transcript of their conversations could be made available anytime they were within one parsec of a receiver (and they were *never* more than a million miles from one of his receivers).

Therefore, when he became aware of their intentions of awarding him the Galactic Meritorious Service Award as a prelude to his forced retirement, he made plans. He knew that they intended to replace him with that *chair-borne* lackey Kor-Zem had been grooming and promoting for the past five years, General Slar. He made plans. General Slar had been assigned as liaison officer with the Directorate for the past two years and effectively out of Ferr's control. However, plans had been made.

When the emergency that sparked the imposition of martial law erupted, all power reverted back to the military. It was one of the few residuals of the Carbon Jihad, which had remained unchanged to date. During those war days, millions of lives had been lost as bureaucrats attempted to legislate a war. Decision by committee damn near lost the campaign—until an unlikely event happened. The politicians made a right decision, even if for all the wrong reasons. They saw that the flow was turning rapidly against the Federation and that there was a very real danger they would LOSE. Beyond all else they didn't want the blame for that devastating loss to land in their laps. So they created the Mandate:

In the event of attack or clear military emergency, all powers and authority would revert to the supreme military commander. He would have absolute control to make any and all decisions to protect the Federation for a period of not less than thirty days. No vote shall be necessary. The supreme military commander shall invoke martial law when, in his irrefutable estimation, all the elements of emergency status are observed (See Annex A). He shall be required to provide a courtesy briefing to the Directorate within twenty-four hours of the invocation of martial law to share what information he chooses to. The entire Directorate and their staff will be sequestered in protective custody until it deemed safe to move them to their planets of origin. This law shall be absolute and unconditionally irrevocable for a period of not less than one hundred years, and then only by a unanimous vote of the entire Directorate.

General Charles-Henry Ferr collected his intelligence, and he made his plans. Now his plans were being put into effect. The Federation was under attack from unknown aggressors in four quadrants. Merrill-2 was under siege, and General Ferr was under control. Oh, was he under control. General Slar, who had never seen any action other than reports on a vidscreen was about to lead his first combat foray. Ferr had already written the posthumous citation for his Medal of Valor. Arkell had been named Ferr's deputy commander and would assume command in the event of General Ferr's demise or impairment. The *courtesy briefing* Ferr would deliver to the Directorate had been written for six weeks and would doubtless rattle more than a few cages. Old Kor-Zem and Isaac were about to learn a painful lesson in the true ruthless exercise of power and authority. There was an old twentieth-century saying that came to mind as Ferr scanned his notes: "Payback is a Bitch." Somehow, the saying seemed to fit the circumstances.

Chapter Ten

Lord Dolfin and the remains of his troops approached the gates of the city. Dolfin turned to his cavalry commander, Kel, and said, "Leave a squad at the gate to escort the demon and his beast to me when they arrive. And bring the bodies of our soldiers to the kitchens and have Car prepare a feast. I want Vanjar sent to my rooms and have his girl select the women to entertain our guest. Tell them I will want a full report on his pillow prowess, and talk…"

"Yes, my lord," snapped Kel as he wheeled his mount to issue orders.

Dolfin stood up in his stirrups and shaded his eyes from the glare as he looked at the gates. He sat down heavily with a confused laugh. "*Strike that order* for an escort detail, Kel. They are already here. How by Vanjar's spirits did they beat us here?"

Kel looked at *The Two*, standing by the gate looking all fresh and clean, and shouldered his mount up next to his leader. "My lord, I fear no man alive but you, yet these two raise my hackles and disturb me in ways new to me."

"You are wise to feel concern, Kel," Dolfin spoke quietly. "But remember, they *want* something of us, and somehow, despite their skills, they are apparently not permitted to just take it." He smiled as his mind reeled.

"Do you trust them, lord?" Kel asked.

"I trust *no* man, be the demon or beast," Dolfin snapped. Then he calmed himself and added, "But I see a way to use them. Carry out the rest of your orders."

Arkell and Dar were cleaned and refreshed as they stood at the front gate watching the approach of Dolfin and his soldiers.

I don't like walled cities, Ark. You know that. And I don't trust that painted warrior/king.

"It is a tattoo, Dar, not paint." Arkell smiled. "Walk with me into the city. When we reach the palace, disappear. Conduct a detailed reconnaissance of the city. Learn the avenues of approach and retreat. We may need to leave in a hurry. Also, find a quiet spot where you can hide and meditate. Scan the city and find if our astral spy is within. And, Dar, stay in touch with me."

As you wish. You try not to let your balls cloud your mind.

"You question my control, Dar?" Arkell asked with surprise.

Never ... have I questioned your control. It is your appetite I fear. Beware of treachery ... and bed bugs.

Dolfin and his troop approached Arkell and Dar. Arkell stood, his hands on his hips, legs spread shoulder width apart, head erect, and with a smile on his handsome face. Dar sat to his right, immobile and fierce as any gothic gargoyle. His only movement was the occasional blink of his large yellow eyes and the constant swish of his long tail.

"*Ho, demon.* You travel fast." Dolfin laughed.

"We travel as fast as the need be. The wind is our steed. We are now hungry for food and knowledge. And, candidly, I am horny as a three-peckered Minuvian hare. You offered me a sample of your women."

"Food and women are easy to provide." Dolfin flashed his evil grin. "Knowledge costs knowledge and any bargain must favor both parties."

The massive wood and iron gates parted and provided entrance to the returning party and its guests.

Here we go, Ark. Into the jaws of treachery, Dar sighed.

"And into the moist sheaths of women untasted." Arkell grinned as he shared his thoughts with Dar.

A slug ... a mink and a slug ... How can I love such a one, Dar muttered.

"How can you resist?" Arkell smiled.

True. Still it is a topic I should give some consideration, Dar replied.

"While you're at it, be sure to give some thought to how we get out of this fortress if we need to," Arkell said.

Dolfin had the germ of a plan already for how to use this demon and give up nothing of value. He hoped he could use the demon to kill that bastard Lacracken before the infection of rebellion could grow any more. He was confident he could get the demon to kill Lacracken and possibly crush most of his rebel army. But he also felt the very real need to kill this unholy pair and was uncertain how best to try. He hoped Vanjar could gain some insight from his spirits, but lately the spirits had been less than cooperative. Or else Vanjar's powers were failing. The thought had crossed his mind that Vanjar's powers seemed to start to weaken and the insight he gained from the spirits lessened all about the time he took to pillowing with that little Petal morsel. Perhaps his increased sexuality was eroding his magic. He would think more on that and discuss it with Vanjar later. Now, he needed information on how to handle this dangerous potential ally which was the Two-That-Are-One.

Chapter Eleven

The Directorate was anxiously awaiting the arrival of General Ferr, who was scheduled to deliver his courtesy briefing to them anytime soon.

Kor-Zem was busy bridling his fears and plotting new plots. General Slar had been called away before Kor-Zem could talk to him. The prime minister had wanted to suggest that Slar should simply kill Ferr at the first opportunity before he had a chance to do anything. Then, again, it was probably just he didn't have time. Despite what his gut said, Kor-Zem's mind knew that Slar could no sooner kill Ferr—despite desire—than President Jobikan could deliver a spanking to Dar. Both men lacked the skills and determination to do such things. Gods, how he hated what was happening. Power and control were Kor-Zem's sustenance. To so suddenly lose both the momentum *and* authority for his marvelous plans was maddening. *One more day* and he could have had it all. Now he had to wait like some mid-level lackey to receive whatever crumbs of information the great General Charles-Henry Ferr chose to share with the Directorate.

That damn red light kept blinking over the control vidscreen, which was blank, giving pulse to his frustration and anger.

As the prime minister pondered amid all the red blinking annoyances, in walked General Ferr with a benign smile.

"Good morning, gentlemen." They all started to crowd toward him like iron filings to a magnet. "I'll keep this as brief as possible and tell you what I can, which will not compromise either the campaign or your individual personal safety."

"General, we would appreciate as detailed a briefing as possible," Kor-Zem said as he attempted to assume control again. "We have important plans that must be implemented as soon as possible."

Ferr looked directly into the eyes of the prime minister and fought to keep his face blank, although a lesser man would have been forced to smile. "Mr. Prime Minister, gentlemen, this briefing will be *brief* and in accordance with the policy of the *Mandate*. Unfortunately, it will also be lacking in many details I am sure you prefer. Please sit down. We haven't much time."

Nervous glances were exchanged between the power elite of the Directorate as they all quietly moved to chairs around the large conference table they had commanded just a day before.

"A state of martial law currently exists within the entire Federation," Ferr began. "Simultaneous probes were launched against us yesterday in four quadrants by Omega class battle cruisers. This habitat suffered minor damage to our screens, power plant, and two launch sites. I will now state the situation, primary mission, and my concept of the operation." He flipped his small handheld computer screen open and plugged it into the input receptacle of the main vidscreen hanging from the ceiling near the end of the table. "It has been judged unsafe to attempt to relocate you to your home planets for the time being. The scout ships we tasked yesterday in the wake of the attack have not returned and are assumed lost. Heavy fighting has been reported throughout the Merrill group. The enemy situation is being evaluated, however. Here is what I can tell you now: it is assumed, although not yet confirmed, that elements of the Andromeda Cartel have launched preemptive strikes at approximately one hundred seventeen locations. Thus far, the probes have been contained and lack battle class organization. We have destroyed several cruisers and dozens of scout craft. However, we have yet to take any prisoners. There has been no verbal communication by the aggressor. All combat intelligence has revealed thus far is encrypted digital communication. I have assigned an Empathic Observer to each patrol and hope for greater information within the next rotation. The aggressor seems to be assembling a major battle group that is tracking in the direction of the Mars colonies. Since two of our major logistics commands are on Mars, and it is so close to Earth Prime, it is assumed to be a prime target. I have sent three Federation battle groups to intercept and defend.

President Jobikan interrupted with a question. "Will *you* command that task force yourself, General?"

"No." He smiled to himself while keeping a blank face for his audience. "I will coordinate the battle from here. After it is concluded,

I will then establish a forward command post at a sight to be designated." He paused and glanced at his notes. "General Slar will command."

Kor-Zem went pale. He tasted bile rise to his throat and fear mingled with rage. Before his mind could stop his mouth, he complained, "He has *no* battle experience. He is *unqualified* for such a command." He immediately regretted his words as the others of the Directorate looked at him with shock.

"He is a full general in the Federation, Mr. Prime Minister," Ferr stated quietly in his most bland conversational tone. "The speed of his promotions and opportunity has not provided him the chance to yet command in battle." He paused and then continued, "That is not General Slar's fault, but ours—by our success in maintaining an environment of Peace. You of all people, Mr. Prime Minister, must know of the man's depth of knowledge and albeit untested exceptional potential. Despite our contempt for battle, this does provide a suitable forum for General Slar himself to prove worthy to succeed me." He paused and glanced at the faces staring at him. "Don't you agree, gentlemen?"

Kor-Zem slumped into his seat. *Omega's left ball, Ferr* knows. *We are screwed, blued, and totally bonked. We have lost. Should we have moved slower or faster? Can we regain the initiative? Is this luck or the result of a superior plan to ours?* Kor-Zem thought complex and evil thoughts and struggled for some grasp that eluded him.

The Archbishop raised a tentative hand and asked a question. "Charles-Henry, may I ask two questions?"

"Certainly, Your Eminence." Ferr smiled.

"How long before you assess we can be moved? And have you designated the battle chain of command?"

All eyes moved from the Archbishop to General Ferr just as the communicator on the general's wrist beeped twice. He touched his left ear where he wore a receiver. He nodded to himself twice, lifted his wrist, and spoke two words. "Acknowledged. Ferr out. Gentlemen, I am afraid I must cut this briefing off now. I am required in the TOCC. In answer to your questions, Your Eminence, you can expect to be detained here no longer than thirty rotations. And, yes, I have established and recorded the chain of command. Now if you will excuse me."

"Wait!" Kor-Zem was on his feet. "Is that *it*? We know no more now than we did before. We *demand* more information and answers to questions yet unasked, General."

Ferr was oppressively calm as he looked directly at Kor-Zem and responded, "Mr. Prime Minister, you will *demand* nothing of me until the crisis has been contained. I refer you to the 'Lessons Learned Annex to the Mandate,' which details specific lessons you gentlemen will recall from the Carbon Jihad. You will be provided every comfort and courtesy during the remainder of the crisis. But neither you, Mr. Prime Minister, *nor* the Directorate could demand anything of *me*, except my duty, which I am off to attend to now." And General Charles-Henry Ferr turned on his heel and left the room full of confused, angry, frustrated, and frightened men.

****

Vanjar sat in his room in a trance while he communicated with the spirit of his grandmother. He was frustrated and frightened. For years he had been the steadying calm controlling the force of Dolfin's storm. His precise advice and counsel had guided the realm. He had held the quiet control in his steady grasp like reins in the practiced hands of a jockey. Now all was turmoil. He received incomplete or no information from the spirits; Lord Dolfin was questioning his abilities. Dolfin had even gone so far as to suggest that his powers were weakening because of his increased sexual activity with Petal and that if he could not improve his performance with the spirits, he would be commanded to cease his performance with Petal. Now, even his most dependable spirit guide, the spirit of his own grandmother and teacher was reticent to help him.

Grandmother, why do you torture me so? he asked. *You know my very real need. If I fail to perform for my lord, I will lose all. And if I truly incur his wrath, I may find myself in the stewpot.*

It would be good for you to give him indigestion, his grandmother responded.

Grandmother, how can you joke so when my need is so great? At least tell me WHY the spirits shun me, he pleaded.

That I can do, she replied, *although you should realize that even if we of the spirit world have been deprived of our earthen vessels and pleasures, our humor remains with us. You have but to ask the right questions in the right manner and I shall answer all. As to why you find silence and riddles where you once found clarity and direction, the answer is in your use of your insights.*

I don't understand, Reverend Grandmother, Vanjar replied.

I know you don't understand, and that is more the pity. When you revealed the location of the rebel base to Dolfin, he used that to destroy the village. When he did that, he raped, sodomized, and killed a woman who was in Doutrin. Her spirit is trapped on this side unnaturally. It has greatly upset the order. That alone angered the Gods and those of us who serve them. That she was most favored by us compounded the injury. As the old legends say, "the Gods are angry" with Dolfin and, my son, with you.

Grandmother, Vanjar pleaded, *what can I do as penance to restore myself?*

You can only do what you must do, and that is not for me to instruct.

Grandmother, please ... *don't leave* ... *What must I do? Tell me and I will do it.*

You must do much and lose much. First, you must turn against your evil lord and cast your fate with the two strangers, the Two-That-Are-One. If you do that, you will see a way, the fate of the lost soul. Her name is Amelia. She is on your hands. Until she is freed and the evil of Dolfin ended, you will find no succor from the spirits ... or from your mother's mother.

Vanjar was suddenly awake and trembling on his furs. A cold sweat covered his thin body, and nausea rested in his gut. He wept openly like a child and pulled the sweat damp furs about his frail old body. Oh, how could he do what he must do? He was never brave or strong, either in flesh or in spirit. How could he turn against his liege lord and side with a demon and a beast? Dolfin would surely kill him. What of that woman, Amelia? How awful it must be to be trapped out of your body when that body is killed. Such a short time ago, he had everything a man could want: power, money, favor, and Petal. Now he risked having nothing. And if he did what his grandmother's spirit instructed him to do, he would have less still.

There was a knock at his door. He stood on shaky thin legs and walked over to open it. The scribe of the court was there and obviously taken aback by the gaunt appearance of the magician.

"Your Eminence, Lord Dolfin requires your presence at feast. Please hurry," the scribe said as he backed out of the room.

Left alone with the door closed and the echo of its closing ringing in his room, he stood shaking for a full thirty heartbeats.

"And so it begins ..." he said to his empty room as he moved off to refresh himself and dress for the feast.

****

General Slar was reviewing his operations order and silently bemoaning the fact that the quality of soldier he wanted for his combat debut were not available to him. He would even have taken Arkell and his monster other half if they had been available. But if they were available, they would be commanding this mission instead of him. Omega's left ball, this was frustrating. Just as he was giving thought to composing a death haiku, there was a buzz at his door.

"Yes," he snapped. "*Who* is it?"

"Command Sergeant Major Burn, General," was the answer.

Slar's heart leaped to his mouth. Command Sergeant Major Lee X. Burn? This was too good to be true. Next to Arkell and General Ferr, he was the most decorated and experienced soldier in the entire Federation. *Exactly* the kind of man he needed for this outing.

"Enter," he said a bit too anxiously. *Control yourself, Slar. Maintain your dignity. Remember, YOU are the general and he is only an NCO ... only an NCO? Worth any hundred other NCOs or officers for that matter.*

Burn walked in and stood at attention while he saluted crisply. "General Ferr thought I might be of some service to you, sir," he calmly said. "IF you want me, that is, sir."

If I want *him? He is a godsend.* "At ease, Sergeant Major. I didn't realize you were on habitat. Yes, I believe you could be of some service to us in this campaign. Have you been briefed yet?"

"No, sir, I was just here to receive some silly thirty-year medal when the attack occurred. General Ferr said I could go with you if I wanted, and *naturally* if you wanted me." He remained empty faced and deferential despite a commanding presence and an almost supernatural confidence, a confidence antithesis to the doubt Slar felt.

"I would welcome the opportunity to command a soldier of your experience and skills, Sergeant Major. Please"—he gestured toward a chair—"have a seat. Perhaps you can even help improve on my op order." Slar was frankly rather proud of his work. It had been a long time since he had had to write an operations order, but he felt good about this one. He had given it special care since his life literally depended on it. It was an excellent opportunity to impress Burn with his general's knowledge.

"Very good, sir," Burn sat down and immediately started to review the material on the screen between them. "The general may want to consider a less direct route to the checkpoints, perhaps two more jumps, and perhaps we could add a couple of alternate routes just in case we encounter any aggressor activity in route."

Gods, those were exactly the kind of details he was hoping to avoid missing. With this man as an aide, that death haiku could wait. Ferr had inadvertently handed him the one tool needed to succeed in this mission and return a conquering hero, qualified to occupy that precious command chair. Burn continued for over an hour making suggestions on the movement plan, the recon, the table of organization and equipment, logistics, and a dozen contingencies at the objective that Slar would frankly never have even considered given a dozen rotations to ponder. Finally, Burn sat back and straightened his tunic.

"That should about do it, sir," he said. "You already had a fine outline. I trust my few embellishments are of some help."

Slar looked at the final order and sighed. This was good … and bad. The plan was superb. A tactical masterpiece orchestrated by a maestro. What was bad was that Burn now obviously knew his commander was inept. That would never do. Time to put this hero in his place.

"Thank you, Sergeant Major. Naturally, most of those suggestions were already in the computer under annexes, but you *were* able to offer a *few* potentially useful tidbits." He smiled condescendingly. Then he glanced at the timepiece display on his desk and said, "Why don't you go draw your gear and meet me in the briefing room in ten minutes." Slar knew no one could draw full battle gear in ten minutes. Burn would be late for the briefing, probably arriving halfway through the concept of the operation.

"Yes, sir, General." Burn nodded as he rose to his feet. "Am I dismissed, sir?"

"Dismissed," Slar answered as he returned the Sergeant Major's salute!

Eight minutes later, after admiring the final product, General Slar walked into the briefing room to meet with his subordinate commanders and NCOs. When he walked through the door, a voice yelled.

"On your feet! Atten-shun!" It was the voice of Command Sergeant Major Burn echoing around the room.

Slar was startled. Worse yet, he let it show.

"Sergeant Major, have you drawn your battle gear?" Slar asked in an accusatory tone.

"Yes, sir! I did all that before I came to your office. It took considerably longer to draw my equipment than to rework that op order, sir," he replied with a straight face.

There were subtle snickers around the room. These men knew what had almost happened and that their general had been caught trying to get credit for the work of Burn. Slar let it slide and marched to the front of the room.

"Take your seats, gentlemen. Here is *my* plan." He then proceeded to brief the men in the room in his best briefing officer manner. This was a task he *was* experienced and comfortable at—presenting other men's work. The big difference this time was *he* would have to execute *this* plan.

Chapter Twelve

Dolfin was livid. The feast was laid, the dancers were dancing, the musicians were playing, and that damnable demon and his monster beast were keeping him waiting—*him*. Lord Dolfin, ruler of the entire world. Nothing like this had ever happened before in all his years. He would kill any other man for such an insult. Additionally, he had just learned of Lacracken's raid on the granaries. It was an act of insult, as well as promise of hardship for the winter. Maybe he should cancel the feast, or maybe he could poison this freak and his pet. *Is he intentionally trying to provoke me? Perhaps his customs are different.*

"VANJAR!" Dolfin barked.

"Yes, my lord?" the trembling magician answered with a diffident bow.

"What news say the spirits of this unholy pair?"

"My spirits give conflicting information, my lord." Vanjar quivered. "One says he is a demon from a far-off world sent to confound us and spark us into costly errors. Another claims he be no demon at all but merely a very skilled man of the Warrior caste. Still another claims he is not real but an illusion created by a witch you once raped.

"Magician, you and your spirits start to annoy me. Confound us he certainly does, and errors *have* been made. No mere *man* could slay fifty of clan T'sui as he did despite his skill ... and if he be illusion. Tell that to the fifty dead warriors whose meat we eat this night." He growled.

"My lord," Vanjar whispered.

"Silence, mage! I have two orders for you and you will obey them fully or be impaled. First, observe this demon/man/illusion and report to me all your thoughts and feelings. Engage him in talk and learn all you can learn, if you still have *any* skill. Second, you are hereby *forbidden* from exercising your short sword until I say otherwise. You will abandon your little whore and avoid even the comfort of your own hand until I give you leave to do otherwise."

"B-b-but, my lord ..." Vanjar started to complain.

The two large doors at the end of the banquet room swung open and in marched an odd procession of three dissimilar figures. Petal led the column with her hands clasped in front of her lap and her head demurely bowed. Arkell marched in behind her, head held high, big smile on his face, and arms swinging like twin pistons of corded cable. Dar followed walking on all fours with his long tail swinging from side to side in counter rhythm to his head as it moved from left to right observing all. Those in attendance who had not seen the two were visibly shaken and impressed. The dancers stopped dancing, the musicians stopped playing, and the crowd all receded to the walls noticeably.

"Ho, Lord Dolfin! Are we late?" Arkell smiled. "It seems you have started the party without us."

"In *my* realm, I wait for no man *or* demon," Dolfin scowled.

"Little matter." Arkell grinned. "As long as there is ale, food, and women still to be had," Arkell said as he turned to accept a horn of ale from a serving girl.

"You will need a blade to cut your meat." Dolfin grinned. "Here … *catch*!" he said as he fired a double-edged dirk at Arkell's chest.

While drinking with one hand, Arkell easily caught the knife by its handle and stopped it inches from his chest as he calmly answered, "Thank you, lord"—Arkell threw the knife back, nailing a small, hard sweet nut to the table in front of Dolfin—"but I have a blade of my own." He smiled.

There were reciprocal gasps at each knife toss. Then the room fell to absolute quiet as Lord Dolfin glared at Arkell. There was an awkward pause broken first by Arkell's belch, and then Dolfin's laughing out loud.

"Ha-ha-ha-ha-a-a-a! Well done, my tall, handsome demon!" Dolfin shouted. "Come sit next to me … *yoh* … *music*. You entertain me, Arkell," Dolfin said to his guest. "You are as cool as the mountain snow …"

"… and faster than the swiftest arrow," Arkell interrupted him.

"Ha-ha-ha-ha. Yes, that would seem to be true also," Dolfin answered, struggling to keep the tone light and hide his boiling rage.

"And don't forget it, Dolfin." Arkell smiled. No "lord" or titles; no hint of respect. Again, the silence fell like a heavy, wet wool blanket.

I think you just succeeded in pissing him off. Methinks the blood will soon flow swifter than the wine. Dar stood up on his hind legs next to Arkell and stretched his arms wide while yawning loudly into the stillness and making sure to bare all his fangs and talons.

Dolfin looked up to the towering Dar and back to the grinning Arkell. He leaned forward into Arkell and spoke in a soft voice laced with venom.

"Why do you intentionally try to provoke me, demon? If you want to fight me, just ask. *Just ask*." His rage was boiling to the rim, and the blood vessels in his tattooed head pulsated.

Arkell rested his horn on the table and leaned down close to his host. "I have no immediate desire to kill you, Dolfin, old man, *nor* do I choose to play games with you for the benefit of your court and your inflated ego," Arkell spoke softly. "That you would fight me is to your credit. It at least shows that you have much courage, and I value courage, especially knowing as we both do that I *can* kill you anytime I so choose … and that you have no chance of harming me. Not to mention that if you were to get *incredibly* lucky and land a blow of some insignificant value, my other half here would be most annoyed."

Dar placed one paw gently on Dolfin's shoulder and slowly bared his claws, sinking them shallowly into his flesh. Dolfin winced but let out no cry and made no move.

"*Now*, you invited us to a feast and a party." Arkell smiled and spoke in a more conversational tone, "We can have fun and laughter … or blood and death. Do *you* choose to die ripped to shreds in front of your adoring court of lackeys, or do you prefer to play the civil and courteous host? What do *you* want, Dolfin? Just ask." Arkell had delivered the last speech quietly and calmly into the ear of his host.

All eyes were on Dolfin. All guards had hands on weapons, unsure of to what to do and fully expecting to die. Dolfin stared deep into the eyes of Arkell and he saw his own death. Never had he felt so helpless. Oddly, it was Vanjar who came to his rescue.

"May I propose a toast!" shouted Vanjar as he rose to his feet. His action startled the crowd and momentarily diverted their attention to him and away from the quiet, although obviously deadly, confrontation. "To the Two-That-Are-One, Arkell and Dar, who have demonstrated power and restraint, and to our liege lord and ruler, Lord Dolfin the Conqueror, who has brought this mighty pair under the protection and hospitality of our grand city. May a mighty alliance result!"

Arkell stood up and held his horn high as he said, "To Lord Dolfin the Conqueror and his hospitality to off-world ambassadors!" shouted Arkell. Dar released his hold and gently helped Dolfin to his feet.

Dolfin grabbed a chalice and shouted, "To the Two-That-Are-One, may their journey bring them all they deserve," Dolfin added.

Everyone drank and the music started again. The dancers started dancing and the guards all let out sighs of relief.

Arkell sat down and leaned over to Dolfin. "We can discuss our differences in the morning. For now let us share drink and food and choose women for each other. I do not mean to undermine your authority, sire, *but* I will not permit you to offer insult unchallenged to either Dar or myself. Save your petty little games of power and ego for the lesser men you command and bully. You do not command us … and never could."

Dolfin was living the personification of a dilemma. He desperately wanted to kill someone or something, preferably Arkell. But he now believed this giant when he said it was not possible … yet, so he would learn to master patience and plot for a way to flay this arrogant man/demon and send his lion/bear to the taxidermist.

"Tonight, we will enjoy the pleasures of the flesh. Tomorrow, we will discuss affairs of state and petitioning ambassadors." Dolfin grinned through clenched teeth. "*Yashida,* you will service our guest after he has eaten."

Yashida was taller than the average woman present, with long black hair and emerald green eyes. She had huge firm breasts with large hard nipples that pressed against her scant gown and a very narrow waist leading into full firm hips and buttocks. She had thick full lips and sparkling white teeth, which she flashed when called.

Petal, who was hidden behind Dar, leaned forward and whispered in his furry ear. "Tell Arkell to beware of Yashida. She once bit off a soldier's manhood on a bet and kept it under her pillow until it rotted. Tell him."

Ark, little Petal warns you to beware of where you bury your short sword with that one.

I heard her, Dar. Thank her for me. I will be careful.

Dar turned his head toward Petal and was surprised that she did not startle or turn away. He leaned down and gently kissed her cheek with his soft flexible lips. He backed up slightly and smiled his strange smile as she ran her small hand down the long length of his hard back. No one saw this exchange, except Vanjar.

****

Prime Minister Kor-Zem and President Jobikan were sitting in a corner of the large recreation room playing Go. Kor-Zem was apparently winning but still in a foul mood.

"I tell you that sonuvabitch freak Ferr *knows*," he fumed.

"K-Z, you and I both know that is impossible. You and I are the only two who actually know the form, substance, and details of the plan. We have been most careful to communicate those intentions and details *only* in sign language, in isolated locales, and under a stealth shield. We have not even written anything down," Jobikan said as he carefully studied the board.

"I'm no bonking empath, but I tell you I *feel* he knows," Kor-Zem muttered. "Are you *sure* you didn't tell one of your little girls or boys?" he asked accusingly.

"I haven't lived this long in public life by making such foolish indiscretions, Mr. Prime Minister. Perhaps *you* bragged to one of your more unsavory agents," the president responded.

"Nonsense. You know me better than that."

"Is it so impossible to accept that this attack is unrelated to our covert plans for the military?" Jobikan asked. "Even General Charles-Henry Ferr would never start a galactic for-real shooting war for mere politics or to protect his own scarred hide. Oh, *you* or I would do it in a nanosecond ... but not Charles-Henry," he said as he made a move and took one of his opponent's stones.

"I don't know. If Arkell and his monster half were here, I'd be certain this was some military set up designed to undermine our authority and protect Ferr. But as sudden and apparently complex and in SO many quadrants, NO ... Ferr would never risk other lives to save his own," Kor-Zem muttered almost to himself. "I bonking *hate* coincidences, especially such *convenient* coincidences. Did you see how he avoided telling us anything of what is really happening?"

"K-Z, we *are* under attack damn it. You know the provisions. You know how we politicians nearly bonked up things during the Carbon Jihad. *Look*, consider it a blessing in disguise. If we *do* have a genuine military emergency, as I believe, and as we apparently do, who is better suited for dealing with it than Ferr?" Jobikan asked. "Would you really want that spineless wuss Slar to hold the reins right now with full *mandated* authority?"

The prime minister leaned over the board and looked hard at the president. "At least we can *control* Slar. He'd communicate with us if only out of fear and despair."

"Sure, exactly what we'd want in a full-blown shoot-'em-up military emergency—a commanding general guided by fear and desperation, unable to make an independent decision," Jobikan pondered over the board and added, "I've told you all along, Slar was the wrong man for that position."

"All those years of grooming, training, conditioning ... we may need to find another anyway," Kor-Zem babbled. "If Ferr were ever to send Slar into combat, it would be his death warrant."

"Don't be ridiculous. Charles-Henry is many things, but he is no fool," Jobikan chided. "He would never give Slar a combat command."

"And who else?" Kor-Zem asked. "Slar is the only other general here; *we* saw to that. It was part of our plan. Omega's left ball man—Ferr *has* to have Slar do something during such a crisis. Arkell is off doing who knows what on that feudal planet. Zen is with that archeological group on Pluto, freezing his balls off. Rath is having a leg replaced on Earth Prime. Who else with appropriate rank does he have in the entire bonking quadrant?" Kor-Zem fumed?

"You overlook the obvious, K-Z ... and the man."

"Oh, *really*? Well, enlighten me, you perfumed fop."

"Ferr will command any major combat force *himself*. He loves that kind of shit, he's good at it, and he will therefore have to leave General Slar *here* in command of the TOCC." Jobikan smiled.

The prime minister actually looked excited at the prospect. A smile erupted from his scowling jowls, and hope danced across his fat flat face.

"You *think* so." He grinned. "*Gods*, that would be too good to be true. But I do have to admit there is a logic to what you say." He paused and ran his stubby fingers through what little hair covered his bald pate. "Ferr wouldn't want to sacrifice a real battle group to the inexperience of Slar"—he paused and turned hard to Jobikan—"but would he *really* give Slar the TOCC? That would mean overall control of the war?"

"Ferr is facing as great a dilemma as we, my friend. He has supreme command. He has military decisions to make. By now he no doubt has a detailed plan full of myriad contingencies. A computer could probably manage most of the battle from now on. That's what battle computers were designed for. I'm sure Charles-Henry would feel that the safest place for Slar would be *here*, implementing the plans and contingency plans already designed and programmed by Ferr. He would figure that at least here, Slar can't get into any trouble and potentially cost soldier lives and lose expensive hardware."

Hope was struggling to gain a hold on Kor-Zem. "If only it is true."

"Relax and concentrate on the Go game, old friend." Jobikan smiled. "The next time we see General Ferr, it will be announce he has turned command of the TOCC over to Slar and that Ferr is leading some battle group off to new glories. I am sure it would be a simple matter for Slar to then arrange to have the returning Ferr *accidentally* run into a particle beam on reentry."

"Ha! If that were to happen, at least we already have the medal to present at his memorial service." Kor-Zem laughed.

The two men returned their concentration to the game board as the Archbishop approached them.

"Excuse me, gentlemen, but as I was praying for a safe and quick end to these hostilities, I remembered something I saw yesterday that perhaps you two could explain to me."

Jobikan smiled his best pearly white politician campaigning smile as he responded, "Yes, of course, Your Eminence?"

"Well, it's just that it struck me as *odd*, although, I guess, under the circumstances most fortunate, that I would see Command Sergeant Major Burn here at this time." The cleric lighted his pipe and continued, "It just seems a strange coincidence that a warrior of his caliber should arrive *here*, where he has never been before, on the eve of such an attack. Are you gentlemen keeping something from the rest of the Directorate that perhaps you could share?"

The prime minister and president exchanged worried glances, which they battled to repress as they responded in unison.

"Strange coincidence indeed."

Omega's left ball! thought Kor-Zem. *That bonking freak* does *know*.

****

General Slar was seated in the command chair of the control on the *Flagship* battle cruiser. They were awaiting final launch orders, and he was sweating profusely despite the coolness of climate control. He appeared outwardly confident and in control. However, it was a thin mask that hid his terror and utter lack of confidence. Thank the Gods Burn was here. That was a bit of luck he could have never even prayed for. Yet despite that apparent good fortune, he was wrecked with doubts. If only he could have communicated with the prime minister or the president before this launch. That, however, was forbidden by the Mandate and by General Ferr.

Command Sergeant Major Burn stood at a relaxed yet stiff parade rest one step behind and to the right of General Slar. His mind wandered as it drifted back and forth between routes to the Stargate checkpoint and a hunt he had shared with Arkell and Dar many years ago. Despite the filtered high-tech air, which caressed his nostrils, he could swear he smelled the sweet, heavy musk of Dar drying his wet pelt on a sun-soaked rock.

Chapter Thirteen

The party feast was in full swing. Naked dancing girls swirled around the tables. The music had increased in intensity with the wild erotic movements of the women, their bodies shimmering with thin coats of sweat and their breasts undulating with the music. Dar was prone behind Arkell and was finishing a quarter of a gor, a native elk-like animal. He had stripped and consumed most of the meat and was now licking marrow from a cracked leg bone. Arkell had eaten three large fowl and was wiping the grease from his chin when servers brought in several large trays with more meat.

"Now"—smiled Dolfin—"we eat the flesh of the warriors you killed so that we might gain their strength." He reached for a large piece of steaming loin.

"I eat no human flesh," Arkell said.

"But it is our custom, and the meat is sweet." Dolfin grinned as he bit into his first helping. "It also shows honor to those we have killed in battle."

"Why should I eat the flesh of weaker men than I? It offers me no greater strength to consume a defeated foe. In fact, it may well weaken me," Arkell said as he looked seriously at the monarch.

"You eat birds? You eat gor—base animals, lesser beings than the men you have killed." Dolfin smiled. "If your logic were sound, you could eat no meat other than the one who would kill you. And then it would be too late eh?" He laughed as he pushed a plate of meat in front of Arkell.

"I eat the flesh of wild animals, nature's fruits and vegetables, because they hold the spirit of freedom. Though they be weaker than Dar and I, they serve no man. They are shackled by no oppressor. When they give their lives to feed others, they pass on their life essence, which has been unfettered and wild. I eat the flesh of no man who has bowed to another," Arkell said.

Dolfin frowned and paused as he pondered those words. "Your ways are indeed strange, Arkell. But just as I would reject your customs, I accept your rejection of ours." He laughed and grabbed for another chunk of man flesh. "Your refusal just leaves more for me and my warriors." Dolfin leaned closer to Arkell and whispered, "You will not provoke me with your rudeness, demon, though you would be well to remember that I *still* hold something which you desire."

"You do indeed possess what I seek, Dolfin," Arkell responded quietly, "but do you truly *hold* it? We will speak of this on the morrow."

The balance of the feast was more food and drink. Couples started to drift off to their own private corners. Three girls hung onto Dolfin in various stages of intoxication. Yashida sat next to Arkell and ran her long nails up and down the inside of his leg. It was having a noticeable effect.

Vanjar drifted over to Petal and spoke in her ear. "I have been forbidden the nectar of your loins until I serve our lord better, but I would have a word with you in the meantime."

Petal was shocked but struggled to hide it, as well as the savoring of the news. "He has forbidden *you* sex while wallowing in it himself?"

"He is liege lord. Rules are of his making," Vanjar responded. "But I need a *word* with you in private."

She glanced around to be sure they weren't being heard. "Meet me in the hall after Lord Dolfin leaves for the harem," she whispered.

Arkell stood up and stretched. Yashida clung to him like a cobweb. Dar turned his head and looked at Arkell.

"I have had a full day, Dolfin. I will take your gift to my room and sample her bliss. If she tires, I will send for more. We can discuss my business with you in the morning." Arkell smiled.

"Your beast seemed to enjoy the gor." Dolfin slobbered. "We will hunt more tomorrow. We can talk while we hunt, provided Yashida leaves you the strength." He laughed.

"Sleep well, lord tyrant, dream of profits and compromise," Arkell said as he scooped Yashida up under his arm and walked from the room with Dar in his wake.

****

When they got to his room, he kicked the door open with his boot and threw Yashida on the bed.

"Get naked, woman. I will wash before we dally."

Dar lay down on the threshold of the balcony and rested his powerful jaws on his two front paws.

"I lo-o-o-ong to have you inside me, my lord demon." Yashida smiled as she licked her full lips.

"Before this night be over, woman, you will long for celibacy." Arkell smiled as he moved to the wash alcove.

A mink and a slug, beware she doesn't make you a eunuch as well.

"You have a job to do, furball," Arkell responded. *Go explore the city and find us our egress.*

I will. But first, a nap feels right.

As long as you prowl before light. We get to hunt tomorrow.

That gor is tasty meat, Dar responded.

And so was Petal, Arkell answered.

You have new fields to plow now, Ark.

And so I shall.

When Arkell went into the refresher alcove, Yashida took off her baggy pants and soft blouse. She took out a small dagger and coated its blade with the contents of a small vial. Then she placed both under the pillow and stretched out under the half closed gaze of Dar.

Arkell walked back toward the bed and dropped his tunic in a pile by the side. Yashida stared at his naked body and smiled.

"Come, my lord, and I will show you bliss such as you have never tasted before." She smiled.

The pillow under her head cradles a poisoned dagger, Ark. Beware more than the bite of her teeth.

Arkell walked over to her side of the bed and looked down at her and smiled. He took her long black hair in one ham-like fist and lifted her mouth to his. As they kissed, he reached under the pillow and palmed the blade. He released her hair as the kiss broke and looked down onto her panting form. He walked away from her, poured a goblet of wine that he used to rinse out his mouth, and then spit on the floor. Then he casually threw the dagger at the massive wooden door, burying it to the hilt.

"You won't be needing any poisoned daggers this night, wench." Arkell smiled. "And you best not consider sinking your teeth too deep into my flesh. If you so much as leave a scratch on my body, I will have Dar skin you alive with his claws and crack your skull like a sweet nut."

She was terror-stricken as she looked alternately at the knife in the door, Arkell's naked form, and Dar stretching his talon-like claws.

"Oh, *forgive me*, lord demon." She sobbed. "It was Lord Dolfin who ordered it. He said to test you in order to judge you worthy." She was sobbing uncontrollably. "*Please* … don't kill me, lord. I am most skilled and will bring you much pleasure. P-p-p-please don't kill me or give me to your beast.…"

"Then prepare to give me pleasure that I might judge YOU worthy of life." Arkell smiled and looked down at her naked form.

Indeed a mink and a slug.… Dar shook his massive head. *I'm leaving now. I'll take my nap elsewhere where it will no doubt be quieter.* Dar stood and leaped from the balcony to the roof next door and disappeared into the shadows.

Arkell advanced to the bed and proceeded to ravish Yashida in ways that made the Kama Sutra of old Earth Prime look like an old etiquette book by the ancient Emily what's-her-name.

Four hours later Yashida lay trembling and sobbing. "No more … please, Arkell … no more. I am sore and dry and I need to rest.…"

"Ah, Yashida, skill is useless without stamina." He smiled. "You have much to learn in pleasuring it would seem. And we have many hours yet before daylight."

His mind was touched by the essence of Dar. *If you'll not show the slut any mercy, at least give* me *a rest, will you?*

What mercy can a mink and slug give to one as fearsome as you, Dar? Arkell responded.

I take it back, okay? You are the king griffin and envy of the Gods. Now, *will you rest that slab of meat you torture that woman with?*

Arkell smiled and stretched like a big cat.

"All right, Yashida, perhaps a short rest would be good. You may rub oils on my body, and I will then reciprocate to you. Then a brief rest … but we are not through with probing the depths of your passion."

"Most men find me a deep ocean beyond their skills to navigate," she sighed. "To *you*, I am but a shallow puddle in an alley."

"On some world's woman, even the faintest puddle is an oasis. You have brought me some relief … and for that, I will grant you a brief respite," Arkell responded. "Now, oil my back." And he rolled over to receive a massage from the fatigued and humbled harlot.

As Yashida dug her fingers into the knotted muscles of Arkell's shoulders, Dar reached out and touched his mind.

Ah-h-h-h, thank you, Ark. That feels good. I have finished my recon. Now *perhaps you will let me get on with that nap.*

Enjoy whatever rest you can find, sweet Dar. Before dawn the tide will again rise in my loins and need release.

****

The battle group under General Slar had just completed the third dogleg of their approach to the Xeres checkpoint. They had but two more jumps before they could be in position. Throughout the trip, Slar had been both willing and glad to delegate the tacit command of the movement to Command Sergeant Major Burn. It had soon become obvious that although Slar held the rank, Burn held the respect and awe of the command firmly, let casually in his powerful hands. This created an awkward dilemma for Slar. He wanted and needed Burn for a while, but he was loath to share the glory that valuable tool could bring him. Also, after the initial wave of joy at having so competent a tool, Slar had started to have doubts about Burn. It was no secret he was Ferr's man. The coincidence of Burn having been on the station when the attack occurred was starting to itch like a fungal rash. Was Burn a blessing or a curse? Whatever, Slar had already decided this would be Sergeant Major Burn's last mission. The man had already seen too much of Slar's weaknesses, and that affront to the general's dignity in the briefing could not be allowed to go unpunished. No, he would have Burn killed. The only question now was, *how* and *when*?

Burn stepped to the command chair and said, "By your order, sir. We approach the next jump. We should alert the attack force, General."

"Very well," Slar responded with a brief wave of his hand. "Engineer, prepare for jump to hyperspace. Navigator, I want the variance as soon as we exit the Stargate. Sergeant Major, dispatch my message to the squadrons."

Decades of statistics flooded into Slar's overworked mind as he computed the areas of maximum risk into which he could send Burn. So much depended on the timing and the enemy. *Who* were they? He could send Burn to lead the diversion force. That would be good (and probably fatal) if the aggressor were Stoellean. They would shoot first and worry about the details after. However, if it were a Cartel commander, they would follow the diversion, contain it, and triangulate on the source, saving their forces and firepower for a coordinated attack on the *Flagship*. Of course, he had prepared for the Cartel alternative by moving the flag from the *Omega Star* cruiser to this *Hercules* destroyer. If the enemy *was* Stoellean, he could sacrifice Burn and isolate the attackers for an easy particle beam assault. However, if it *were* the Cartel, he would want Burn here on the bridge beside him. And what if it were some other unknown aggressor? What was *their* battle doctrine? What would *they* do? All these strategic considerations were starting to give him a headache. He wanted the power being offered him by the Prime Minister Kor-Zem, but he didn't want these responsibilities *or* the inherent dangers. One thing for certain: this would be his first and last combat mission. Charles-Henry was a dinosaur. Generals belong in the seat of power where larger plan considerations were decided, not in the front lines with the fodder. Ferr ordered his officers to lead by example. Slar preferred to lead by long distance.

"General." It was Burn interrupting his thoughts.

"Yes?" Slar responded, looking into the face that showed all the emotion of a sheet of plasteel.

"I have a Priority One message for you from General Ferr. It asks that I take you to the Stealth Cone for decrypting before we make the jump," Burn said.

"Omega's left ball, man, what is it *now?*" *Control yourself, Slar. Calm down. Perhaps Ferr has identified the enemy. This may be the clue you need.* "Very well, Sergeant Major, let's get it over with." He turned to the bridge as he rose from his chair. "Navigator, beep me on the comlink TA when we are ten beats from the jump point."

"Yes, sir, General," the Navigator responded.

The two men walked down the corridor to the stealth cone in the communications section. General Slar's thoughts were scattered. Command Sergeant Major Burn's thoughts were focused. Slar looked down on the back of the head of the shorter man and wondered how such a small body could be so deadly. He had no doubts about Burn's ability. He had read all the reports over the years. He had even had to write one of the commendations for an exceptionally bloody battle in which the only survivors were Arkell, Dar, and Burn. At this moment, Slar would gladly have traded places with the *Odd Couple.* They were supposedly off negotiating for mining rights with some backward barbarians while he, the MASTER of negotiation, was about to go into battle, the principal thing Arkell and Dar were created for in the first place.

They reached the communications section and Burn placed his hand on the clearance monitor. It blinked green with a display of his name, rank, and service number. General Slar did likewise and received a similar response. The two men walked into the small cubicle and activated the Stealth masking device, which isolated them from any and all surveillance.

"Decipher the message, Sergeant Major," Slar snapped.

"Yes, sir," Burn stoically responded. He inserted the message disk into a receptacle and punched in a series of coded letters and numbers. After a brief moment, the face of General Ferr appeared on the vidscreen and smiled a greeting to the two men.

"Honors, gentlemen. I asked that Sergeant Major Burn be present for this briefing for a couple of reasons, which will soon become clear. General Slar, your career advancement has indeed been rapid. That synergistic rise, compounded with your attachment as liaison officer to the Directorate, has unfortunately precluded you from many of the routine advantages of a normal military career. General, these are hard times for the Federation. Time seems to have eroded our insight of the Lessons Learned from our mistakes of the Carbon Jihad. I won't go into great detail of events you no doubt are more intimately familiar with than I. However, I will cut to the quick of the matter. I have known for some time now of the prime minister's plan to rapidly promote you into a position of succession, and then retire or assassinate me."

Slar felt the color rapidly drain from his face. His heartbeat increased and slowly started to reach for his laser, only to find the tight grip of Burn already removing his weapon.

"You and your brother political conspirators suffer the tragic flaw of most conspiracies, Slar. Your reach exceeds your grasp. This entire campaign—the attack, the casualty reports, the missions—are all a sham. A TEWT—a tactical exercise without troops—was designed, planned, and implemented by me to spark the Mandate and pull the teeth of your powerful coconspirators. You learn of this now. They will not know what is to happen to their plans for glory and control until much, much later. I have designated Colonel Arkell and Dar as my second in the chain of command. They will soon enter the game, albeit after you depart. Slar, after over a decade of avoiding your duty to the uniform you wear, you are now faced with a combat command and the decisions and responsibilities that are inherent in such a command. Fortunately for you, that also, like your military career, is sham. None of the brave and loyal men in this battle group need to potentially die because of your gross incompetence. However, all sham is theater, and in the spirit of all the great ancient theater, our sham shall include epic confrontation, tragic flaws, heroes, and death. *your* death has been ordained for years. How you meet that death will reveal the part you play in our little drama.

"This galactic *emergency* is, as I have explained, a mere TEWT. However, I have arranged for your battle group to converge with a real shooting adversary. A small squadron of pirates from the Belt will arrive at your checkpoint shortly. I offer you an option you are not worthy to receive. However, you wear the same uniform I do, and although you have disgraced it, I give you two options from which to make a command decision—perhaps your last command decision, but one that may offer you some hope. You may take a single scout craft manned with two androids and yourself and provide the bait for the Belters. The odds are slim that you would survive, but there *is* that possibility. *Or*, if you so choose, Command Sergeant Major Burn will give you an ancient Earth Prime poison pill called Hemlock-Zero with which you may take your own life. The pill offers certain death; the mission, probable death at the hands of phasers of Belt pirates. You may give your decision to Command Sergeant Major Burn in fifty heartbeats. Oh, one last small item, Slar. Should you manage to choose the honorable death and manage to survive, Arkell and Dar will know all. Ferr out." And the screen went black.

Slar felt incredibly cold all over, yet he was sweating like he was in a steam room. His hands were shaking and he stared at his feet and the high gloss shine of his boots. He was contemplating his distorted image in the toe of his boot when a single tear splashed down and woke him from his funk. *Damn* Kor-Zem. May he rot from the inside out. This was a result of HIS plotting. It isn't fair—Belt pirates or suicide? How did Ferr find out? *Jesus, Corbel, Xing, and Omega, is there* any *escape from this trap Ferr has thrust me into?*

"How could he have known? How could he know?" muttered the pathetic General Slar.

"A good commander knows his enemies and plans for their plans," Burn interrupted. "Governor General Ferr is a good commander—the *best* I have ever served with. And I have had the privilege to serve with the most elite. What is your decision, General Slar?" Burn asked.

"What if I do *neither*?" A plan was taking root in his mind and fueled by his own ego. "What if I choose neither and have *you* put under arrest? What then, Command Sergeant Major Burn?" Slar barked out his name like an empty threat.

Burn remained blank-faced and calm as he responded, "General, you have your orders from General Ferr. So do I. You are not to return to the bridge. If you choose the pirates, I will escort you to a scout craft, which is already prepared. The androids are programmed for the mission, and you cannot countermand their orders. If you choose the pill, I am to give it to you and watch you die. If you attempt any other action than the two prescribed by our commander, I will kill you with extreme prejudice." Burn paused and then added. "What is the general's pleasure?"

Slar looked at the rock-hard face of Burn and for a brief moment considered jumping him. The brief moment passed quickly and he collapsed to his knees and started to cry uncontrollably.

"I don't want to die … I don't want to die … oh *please* … I'm not supposed to die … I don't wanna.…"

"General," Burn calmly replied, showing no emotion at all, "I can wait no longer. Choose your fate, or I shall be forced to choose it for you."

"The p-p-pill. The pill …" Slar blubbered without looking at Burn. "Give me the bonking pill."

Burn bent down and handed Slar the oblong black pill. Then he returned to a stiff Parade Rest as Slar first looked at the pill, and then plopped it in his mouth and swallowed it. In less than five heartbeats, he grabbed his chest and his eyes bugged out. He tried to scream but nothing would come out. He fell forward, smashing his head on the pastel floor and breaking his once proud nose. His body twitched twice and it was over. He was dead.

Burn checked his vitals to be sure he was dead, and then turned and erased General Ferr's message disk. Next, he turned to the comlink and sent a two-letter encrypted message to General Ferr on a Warp-20 secure line. When received and decoded by General Ferr, the message would read "SD" (for Slar Dead). After the message was sent, he hit the emergency internal comlink and announced in a loud, clear voice, "Code Blue. Med team to com section now!"

As he waited for the med team to arrive, he looked down at the distorted shell of the would-be soldier/politician and noted that the impeccable General Slar had just voided his bowels and bladder.

"Well, General, as usual, you took the easy way out. The fact is even *you* could have probably handled that small squadron of two pirate ships. That scout craft outguns the pirates six to one, and it is four times as maneuverable. With the combined capabilities of your craft, androids, and the battle computer, you could have actually been a real hero. Now, I get to have all the fun."

Chapter Fourteen

Vanjar paced in the hall in the shadow of Lord Dolfin's larger-than-life statue. The statue had been commissioned on the second anniversary of his assumption of power. It was carved out of the rock-hard wood of the tue tree. Everything about the statue was exaggerated: the muscle definition, the cheekbones, the nose, the glare of his eyes, the tattoo on his head. Even his genitals (especially his genitals) were proportionally out of proportion. Dolfin loved that statue. And all his retainers oohed and aahed over how exacting in detail it was to their liege lord. More than one court slut was disappointed when given the opportunity to compare the reality to artistic hyperbole. Not that any of them would ever say anything. Actually, one did once say something in ill-fated jest to her lord lover. He raped her with a lance after splintering the end across her knees. Then he had her impaled naked body set in the harem with the simple warning that "the bitch displeased me with her speech." After that little incident, his women were as silent in their speech as they were ardent in their efforts to please him. Vanjar was trying to remember the face of the dead girl when Petal rounded the corner and walked up to him.

"Did Lord Dolfin *really* order us apart?" she sighed.

"Yes, child." He nodded.

"Why?" she asked. "What have we done to earn his anger?"

"It is what I have *not* done, child. He claims you are draining all my energy on the pillows, and that is the reason the spirits taunt me."

"That could not be true, could it?" she asked.

"No. That is not the reason. But were I to tell him what I have learned is the true reason, it would be much worse."

She looked at the floor and said, "I was ordered to give pleasure to the man/demon Arkell."

Vanjar just stared at her. He was confused by conflicting feelings of regret, envy, jealousy, and hope.

"Did he hurt you, child?" Vanjar asked.

"Oh no, my lord. He was a most excellent and virile partner. He was demanding yet strangely tender."

"He must have been a pleasant change for you after having to sleep with a wrinkled, thin old man of limited vitality."

"What you and I share is more than just the animal joining master." She reached up and touched his hand gently. "I shall miss you ... and pray for our reunion." She kissed his hand.

Vanjar felt a pang in his throat and a strange wetness in his eyes. "You are a kind child and a poor liar, Petal, my sweet. But this may be for the good in the long run. What is he really like? Can he be trusted?"

Petal now looked at the magician with a mingling of confusion and concern. She believed Arkell could be trusted. He promised not to share his knowing of her astral wanderings, and that was something she had kept even from Vanjar. Yet now she questioned how much she could trust her old lover. He was out of favor with Dolfin and striving to repair that damage. She must be careful what she shared with him while still maintaining him as a source of future information.

"I believe so, my lord. He has many wants and needs besides sheathing his short sword. And I know he does not trust Lord Dolfin and expects treachery."

Vanjar pondered for a long moment as his thoughts raced. He thought of the words of his grandmother's spirit, the soft feel of Petal, the churning release of sexual climax, the size and power of Arkell, and the awful terror of Dar.

"Petal, I need you to do me a service," he said quietly. "But it *must* be a great secret between just the two of us."

"Anything, my lord," she said. What does he want? Would he turn against Dolfin over a mere girl? Or was there more? For many weeks now, even before the arrival of Arkell, he had not shared the details of his conversation with the spirits, although he used to give her a word-by-word recording of everything he was told.

"I need to speak to Arkell ... in private. Preferably away from the city if at all possible. Tell him for me—and *only* him, child—not to trust Dolfin in anything and to always protect his flanks. Dolfin may strike him from any direction. And I need to know what our lord asks you to do for him."

She stared at him with wide curious eyes.

"This is *important*, child," he stressed. "A very great deal is at stake. You're very life, my life, Arkell and his Dar, and perhaps thousands of others as well."

"I will do as you ask, my lord," she responded. "And none shall learn of this except you, me, and the Two-That-Are-One."

Just then they heard the approach of footsteps down the hall, and Petal ran off down the corridor in the opposite direction. Vanjar stood still in the shadow of Dolfin's statue and bowed his head in deep thought. An old man and a girl and a warrior/demon and a beast against a tyrant and the armies of an entire world.

****

Major Gos led the detail into the stealth cone and looked down on the body of Slar and then up to Command Sergeant Major Burn.

"What happened, Sergeant Major?" Gos asked.

"Suicide, sir," Burn said from the position of attention.

"How?"

"Some kind of pill. He had just received a message from General Ferr. After the message, he just reached in his pocket, took out the pill, and swallowed it. I thought it might be a stimulant or some kind."

Gos looked again at Slar and grimaced. Gods he stank. That once elegant shell, who was once called the *best looking clothes hanger a uniform ever had* had released noxious odors viscerally upsetting to everyone in the small, close-packed room, except (apparently) Burn. But then Burn has smelled more death on more worlds than almost anyone in the Federation. No wonder he had become immune to it.

"What was the content of the message, Sergeant Major?" Gos asked.

"Sir, I regret to inform you that the contents of the message were classified most secret for General Slar's eyes only. It will not impact on the conduct of our mission and is of no tactical value to our situation."

Gos stared at Burn but quickly realized the futility of probing any further. A lesser soldier could be bullied by rank and pressure. Burn cared little of rank and less of pressure of that kind. Gos knew he could learn nothing else from Burn. If the message could affect the mission in any way, he knew Burn would share that portion with command. Curiosity would not be served by Command Sergeant Major Burn.

"Very well then, Command Sergeant Major. Save it for your report at the inquiry. You can tell General Ferr what you won't tell me. In the meantime, we have a battle to fight. We'll be at the last Stargate in very short order." Gos turned to the med team. "Get that body out of here and have someone clean up this mess. Put the general in a cooler. I'll file an interim report here and complete the summary court papers after the action."

As the med team shoved Slar's body into a plastic bag, Gos leaned over to Burn and covertly asked, "In your opinion, Sergeant Major, will this help or hurt our mission?"

With a stone-straight face, Burn replied, "Major, you know a lowly NCO wouldn't know diddly about the business of generals." And then he grinned a faint grin.

"Come on top. Give me a hint, will you? This entire campaign smells as bad as the late general's bodily leavings."

"Sir, I don't know what you're talking about," Burn replied. "My sinuses have been *fubar* ever since they got fried on Merrill-2."

Gos gave up and straightened himself. "Okay, Command Sergeant Major Burn, later. In the meantime, who did the general want to command the diversionary probe?"

"No idea, sir," Burn replied. "However, if I might be permitted to offer a suggestion ..." Burn said.

"Yes?"

"Why don't you send *me*? I've got nothing else better to do, and frankly, sir, I'm getting bored."

Gos smiled. "I was kinda hoping you'd suggest that. If their advance element is more than two ships, I'll give you particle beam fire support from the destroyer."

"Thank you, sir. But like we used to say at the Academy, 'You don't use Dar to pick flowers.'" Both men smiled as the warning came on announcing approach to Stargate.

****

Yashida was totally exhausted and completely terrified. Her insides were raw, and the hard muscles in her legs and hips ached. Her hair was matted and she could feel the cool breeze from the balcony doors drying the sweat on her body. If she had been turned over the cavalry at this moment, they would have considered her "rode hard and put away wet." Arkell by contrast was refreshed and rather merry.

Dar landed on the balcony with a soft thud and sat on his haunches as he glared at the two on the bed.

I take back any nice things I have ever said about you, you hairless, brainless gibbon. Dar plopped down prone and rested his huge head between his two outstretched front paws. You are the lewdest of the lewd mutant-breeding minks, and the basest of the base death swamp slugs. Your frolicking forced me to leave slimy pools of semen in my wake that could drown a navy and dehydrate a Xighian land lizard. If I could, I would stop loving you and bond with a Xighian desert coral.

"But you can't, so you won't," Arkell replied as he threw a pillow at the resting beast. "Did your recon reveal anything beyond your bodily excretions?"

It revealed that walls do not a fortress make. This walled anachronism has more loopholes than a galactic bank contract. Should we need to, we can leave when we choose.

"Fine," Arkell responded. "Sometime during the hunt today, I need to break away and contact General Ferr. But first, I want to see Petal."

Gods, man! Haven't you had enough? Dar moaned as he moved his two front paws over his snout.

Arkell smiled and responded, "Yes, for now. I need to see her to *talk.* We both know Dolfin has no intention of giving us what we need. He would kill us outright if he could, or thought he could. But as dumb as he is, he is experienced enough to realize he may have more than a little trouble disposing us off."

Dar pawed at his snout and then rolled over onto his back and lay supine with all four massive legs pointing to the ceiling. *Let's just kill him outright and deal with someone else. That magician perhaps?*

"No. Not just yet anyway," Arkell answered. "I doubt these people would ever accept a magician as ruler, especially one as old and apparently frail as he. Perhaps Petal's rebel brother. But I need to see him first and judge his potential."

Yashida stirred on the bed and awoke as if from a bad dream. "M-m-may I go now, my lord?" she whispered.

"Yes, you may go," Arkell replied. "Report to your master." He smiled at her almost gently. "And thank you for the brief sample of your wares."

Sample? she thought. She felt as if she had been gang raped by an entire army. She would seek out the priests and beg that she be allowed to enter a cloister for at least as long as this demon remained on this world. She staggered and limped to the door, stopping only briefly to stare at the six-inch blade buried in the hardwood door. The hilt was also buried to about the depth of her first knuckle. She shuddered and hurried as best as she could out of that nightmare room.

The nice *little one you wanted is on her way. She feels troubled and confused.*

"Let's see what she wants then." Arkell opened the large doors just as Petal was about to knock.

"Enter, Petal, we haven't much time." He closed the door behind the confused young woman and led her to the table. Dar walked over and nuzzled her leg with the side of his snout. She smiled and scratched him behind one big ear.

"You are no longer afraid of my beast?" Arkell smiled. "There are *very* few people in the entire galaxy who would dare attempt what you do ... and less than a handful who could survive it."

Petal smiled. "Dar is sweet. He may appear fierce, but I *sense* a gentleness in his nature. Besides, if you two truly share thoughts and feelings, he has already enjoyed more than just an ear scratching from me."

This one is special, *Ark. Even I like her. You may tell her I like her.*

"Dar says to tell you he likes you." Arkell smiled. "In fact, he thinks you are rather *special*."

"Thank you, sweet Dar, but I am but a weak shadow of my lost mother. Now *she* was truly special…" Petal drifted off for a moment in deep introspection.

"We will deal with that problem later, girl. First, we need time to be alone undisturbed so that we may contact your brother. I want to discuss matters with him," Arkell said.

"We have time now," Petal responded. "You don't leave for the hunt until after the noon meal. But first, there is someone who wishes to speak to you here."

"Who?" Arkell asked, striving to hide his curiosity.

"Magician Vanjar," she answered. "I know not what he wants of you, but it must be important. He has been ordered by Lord Dolfin to avoid me and *all* sexual intercourse. Yet the magician sought me out even in the wake of such an order to seek an audience with you. It is most unlike him to go against even the slightest whim of Lord Dolfin. For him to seek me out to arrange a meeting for the two of you is most extraordinary." Petal said all this while nonchalantly stroking Dar's back, eliciting a low rumbling, purring sound.

"Where is the magician now?" Arkell asked.

"He awaits word in his chambers. I cannot go there, but I can send word."

"That is not necessary." Arkell grinned. "Here is what I want you to do." And Arkell explained his brief plan to Petal as Dar purred deeply like a rumbling turbine. When he was finished, he kissed her lightly on the mouth and patted her behind to send her on her way. She started for the door and stopped. She came back, and taking the massive head of Dar in both her dainty hands, she kissed him on the top of his wet snout. Then she turned and left the room.

Ark, my friend, that *one is truly* special. *Let's be sure to keep her alive.* Dar purred.

"Agreed." Arkell nodded as he turned and walked to a cluster of furs and pillows on the floor at the base of his bed. He sat down in a lotus position and rested his upturned hands on his knees. "See that I am not disturbed, Dar."

Your shell shall be safe even if General Ferr were to call me to the final battle.

Arkell drifted off into a deep Doutrin trance and felt his astral spirit rise from his body. He looked down on his resting body and the massive Dar seated next to it, facing the door like a sphinx.

Safe journey, hairless one. Fear not for your puny body. Dar the terrible shall protect it, as always.

Arkell drifted out of the room and floated above the palace as he allowed his essence to absorb the feelings of the city. He quickly cataloged the feedback he received: fear, submission, fear, anger, fear, desperation, fear, duplicity, fear, betrayal, and always and everywhere—fear.

He followed his hunter instincts and sought out the essence of Vanjar the magician. He found the man supine on a prayer rug in converse with the spirit of a very old Crone, his grandmother's spirit it seemed.

"Grandmother, your riddles are driving me *mad*. I already have asked Petal to speak to the Two-That-Are-One for me, but I know not yet what to ask of them."

Vanjar, the old spirit responded, *I can help you no more than I have. For what you must say to Arkell, you had best decide soon, for he is here with us now.*

Peace and contentment, Reverend Mother, Arkell responded.

Honors and joy, great warrior. My grandson awaits you, she replied.

A moment, Reverend Mother, if you please. I seek knowledge of a lost soul called Amelia in her worldly life. She has been trapped on the astral plane in the wake of a terrible tragedy. Do you know of her?

I know of her, was the response.

I would help her if I could but find her, Arkell replied.

She is beyond help from any but a master of Doutrin, and none such exist on this world. If you can find such a one, there may be hope. Otherwise, she is lost.

I am such a master, Arkell answered.

Impossible! You are too young. But she probed his essence and expressed shock and surprise. *By the comingling of Gods' blood, you are such a one.*

Yes, Reverend Mother, can you help me help her?

Perhaps. I will seek what I may find. Meanwhile, do what you can for this poor wretch of a grandson of mine, master. He is tainted but his fate may yet erase that stain. She winked out of existence in half a heartbeat, leaving Arkell's spirit alone with Vanjar.

Vanjar, this is Arkell of the Two-That-Are-One, speak to me. What do you seek?

"How … h-h-how can it be? You are alive still, yet you move with spirits and come to me in this way. How?" Vanjar had made a rapid transition from frustration to wonder to fear.

Worry not on the how of things, magician. I have little time to instruct old men. Speak of what you want. As a courtesy to your grandmother, I shall listen and give it thought.

Vanjar trembled. For years he and Dolfin had been the perfect combination for the controlling of the planet. Dolfin had no equal at arms, and Vanjar had no equal in dealing with the spirit world. Here now was one man clearly the superior to each of the two most powerful men on the planet.

Speak, magician, I have little time and much to do, Arkell growled.

"Oh, master, lord demon, I need much time to talk with you, but speed be a concern now and I shall try to be brief. Do *not* trust, my lord Dolfin. He means you grave ill.

I need no dried up old mage to tell me that. He fears me. And to a man who has never known fear, it is a dangerous situation. I know he would kill me if he could, but he couldn't. He would use me if he could to his own selfish ends, but he couldn't. He faces dilemma he would turn to his advantage, but he couldn't.

Vanjar had hoped to ingratiate himself to Arkell and Dar by providing them with insight he could barter for deeds. He now realized he had no leverage and was doubly confounded.

"Master, for my entire life, I have served my lord Dolfin. I have been his eyes and ears and given him what he needed to conquer and rule…"

He apparently has done both badly, Arkell interrupted.

"Indeed he has, and in so doing, he has cursed me in the eyes of the spirits. I am ordered by the spirit of my grandmother to aide you in retrieving the lost soul of Amelia, but I know not how."

107

Arkell looked down on the trembling sweat-covered body of the frail old magician and immediately hatched a plan.

Magician, I will do you a service, and you may choose what it is to be. I can either have Dar come to your room and disembowel you, or you can swear an oath. If you break the oath, I will personally hurl your soul into the abyss while you yet live and disintegrate your earthen shell. My time grows short, choose.

Vanjar didn't need to hesitate a moment. "The oath ... any oath of your choosing."

Very well then. Repeat after me: I, Vanjar ...

"I, Vanjar ..."

... swear true faith, fealty, and total obedience ...

"... swear true faith, fealty, and total obedience ..."

... to the Two-That-Are-One.

"... to the Two-That-Are-One."

I hereby forsake Lord Dolfin ...

"I-I hereby forsake Lord Dolfin ..." He shuddered.

... and pledge my life and soul ...

"... and pledge my life and soul ..."

... to aiding in the recovering ...

"... to aiding in the recovering ..."

... of the soul of Lady Amelia ...

"... of the soul of Lady Amelia ..."

... and the establishment ...

"... and the establishment ..."

... of the new order.

"... of the new order."

Arkell reached his astral hand into the chest of the trembling Vanjar and touched his soul. Vanjar felt a stab of ice into his chest, and then a warm glow throughout his body.

It is done, Arkell said. *I will come to you this evening before we eat, and we will take counsel and discuss plans for a new beginning.*

Vanjar suddenly blacked out into a deep restful sleep, and Arkell drifted off to his next meeting.

Chapter Fifteen

Sergeant Major Burn was sitting in the small scout/attack craft awaiting clearance to take off. The two androids accompanying him on this mission were seated directly behind him and linked with the battle computer and fire direction control.

Whether it was a one-on-one physical confrontation with another soldier or a task force attack formation, Burn always experienced that precontact adrenaline rush, which was both his narcotic, and probably the reason he remained in uniform years after he could have collected a pension and retired to Auellos-9 and a daily agenda of drink, smoke, and fornication. He had met few who shared his feelings in this long and distinguished career: General Ferr for sure, Arkell, and Dar (although that big hairy fighting machine was bred for this).

The green light blinked on, and a voice spoke the spark which would ignite him.

"Go!" the voice said. And he did.

Immediately, he was clear of the ship. His battle computer winked on to display data: bogies, range, azimuths, weapons systems status, fuel, etc. He had already decided on an attack plan. Yes, he had no intention of mere reconnaissance. He didn't yet want the major and the others on board to know who these aggressors were. General Ferr had arranged to deliver those Belt pirates into this quadrant as a clever *red herring,* and it was Burn's job to eliminate any telltale smell of fish.

On the bridge, the major monitored the sergeant major's progress.

"Status," he asked, rehashing the plan for Burn to hide behind a small group of asteroids and report an updated situation report to the con.

"He should be in position in about three zero beats," responded the navigator.

Burn punched in two sets of coordinates into the computer and received a warning from one of the androids behind him.

"Error. Error. Incorrect coordinates. Light drive *not* programmed," the android said.

"Countermand code: two-nine-zulu-ferr," he responded.

"Confirmed. By your order," the android came back.

"Bonking-A by my goddamn order. Prepare to jump. Jump!" He pushed the button that drove the small craft into hyperspace and blinked them back into real time a few thousand miles *behind* the pirate craft.

On the bridge, the navigator stared at his screen.

"Omega's left ball, they're *gone*!" he shouted.

"Who's gone? The bogies?" the major asked.

"No, sir, Sergeant Major Burn is gone. He was there … on the proper azimuth … then … *he's gone*?"

"Could he have been hit?" Major Gos moved to look at the screen himself.

"No, sir. Bogies are still out of range, and I can't find … *hey* … wait a bit … *there* … *behind* the two bogies … a small craft … *phlegm* … it's him, sir." The navigator turned and looked up at the major.

"He went hyper and dropped in behind them …" Gos mused. "Son of a bitch. What is that old war horse up to?"

The navigator, ruffled and confused, said, "They'll pick him up on their rear screen and zap him for sure."

"No, they won't." Gos smiled. "They'll have all their power diverted to the forward screens to keep track of us, and Burn *knows* that. I don't know whether he's brilliant, bonking crazy, or just plain foolish."

"Sir, the command sergeant major is *not* noted for being foolish," the navigator added.

Burn knew the design of the pirate craft well. If they were approaching a prospect target, they would have shifted their scans to full power *forward*, leaving him and his small vessel in the wake of unskinned darkness in their baffle. He gently increased his speed to close the gap between himself and the pirates.

"Get ready, fellas, it's about to get busy." He grinned. "Grumpy," he said to one of the androids, "prepare a proton enema for *bogie right*. As soon as the shot is fired, I need two equidistant hundred-mile doglegs. Stat, turn left. Sprint, turn right. Sprint, I want us to end up with *boggie left* between us and the explosion of *boggie right* before the burst dissipates."

"There will be a two-second delay, sir," the navigational android replied.

"You make it *one second* or I'll turn you into scrap."

"I can make it simultaneous, sir, but *you* would suffer a negative physical reaction that would debilitate you for at least ten seconds."

"Then *do* it, goddamn it. I'll give you twenty seconds worth of commands before we fire."

"Is it our intention, sir, to cripple *bogie left* and take prisoners?"

"No, you metallic sewer coupling. It is our goal to blow that bonker into oblivion," Burn responded.

"Yes, sir, confirmed," the android replied.

****

Arkell's astral spirit was drifting in suspension over the high mountaintops of the northern range. He had found Lacracken seated in a hide-covered tent contemplating the heart of a sweetened. The astral Arkell touched the mind of the rebel chief and called him to the astral plane. Lacracken was startled but recovered quickly and posted guards at his door as he struggled to settle himself into a trance. Moments later his spirit was drifting above his tent and confronted by the spirit of Arkell.

Are you the Two-That-Are-One that my sister spoke to me of?

I am but half of that oneness. You may call me Arkell.

Then what are we to speak of, Arkell?

Simple things would be best: power, glory, ridding your planet of fear, and Lord Dolfin.

That should go without saying. One assumes the other. What are your terms?

Hard, Arkell replied. *Honesty, integrity, fairness, the greater good for the greater number, and the introduction of a profitable commerce and alliance that will speed your civilization centuries into the future.*

Speak to me that I may comply, Lacracken responded.

****

The officers and men on the bridge of the battle cruiser were charged with anticipation in a sea of total silence. The silence was broken when one of the technicians cracked his knuckles.

Major Gos turned from the screen and asked, "What the bonk is that old Noy dog doing?"

As if in answer to his question, the screen flashed and the windows erupted in white light as *bogie right* exploded. The eyes of those watching barely had readjusted and shifted to the screen when the second craft, *bogie left*, joined its sister in oblivion. For the brief second before the second explosion, the sergeant major's small craft had appeared to shift positions from behind the first Bogie in front of the second, then it too winked out of existence.

"Omega's left ball!" Gos exploded. "Why in the nebula did he do *that*? Where is he?"

"I don't know, sir," the navigator answered. "I would assume his craft was destroyed within the second explosion. He *seemed* to be awfully close. How he got there I just can imagine …"

"Could he have tried hyperdrive jumps?" Gos asked.

"Impossible, sir, not enough room. And if he pushed the scout to its maximum, he *still* couldn't have made it to where he appeared without scrambling his insides."

"Fine," Gos muttered. "And just what am I supposed to write in the bonking smegma log?"

****

After Arkell had concluded his astral meeting with Lacracken and made the necessary plans, he made one more stop to a very special place in the *Never Never Land* of the spirit world before he returned to his room.

He had just entered his body and was experiencing the heightened awareness of the normal six senses when Dar's thoughts touched him. *Well, you cut that close, my hairless brother. A frightened messenger just announced through the door that you are to meet the great Lord Tattoo Head in the arms room in twenty minutes. So brief me quickly before we go sporting with Dolfin the vain.*

Arkell settled his breathing and exhaled deeply. "Thank you, my sweet, but I will be hunting with our host alone today. I need you to do another more urgent errand."

What could be more urgent than hunting food, except perhaps dismembering our host? Dar asked.

"I need you to go with Petal some distance to join up with her brother, the rebel leader Lacracken, from whom I have just come." Arkell stood up to his full height and proceeded to go through a short series of stretching exercises. "I need her to guide you, and you to protect her as you would myself. I will deal with Dolfin and lay the stage for the next act."

I don't like you being alone with that psychopath, Ark. His duplicities have duplicities. He would bugger you the first time you bend over.

"Come now, Dar, you don't really question *my* ability to deal with the likes of a Dolfin?"

Ark, you could deal with a thousand Dolfins and not break a sweat. Logic dictates that. But

something beyond logic turns my stomach. I don't trust that scribbled on bonker. I have a bad "feeling." Let me come with you.

"Dar, I do believe you are getting old. If it has come time for us to send *you* to pick flowers, we will have to rewrite half the Academy's lesson plans." He smiled and ruffled his partner's mane. "Don't be an old fart. I need you to go with Petal. She has become *crucial* to our success here. Trust *me* to deal with whatever entertainments Dolfin should choose to offer."

So be it, Dar shrugged. *But if you step on your short sword, I won't be available to save your skinny hairless ass.*

"If Dolfin gets the upper hand on *me*, I will personally make a lamp shade of his scalp for your chessboard. Not that it would aid your game any."

Tell me what you require, and be sure to bring me back the livers of whatever you kill today.

Arkell proceeded to brief Dar as he washed and refreshed himself for the day's recreation.

****

Dolfin sat on his man-hide-covered chair with one large booted foot resting on a former enemy's skull. Yashida kneeled at his feet, sitting on her heels.

"Tell me all, slut," Dolfin barked. "Does this demon Arkell couple like men? Is he skilled? How long did it take you to wear him down?"

"My lord," Yashida sighed, "*never* have I ever experienced such an evening. The time you had the entire clan T'sui rape me for punishment was but a mother's goodnight kiss to what I suffered in his service last night. *Please*, Lord, do not send me to him again. Kill me rather, peel my skin from my bones and feed me to gel eels, but please don't ask me to endure his touching me ever again."

Dolfin was amazed. Yashida was an incredibly vain, selfish bitch. She prided herself in her bedroom skills and ability to take into her loins any number of men or lance staffs. She had once worn down over forty men of clan T'sui and laughed at their failure to satisfy her infinite carnal needs. This demon must be more than extraordinary.

"I prayed I had been successful in plunging that poisoned dagger into his hard muscles," she sighed, "but before our first kiss, he had found it, and he threw it into the door with such force that the very hilt was buried."

Dolfin waved a hand in the air. He hadn't expected her to succeed in killing him, but it was a chance worth taking.

"Did he in fact couple with you still?" Dolfin asked, staring in disbelief at this broken mink. "Did he enter you as a man?"

"Oh, lord, he entered me *many* times, although to say it was like a man would be a gross understatement. His short sword (although it be anything but short) assaulted me like a piston in the milling machines. His control was incredible. He played me like a lute and drove me to highs even I never dreamed of. *Never* has any man ever bonked me dry. He turned my insides into a dry sandy beach, and his piston assaulted me still. At first he was *wonderful*. He brought me pleasure upon pleasure, bliss upon bliss." She halted and rested her head on the cool stone floor. "My lord, there truly *is* such a thing as *too much of a good thing*. My bliss turned into fatigue, my fatigue into terror, and *still* he continued. *Please*, my lord, kill me before you choose to send me back to him."

"You have done well, Yashida." Dolfin mused on what he had heard. "I will not kill you now, and you need not fear my sending you back to this demon." She let out a great sigh of relief and then started to tremble.

"May I leave, my lord?" she whispered. "I do not feel well at all. May I retire to the harem? I fear I shall be sick."

Dolfin smiled and stood up to look down on the woman. "Yes, slut, you may retire to the harem. I will send Av to tend to you. Perhaps a bath and a long rest will restore you."

"Thank you, my lord ... if I could just sleeeep ... *oh*!" She started and collapsed face-first on the stone floor.

Av stepped forward from behind Dolfin. He was only five two, perhaps a hundred pounds. He had a right hand tattooed with intricate runes with which he felt Yashida's head. "It is to be expected, my lord. I will remove her from your majesty."

"Yes, Av, do so." Dolfin smiled and drank from a chalice to his left. "I go to meet the demon and hunt."

"I would expect within three hours, my lord." Av smiled.

"Very well, see to Yashida." Dolfin smiled and slapped his hand on his thigh as he moved toward the door that led to the arms room.

****

Petal entered the room just as Arkell was returning from a cold shower. She walked directly over to Dar and gently scratched his snout, eliciting a deep, low-grumbling purring sound.

Arkell entered into the scene and smiled. "Petal, I have had converse with your brother. I now go to join Dolfin on the hunt. After we have gone, you will take Dar and depart to join with your brother and his men. Once you arrive your brother will tell you what is to be done. Before you leave, however, you are to visit Vanjar and tell him you will be gone for two sunsets but will return with the *new order*. That is all. Now go and prepare a small bag. You and Dar depart as soon as the dust of the hunting party has faded."

"Yes, sire," she responded. "How went your night?"

"It was entertaining." He grinned. "If not fully satisfying."

"Yashida returned to the harem looking ill. Av, the apothecary was with her when I departed. She was uncharacteristically less prideful than is her wont."

"It would appear that like your lord Dolfin, Yashida of the sheets has finally met her match." Arkell grinned as he pulled on his trousers and boots.

"She looked quite ill, my lord," Petal said concerned.

"I'm sure nothing was seriously damaged, except her pride and abundant confidence." Arkell put on his belt with the long sword and antique Randall knife. Then he tucked his laser pistol in the small of his back. "Now go and pack. Dar will join you in a short while. He has consented to let you ride his back, so that you may make the best time to Lacracken's camp. We are about to enter the endgame, Petal. All will soon be over, and Dolfin will soon be dead."

Petal beamed and yet was frightened. "Arkell, be careful. Dolfin is up to something. *Even* my lord Vanjar has asked that I tell you to protect your flanks."

"Fear not for Arkell, little one. And never fear for yourself while Dar is near. I am entrusting the most lethal weapon on this ball of dirt to your small hands. Dar will see you both safely to your brother and to a triumphant return."

****

Dolfin was in the arms room selecting his spears when Arkell entered. "Ho, demon! I trust you had a good evening." He grinned evilly. "Reportedly, your prowess exceeded even Yashida's excessive appetite."

"She was an entertaining although prideful wench. I would have asked for more, but she badly needed taming. I believe you will find her somewhat less prideful in the future, Dolfin."

"She is fatigued but resting. I sent my apothecary to her," Dolfin noted. "Now, choose a lance that we may depart for the hunt. It is a good two-hour ride to the place we would go."

Arkell looked around the room and selected a lance about ten feet long tipped with an iron broad head. He hefted the weapon and felt its balance. The staff was about three inches in diameter; it felt good in his hand. "This should do nicely. Let us be off."

"Will you ride? Or can you keep up on foot?" Dolfin asked.

"No, I will jog next to you. You have no beast of burden worthy of carrying my bulk."

Dolfin grinned and said nothing more.

The hunting party departed the front gates with Dolfin trotting his horned steed at the front and Arkell easily jogging at his side. They had traveled about an hour and a half in almost total silence when the party stopped for a rest.

"We will be there soon," Dolfin noted. "I sent a scouting party out this morning to locate a herd for us. They should pick us up soon. You may have the first kill, demon."

"Thank you." Arkell nodded. He felt strange. He couldn't isolate what it was that troubled him. A short jog like this should not have affected him at all, but he felt a slight twinge of nausea. He sipped water and quickly conducted an inventory of his body and its secretions. They had moved about another five miles when he felt a sharp pang in his side and finally identified that he had some strange sort of poison in his blood. *Omega's left ball, how did he do this to me and without Dar nearby?*

"Ho, demon!" Dolfin called from his steed. "We approach our scouts."

Arkell stood rock still and struggled to isolate the poison in his blood. He already realized that the running has speeded whatever poison he had in him into his muscle tissue. It would take him hours to isolate the cause and purge it from his body. He estimated he had time to either kill Dolfin or contact Dar. He dropped to the ground and struggled to force his body into Doutrin.

"Ha!" Dolfin shouted. "It works! Av's salve has taken hold. The mighty tree has fallen! Nev, quickly, bind the demon," he called to one of his lieutenants. "Strap him to a litter. We will return immediately to the palace. I want him chained in the tower keep before sunset."

Nev tentatively approached the fallen Arkell and proceeded to bind his legs and arms with heavy metal cable. Then he and three of his comrades quickly constructed a litter and tied Arkell to it. Within twenty minutes the hunting party was beginning their return trip. Dolfin was ecstatic. He laughed and joked all the way back to his capitol city.

Meanwhile, Arkell struggled to calm his body and slow his respiration and heartbeat. It was too late. The poison had done its job. He was totally incapacitated. And he lacked the necessary control to enter Doutrin. He was helpless and totally at the mercy of the merciless Dolfin. When the party stopped for a brief rest, Dolfin dismounted and walked over to the bound Arkell.

"Well now, Arkell, you seem rather less arrogant *now*. I will keep you drugged until I have the necessary controls to fully interrogate you. Later, we will hunt your other half. I will have his carcass sent to the taxidermist so that his form may adorn my trophy room. When I am finished squeezing information from you, I will have you skinned and made into a nice tunic and boots. I will eat your brains and your heart and feed the rest of your meat to my palace guard. I will make a gift of your liver to Av for his having developed the poison and suggesting the means of felling you." Then Dolfin walked over to the side of Arkell's litter and pissed on his head and in his open staring eyes. Then he pried open the catatonic Arkell's mouth and filled it with the last of his acrid urine, laughing insanely all the while.

****

Petal watched the hunting party depart through the front gates of the city and turned to walk to Vanjar's rooms. Dar followed in her wake, causing those they encountered in the halls to turn and run. She found Vanjar sitting quietly on a cushion with his eyes closed. When she and Dar entered the room, he opened his eyes and smiled briefly.

"You should not have come here, child," he said.

"I have a message for you, my lord magician," she said.

"Then speak it and be gone before someone sees you and reports our being together to our lord Dolfin."

"I have been told by Arkell of the Two-That-Are-One to tell you that I shall be gone for two sunsets but shall return with the *new order*."

Vanjar started and began to rise. Dar snarled a warning and the magician sat back down. Petal turned and rushed from the room. Dar slowly followed her departure. Vanjar breathed deeply and prayed. Truly, fate was playing some cruel game with him. He thought to contact his grandmother but changed his mind, choosing instead to mediate in silence and weigh the potential results of fate's cruel game. Dolfin had gone to hunt with Arkell, and he was to await a visit from Av. He breathed deeply, concentrating on exhaling and praying that his small part in the games of demons and tyrants might result in the survival of one old magician.

Chapter Sixteen

Petal walked to the front gate with Dar at her side. Small groups of people saw the strange pair and quickly moved in other directions. When they came abreast of the front gate, they were stopped by a sentry.

"Halt, girl!" the guard snapped before he noticed Dar and he backed against the wall with his hand on his weapon. "None may leave the city until our lord Dolfin returns," the guard muttered.

"I have been told to take the beast for a walk outside the city," Petal responded.

"I have been told nothing of this," the guard countered. "Return to the palace and take your strange beast with you."

Petal turned to Dar, placed her left hand in his mane, and grabbed a handful of coarse hair. Then she swung her shapely legs over his back and sat on his shoulders. The guard stared curiously at the strange pair in disbelief. When Petal was seated on Dar's back, she grabbed another handful of his mane with her right hand and dug her dainty knees into his hard side. Dar reached his snout back and nuzzled her leg. Then he rose on his hind legs and bolted through the gate and was four hundred yards past the entrance before the guard knew it had happened.

****

They galloped north in long, surging strides. Petal rested her head on Dar's mane as the wind blew her hair straight out like a flag. After the first terrifying lurch, she settled into the bounce and spring of Dar's gait and felt a strange exhilaration. Never had she felt such an awesome sense of unbridled freedom and power. They had covered over ten miles in less than twenty minutes when Dar slowed to a staccato lope and finally to a walk as they entered the woods. He stopped and nuzzled Petal for her to dismount.

"Oh, Dar!" she exclaimed. "I have never felt anything like it before. It is like riding the wind." She turned and looked back at the city's spires in the far distance. "How could we have come so far so fast?" She looked about them and off further to the north. "Our destination is yet another thirty miles that way"—she pointed to the north—"just beyond the saddle of those two mountain peaks. There is a trail that leads into a valley. My brother's camp is on the rise of the mountain to the left, just above the valley floor. If you are not too tired after our run, let us hurry."

Dar smiled to himself and thought, *Dar does not tire from such short sprints, little one. We will continue as soon as I tend to nature's call. When we get to this rebel camp, you and I shall contact Arkell and plan then for the demise of your tattooed fool.* Dar walked off to a stand of trees and marked it with his urine. Then he paused to drink from a stream before returning to his young charge. He nuzzled her leg and coaxed her back onto his back. Once she was seated, he continued north at a steady although less frenetic lope, savoring the smells of the forest through which they ran.

When they arrived at the trail she had spoken of, he smelled men in hiding and could taste the fear and apprehension in the air. He stopped and urged her to dismount. He prodded her with his snout to walk ahead of his, and he faded into the brush. She had only gone about a half mile when two armed men dropped from the trees and blocked her path.

She recovered quickly from her start and announced herself to them. "I am Petal, sister to Lacracken. I come with tidings and a fearsome weapon."

"We have been told to expect you, girl," the taller of the two men said. "Come with us, and we will lead you to your brother. It is a dangerous journey you have taken. The tyrant himself is at large this day."

She made no reference to Dar. Arkell has instructed her carefully in this part of the plan. She knew Dar was nearby and following them. Dar would allow no harm to come to her.

A short time later, they entered a medium-sized base camp on the side of a large hill. Lacracken stood outside a long hut and opened his arms to his sister.

"Petal!" he exclaimed, "Come hug your brother. We have much to discuss."

As Petal was greeted by her brother, Dar circled the camp and came in from the high side. During his stalk he was troubled by a nagging feeling that something was wrong. He wanted to try to contact Arkell but would never risk leaving his body unprotected in these hills full of frightened armed rebels. Perhaps after Petal had talked to her brother, he could get her to make contact with Ark. Perhaps Ark would just kill the tattooed fool, and they could then get off this useless chunk of dirt. In the meantime, he settled in a small shaded area above the camp and waited for Petal to call him. If he had tried to enter the camp before she called, he would doubtless have to kill several of the rebels. Ark said they needed every man they could get for the next battle.

Ark, you take care of yourself, you hairless dung slug, he thought as he drifted off into a half wakeful rest.

****

The men of the Directorate were getting restless. The Archbishop sat in a corner meditating. Isaac fooled with his small computer, adjusting figures and timetables. Jobikan and Kor-Zem sat in another corner brooding.

"We have to *act*," Kor-Zem said to Jobikan, "rather than just react. We cannot allow Ferr to maintain the initiative."

"And just what do you propose, K-Z?" Jobikan asked. "We are shackled by the Mandate. Ferr is the one who now has control. We cannot reach Slar—if he is even still on station—and Ferr has us firmly by the short hairs."

"I have a plan, my friend," the prime minister smiled.

"K-Z, I get very concerned anytime you call me 'my friend,' and I get troubled when I see you smile that wicked smile," Jobikan said. "The combination of the two occurrences promises something I don't think I am going to like."

"Listen to me, you pathetic fop," Kor-Zem growled. "As long as Ferr remains in control, we are hobbled. The longer he calls the play, the less likely we are to get out from under his hand. We have but one chance, and it must be quick." He paused and looked around the room. Then he nudged the president deeper into the corner. Using a series of their private hand signals, he outlined his plan for turning the tide. Jobikan argued vehemently against it but was frightened into finally accepting what was proposed. The turning point in the argument was when the prime minister reminded his handsome president that given time, Ferr would discover their plans, and *if* or *when* that happened, they would both find themselves either dead or on some desolate slab of rock floating out in oblivion.

The plan called for Jobikan to take a direct action against Ferr, something he was loath to do. Ferr was a most formidable adversary. Both men knew that Ferr would never allow Kor-Zem or Isaac to get close enough to him to even casually touch his person. But Jobikan was perceived (and rightly so) as harmless. Kor-Zem gave the president a small signet ring that contained a paralysis drug in a small needle. All Jobikan had to do was gently tap the general on the shoulder with the needle exposed, and he would instantly be drugged into a catatonic state, which would last for over twelve hours. Of course, if Ferr suspected anything, or could act first, he would doubtless kill Jobikan. However, Kor-Zem has convinced him that if he did not act quickly, Ferr would eventually kill them anyway when the general spoke to them again. The fear of uncertainty was overshadowed by the fear of the inevitable, and it was a nervous and sweating president Jobikan, who accepted from Kor-Zem the small ring that he placed on his right center finger.

An hour later General Ferr came into the room and all faces turned to him immediately.

"Gentlemen, if I may have a moment of your time," Ferr asked.

"When can we get out of here, General?" Isaac asked from his rocking sled.

"Soon, Mr. Chairman. A day, perhaps two. But first, permit me to conclude the briefing, which was interrupted."

Jobikan and Kor-Zem walked toward the general who casually moved so as to place Jobikan between himself, Kor-Zem, and Isaac.

"General Slar's battle group has been joined in contact. Two enemy cruisers were destroyed. Unfortunately, no prisoners were taken. Both craft were vaporized. Command Sergeant Major Burn is reported missing in action, assumed dead," General Ferr added quietly.

Kor-Zem felt a rush of relief as he nudged Jobikan, who heatedly walked forward to Ferr.

"Charles-Henry, we are *so* sorry. I know—as we all did—that Burn was more than just a superb soldier to you. We share your great loss," the president said as he took another step forward. The sweat was running rivulets down his back and the insides of his thighs. Bubbles of sweat erupted on his lip and forehead despite the cool temperature of the room. "When does Slar return?"

Ferr looked up from the floor into the oddly nervous face of the president. "I regret to inform you, gentlemen, that General Slar will not be returning. He is dead."

Shock and annoyance danced through Kor-Zem as fear and betrayal rattled Jobikan.

"How?" Kor-Zem asked. *Damn! This is no mere coincidence. Ferr knows. He had Slar killed as sure as I stand here. Well, you won't be so bonking smug for long Charles-Henry.*

"Details are not as yet available," Ferr said. "I have submitted his name for our highest commendation pending further reports from the scene."

Jobikan fought an epic battle with himself as he took one more tentative step closer to Ferr. "Oh, General, what can we say or do?" he said as he slowly raised his right hand toward Ferr's high shoulder.

Why is this fop so nervous? Ferr asked himself. *Something is afoot, but what?* Just as an instinctive warning alert sounded in the old warrior's brain, Jobikan brought a consoling hand gently down onto his shoulder. He felt a sharp pinch and instinctively started to strike. However, rather than strike a death blow to Jobikan, he used his last controlled action to strike the second button down on his tunic. It was too late to kill Jobikan or his confederates but not too late to get off that final last message. He crumpled to the floor in *a totally catatonic state.*

Omega's left ball, you old fool, he thought as he struck the ground without any feeling.

Jobikan, of all people, you would have expected this from Kor-Zem or the nails of that banking pig Isaac ... but not this perfumed popping jay Jobikan. After all these years ... all these campaigns, the great bonking Charles-Henry Ferr falls to failing by underestimating your enemies ... Arkell will be disappointed in you, General ....

"What happened!" the Archbishop shouted.

"Quick! Call the med team," Kor-Zem said. He struggled to hide his smile. Jobikan seemed in shock. Indeed, he had soiled his trousers and could feel nothing except the warm wetness that ran down his leg. "Well done, Mr. President," Kor-Zem whispered in his colleague's ear. "Now collect yourself and regain some dignity. We have much to do."

"K-Z," Jobikan whispered, "h-h-he could have killed m-m-e...."

"He *would* have, could have, should have killed us, my friend." The prime minister smiled quietly. "But not now. Now, WE have the upper hand again."

Yet, even as the med team rushed into the room, the brief encrypted message Ferr had sent was fired to the TOCC's consecution and burst to a relay station at twenty times the speed of light. It no longer mattered if Charles-Henry Ferr lived or died. Only that that message was received and acted on.

"Get him to the midsection immediately." Kor-Zem assumed control of the situation. "Have the next officer in the chain of command informed." He looked at the medical officer who was fussing with the fallen general. "Who is it?"

The med team leader looked up and said, "Colonel Doza was to assume command until the Two-That-Are-One can arrive."

Kor-Zem repressed a shudder at the thought of what would happen if his plan couldn't be completed before Arkell arrived. "Please ask Colonel Doza if the president and I could have a word with him at his first convenience.

****

Kor-Zem and Jobikan returned to the conference room and sought out Isaac, who was mumbling to himself and working on his laptop computer.

"Isaac, a moment of your time?" Kor-Zem asked.

"Omega's left ball, man," Isaac growled. "This situation is totally unacceptable, and not at all as you had indicated, I might add."

"We have no control over a bonking surprise attack, Isaac," Kor-Zem countered.

"Well, you *should have*," Isaac snapped. "What kind of intelligence operation are you fools running anyway? You have spies (*expensive* spies) spread over the entire galaxy like tug jam on bread and you can't get wind of a major coordinated attack?" Isaac spun his sled around to face the two men directly. "Bad form, gentlemen. And why by the Mints Computer could you not have done away with that bonking Mandate shit by now? At least Ferr cooperated by finally running out of fuel. By the way, is that patchwork general dead, I hope?"

"No, Isaac, Charles-Henry is *not* dead," Jobikan responded. "He has had some kind of stroke and is still in a coma." He paused and Kor-Zem stepped forward (being sure to stay out of reach of those long nails of the banking chairman).

"However, *that*, my friend, maybe to our benefit." Kor-Zem smiled.

"I am *not* your friend, Prime Minister. And don't attempt to insult me with your patronizing fawning," Isaac grumbled as he rocked his sled. "If you have a plan, let me hear it."

All the while Jobikan and Kor-Zem presented their plan, Isaac putzed with his computer, apparently only half hearing what they had to say. When they finished, he struck a series of keys and turned off his machine.

"I see," Isaac said. "It is a good plan … for *you*. It *could* be a good plan for me too if I were not the only one at risk." He paused and looked down at his wasted legs and then looked up to Kor-Zem. "Okay, K-Z, you nefarious bastard, I'll play. But mutual exploitation must be mutual. I will carry your plan to this Colonel Doza, but you will have to pay a dear price for my cooperation—and risk."

"Yes?" Kor-Zem asked.

"After the difficulties have been concluded, the Directorate will create a new galactic monetary fund. It will have supernumerary authority to establish and set *all* interests rates within the Federation and its protectorates. I shall be appointed chairman for life with a *voting* ex officio emeritus position in the Directorate. I am to be given full power and authority *without* any annoying responsibilities I do not choose."

"You ask much, Isaac, to serve as a messenger," Jobikan responded stoically.

"I ask much, because much can be won. If I choose *not* to deliver your message *or* to inform the military command of your proposal, you two have *nothing*. Of course, were The Two to learn of your proposal, you *would* have something … something most unpleasant, I would assume."

Kor-Zem fumed. Jobikan bit his lip. Isaac smiled a smile that made Kor-Zem look like a sunset on Jupiter.

"Done," Kor-Zem said through clenched teeth.

"Have it written up and duly authorized"—Isaac grinned—"and *then* I will speak with Colonel Doza." He paused and moved his sled to the refreshment table. "Don't look so put upon, K-Z. Doza *may* choose to reject our proposal and have me killed for treason. You'd like that, wouldn't you?"

****

Colonel Doza sat in General Ferr's office and fondled the reins of command. He punched in a series of *secured* files and reviewed the contents. His stone-cold face broke into a grin, and he chuckled as he grasped the full scope of the situation. As he sat wallowing in his newfound power and authority, a brief encrypted message flashed on General Ferr's screen. He authenticated it, and then decoded it. His smile vanished as his fingers dashed out a response and included a set of coordinates and time/space window.

"So," he said to himself, "the soup thickens.…"

****

Jobikan entered the midsection and nodded as he was escorted into Doctor Ne Brevet Colonel Jawkinslz.

"Mr. President, this is a surprise," the doctor said. "To what do I owe the privilege of a visit from our esteemed president and Directorate vice chairman?"

The guard stood two paces behind the president at a rigid parade rest.

"My bloody sinuses are raising hell with me again, Doctor." The president smiled his most gleaming presidential smile. "One would think with all this multifiltered, purified air we breathe I'd be spared this humility."

"Well, Mr. President, let's have a look." The doctor smiled as he moved closer. "I'll just take a small blood sample and a small beaker of your presidential urine, and then I'll put you on the scope." He turned to the guard. "Sergeant, you are dismissed. You can wait for the president in the receiving room. We'll be about a half hour or so. You can have a cup of something warm while you wait."

"Yes, sir, Doctor," the guard replied as he left the room.

"So"—Jawkinslz sat down and looked at Jobikan—"what is the *real* purpose of your visit?"

"Before the rotation is out, you will be ordered to prepare General Ferr to be moved to the Thompson-9 colony," Jobikan whispered. "Be sure he is sufficiently sedated for at least twenty-four hours."

"But what happens when he gets to Thompson-9? They will put him through a full battery of tests and learn of our subterfuge?" the doctor asked.

"He will never *get* to Thompson-9, you fool," Jobikan snapped. "We are arranging as we speak for his shuttle to suffer an unfortunate *accident*. The tide is about to turn finally in our favor."

"But *how*?" Jawkinslz asked. "Doesn't Colonel Arkell replace Charles-Henry?"

"That mutated anachronism doesn't even know what has happened to his dear general. Doza has assumed command for the time being, and it should be time enough."

"Can he be trusted?"

"None of you uniformed clowns can be trusted," Jobikan snapped. "But it would appear that the good colonel sees this unfortunate turn of events as a blessing he had not dared hope for. His obvious ambition shall be our key to success. Now, prepare Ferr for the move and give me something for my sinuses. They *really* are troubled."

****

Dar was galloping full tilt when he was suddenly touched by the essence of Arkell.

HO, furball! Your gallop feels go-o-od.

Well, you *took your bonking time contacting me,* Dar responded. *Or was it the time you took bonking that got you in the crack in the first place?*

Dolfin is slyer than we gave him credit for, brother, Arkell mused. He explained how he had been incapacitated and jailed. *I intend a little surprise for Dolfin when he visits me in the morning.*

You won't have the chance, Dar responded as he settled into a lope. *I can't allow painted vermin to abuse my sweet defenseless little Ark. I intend to shred him into taco meat before I come to your rescue.*

No you don't, furball. Dolfin must die. But neither you nor I can be the ones to do it, Arkell argued. *I have a good plan that will see Dolfin dead—a new enlightened ruler on the throne and the savior of Petal's mother. But I need you to control yourself and listen to reason.*

Can't I listen to you after *I get some exercise?*

Get your exercise by dragging your balls on this run. You will not *kill Dolfin. Slay as many of his soldiers who are foolish enough to stand in your path, but the tyrant must live so that he may die.*

You will owe *me for this,* boy-who-knows-not-where-it-is-safe-to-stick-his-penis. *Tell me your plan.*

Arkell outlined his plan for the next day as Dar continued to lope toward the city. When he had finished, he reached inside Dar's pulsating body and touched his soul lightly. Then he flew back to his Tower Keep jail cell and entered his body.

He breathed deeply, dragging oxygen into his lungs and his blood to flood his tissues with new health. After a brief moment of breathing exercise, he held his breath and ripped the first shackle and then the other from the wall. Next, he bent down and ripped the two leg irons from the wall. Later, he sat down in a lotus position and proceeded to take an inventory of his body, both internally and externally. When he had completed that task, he removed his trousers and passed the pill Av had given him. He set it on a ledge behind the huge wooden door and settled into a deep rest. He programmed his body to awaken when it sensed the vibration in the stones from entry below.

Chapter Seventeen

Colonel Doza was pacing in Ferr's office. He had difficulty focusing his thoughts. *So near and yet so far.* He walked over to the command console and checked on the status of the most recent SITREPS from the TOCC. His eyes were looking at the numbers and data being displayed, but his mind was far away when the buzzer announced a visitor at the door.

"Colonel, Mr. Isaac, chairman of the First Galactic Banking Commission, is here to see you," a voice announced.

"Send him in," Doza said as he returned to the sanctuary behind the large desk of the commander and chief. He was sitting straight up in his chair with his hands neatly resting on the desktop in front of him when Isaac glided into the room on his antigravity sled.

"Thank you for seeing me, Colonel," Isaac said.

"You have five minutes, Mr. Chairman," Doza said nonplussed. "What do you want?"

Isaac was momentarily taken aback. Men did not normally speak to *him* in this fashion. Nevertheless, he overlooked the petty personal offense and continued in a very businesslike manner. "Very well, sir. I see you are direct. I like that. It makes this easier. I will speak frankly."

"Please do," Doza said.

"Colonel Doza, as you realize, these are difficult and on occasion *awkward* times." He started to slowly rock his sled without realizing it. "There are several key points that present concern to the Directorate. Candidly, this war comes at an inopportune time."

"Is there ever an *opportune* time for a war, Mr. Chairman?" Doza asked.

"Oh, most certainly there *is*, but *you* of course should realize that as well as I. Colonel, here is the litany, and my proposal: This war interferes with critical Federation negotiations that can have dramatic economic effects on all sentient life for centuries. The Mandate prevents those with the *authority* from functioning as is most urgently needed for the good of the greater number."

Doza interrupted, "The Mandate *passes* authority to those who are most capable of preserving the Federation from ruin and destruction, sir."

"Yes, yes, of course, which brings us to my very proposal submitted for your consideration, and hopefully, approval." He paused and moved the sled closer to the desk so that one hand rested on the edge.

"Mr. Chairman, you will remove your hand and its poisoned affectations from my desk, or this meeting will conclude with your immediate death," Doza quietly said as he stared hard into Isaac's watery dung-colored eyes.

Isaac was startled by the threat. But instead of doing what a normal man would do and retreat from such a reproach, he decided to cast the dice in one win or lose chance.

"Fine, you don't trust me, and I have no reason to trust you. Let's cut to the quick and see if we can't either close this deal or die in trying," Isaac said as he backed his sled away from the desk. Doza remained blank-faced and continued to stare at the banking chairman. "I have reviewed your personnel file, Colonel, as well as all your efficiency reports." He paused and waited a two count for some response from Colonel Doza. He got none so he continued. "General Ferr's stroke is a *godsend* to you. You, my quiet blue-skinned friend, had *peaked out*. You had gone as far as you were going to go in the military, and, despite an above average ambition quotient, you had *no* chance of ever getting either a command *or* further promotion."

"I may have been given General Slar's slot had you politicians not interfered with your oh-so-transparent *hidden agendas*," Doza said. His voice was still calm and controlled, but the words showed Isaac some promise.

"Regardless of our positioning of Slar, *you*, Colonel, had reached a dead end. Even your last three efficiency reports made that clear. You have been identified as a competent *staff* officer, *not* a commander of troops, and certainly not a prospect to succeed the great legendary general Charles-Henry Ferr."

"Mr. Chairman, do you have a point? Or is your rambling merely some perverted attempt to provoke me into killing you now rather than later?" Doza asked.

"Colonel, I'm half dead already. Your threats are moot. Listen and decide. I am in a position to offer you this office *permanently*, complete with the governor general title, privileges—the whole bonking enchilada. If you are interested in realizing your lifetime dream and greatest fantasies, pour me a drink and let's continue. If not, and you want to end the act as the expendable little toy soldier, kill me, and may you rot in hell." Saliva bubbled on Isaac's lips, and sweat was flowing freely. He held half a breath and waited for his fate, all the time looking hard as plasteel into the expressionless eyes of the thin blue-skinned manikin who sat behind the huge sea of metal and wood.

Doza rose from his chair and walked around the desk. Isaac struggled not to show the fear tormenting his bowels and stomach. The colonel picked up what looked like a hand laser and pointed it at Isaac, who shut his eyes and waited for death. Rather, Doza pointed the handheld transmitter at the wall behind Isaac and depressed the trigger, opening a small concealed bar.

"What would you like to drink, Mr. Chairman?" he said as he hazarded a thin smile.

Omega's left ball, Isaac thought to himself as he breathed a sigh of relief, *we've got him.*

****

Meanwhile, in the midsection, Doctor Jawkinslz was looking down on the sedated form of General Charles-Henry Ferr. On the table next to the supine general was a series of drugs that the doctor would administer when buzzed. The two men were alone in the room and the door was sealed. Two guards were posted on the other side, unaware that the threat to their legendary leader was greater from within than from outside the midsection.

"The great governor general Charles-Henry Ferr, PhD, CVX, HCJ, SC, hero of hundreds of battles in defense of the Federation of Sentient Planets, savior of the Carbon Jihad, tamer of the Two-That-Are-One, champion of the Stoellean campaign. Arrogant, command-centered, medically pieced together bonking freak"—the doctor was on a roll—"you don't look so all-bonking-mighty legendary *now*, Chuck. You know, I would *love* to kill you myself right now, and I *would*, if it were not for the prime minister's orders and your damnable loyalty conditioning drugs. Omega's left ball, man, the only thing that *has* gone right since we landed on the godforsaken chunk of rock is that *you*, Ferr, have finally fallen. The great sadness is the fact that you were felled by President Jobikan, that Kor-Zem puppet and vidscreen fop, and *no one* can ever know. To the Federation, their great legendary leader will have died in a tragic accident in the wake of his regrettable stroke." The doctor smiled broadly and patted Ferr's scar-crossed chest.

"Actually, we do you a great service you don't deserve Charles-Henry," the doctor continued. "You now get to die during a war (and we all know how you so loved war) in a spaceship (albeit a transport) in a fiery ball of sterilizing flame, a far more fitting death for you really than a boring, quiet death in bed or behind your almost omnipotent desk and computers."

His tirade was interrupted by a high-pitched buzz and a terse command. "Prepare General Ferr for transport."

Jawkinslz looked at Ferr and at his drug tray. Then he administered the drugs and sat down. He had broken out into a cold sweat and his hands were shaking. Was this some symptom sparked by his *intent* to do harm to his commander, or was it a physical reaction to the enormous stress and pressure exerted on him by the prime minister?

Ten minutes later, four guards entered and moved the gurney holding General Ferr to the transport bay.

****

As Arkell rested on the stone floor of his cell at the top of the Tower Keep; General Ferr was being moved to the transport bay; and Dar approached the woods at the outskirts of the capital city Dolfin, a single silent battle cruiser of the Andromeda Cartel settled in an easy orbit around the mineral-rich feudal planet that was about to enjoy or suffer revolution.

The commander of the cruiser was a nine-meter-long insect-like creature named Llers. His golden brown shell reflected the ambient light of the command center as his eight legs remained as motionless as tree branches. His body consisted of three oblong sections and a rounded triangular head with two massive multifaceted disks that served as eyes. The first (or what would be considered the *shoulder*) section of his body contained organs for pumping nutrients throughout the body. The second section contained a respiratory system of sorts that extracted carbon dioxide from the liquids pulsed by the first section. The third section contained a triple stomach arrangement connected to the mandible-framed mouth by a long, flexible *esophagus*, and the fourth section was a waste management/disposal unit that extracted whatever remaining nutrients existed back to be used, and then excreted the inert waste matter through a porous membrane that covered a *tail* and dragged behind the creature, leaving a slimy stinking trail wherever it went.

Llers had trained his entire life for this mission. It was intended to be a shock raid that would result in a massive and total genocide of the population and hasty establishment of a mining colony, which would later be converted into an independently governed protectorate of the Cartel. Llers had been bred, raised, and trained for this one mission his entire long life. It had been decreed by the Most High Queen Mother that he would provide the seed to populate this world. One hundred forty-six earth years he had waited. The curse of his mandated celibacy had been filled with the dream of the glory and continuance of his line. Originally, he had been told he would not be allowed to enjoy his carnal reward until all had succeeded. He was to be allowed to mate only after succeeding in his task. Then his brood would be left on the planet and he would be permitted to return for honors and a ritual death at the mandibles of the Queen Mother. However, during the long flight, he had decided that he would consummate his due at the moment he launched the attack. He would be denied his right not a moment longer.

He had rehearsed the crew for over a month now. They were ready. He slowed the orbit of his cruiser to the minimum speed necessary to prevent the orbit from decaying, and sent the already prepared and encoded message to his superiors. As soon as they received it and responded, he would attack. In the meantime, he took nourishment, rested at his station, and dreamed of the ultimate coupling.

****

Arkell was awakened from his rest when his sensitive nervous system responded to the first vibration of a large door opening many floors below. He was instantly alert and smiling. He walked casually once around the room and did his breathing exercises. Then he stopped at the barred window and looked down at the sun rising on the horizon past the river below.

"Show time," he said to himself. He could already feel the presence of Dar in the woods outside the gates. *This* was going to be fun.

Dolfin was accompanied by Vanjar, Ar, and a platoon of his elite personal guard. The company followed Dolfin up the long stairs. They stopped halfway up the tower on the fifth level in a large arms room and collected certain tools Dolfin would use in his "interrogation" of the demon/prisoner. Then they continued up the next five levels. The only sounds being made were that of boots on stone, heavy breathing (from Vanjar and Av), and an occasional insane giggle from Dolfin.

Arkell had returned to his place on the far wall and held the broken chains in his hands. He placed his feet at shoulder-width apart in front of the broken chains, which had held his feet. His eyes were closed and his breathing shallow.

Dolfin walked into the center of the room and gloated as his company of guards and advisers joined him and closed the door, and then locked it twice. The anticipation and lust for revenge showed visibly on his cruel face. The veins at his temples pulsated and his breathing increased.

"Give him something to stir him from his rest, Av." Dolfin grinned. "I want him *aware* of what I say and what I do." Dolfin was fondling a pair of metal pliers in his hands.

Meanwhile, Dar melted out of the shadows by the front gate and purred. *This IS going to be fun,* he thought. Then he rose up onto his hind legs and *roared*—its sound echoing through the entire city and up to the Tower Keep. The sentry dropped his sweetened wine and held his ears to block out the sound. He looked outside the front gate and trembled at the terror of a pissed-off Dar. He hastily and nervously grabbed a spear, which he threw with all his might and fright at the massive target in front of him. Dar swung a long hairy arm and broke the spear in two as he bared his fangs and talons. The guard soiled his breeches but managed to rush away from the nightmare monster and toward the palace.

Dar dropped to all fours and started to sprint toward the tower. Men-at-arms had rushed out of various building when they had heard his roar. Now they stood frozen in terror, uncertain what to do. Several threw spears, which Dar either avoided or slapped from the air like annoying insects. One platoon of men formed a semicircle assault line and to their credit actually tried to attack Dar. They all soon died in a welter of gore, broken bones, and shredded flesh. Dar continued his rush to the tower.

In the tower, Dolfin lost his smile and turned to his captain of the guard. "Find out what that is," he snapped. Av was two paces away from Arkell and looking over his shoulder at his lord Dolfin.

"It is t-t-t-the b-b-b-beast, my lord. He returns," Av stuttered.

Arkell opened his eyes and smiled as he dropped the chains. All eyes were turned away from him, but the sound of the chains dropping resulted in all men snapping their attention to him.

"Yes, Dolfin"—Arkell smiled—"my other half returns to be reunited with your prisoner."

Av spun and in an act of total desperation attempted to slash at Arkell with a poisoned blade. Arkell blocked the strike and broke the little apothecary's wrist. Av screamed!

"*You* have embarrassed and annoyed me, little man," Ark said as he thrust one extended finger between two ribs and fully through the heart of Av. As Av fell to the floor already dead, Arkell took his soiled finger and put it in his mouth to suck the blood off.

Immediately, the guards swarmed toward Arkell with weapons bared. Dolfin pushed Vanjar out of the way and struggled with the twin locks on the door as his guards died by the numbers before the blur of Arkell. Vanjar retreated to a corner of the room and watched as bodies fell, flew, and died. Dolfin had opened the first lock and was opening the second when Arkell laughed at his back.

"Dolfin, there is an old saying from the ancients of my people," Arkell said as he stepped over the gore he had created to stand in the middle of the cell. "Payback is a bitch!"

Dolfin turned and swung a roundhouse blow at Arkell with the pliers he held in his right hand. Arkell dodged the blow and the force of the swing spun Dolfin completely around. Dolfin fell on his rump before quickly springing back up, drawing his sword.

"*None* can stand before the blade of Dolfin and live, demon," Dolfin roared with an embarrassing lack of conviction. Arkell bowed with a flourish and smiled.

"Then kill me, man." Arkell smiled as Dolfin charged with considerable skill, skill that had cleaved hundreds, and power. Yet, despite his skill, speed, and strength, none of his blows could even come close to the acrobatic dodges and tumbles Arkell executed. Dolfin stood in the center of the room panting heavily, resting his long sword tip on the floor as Arkell stood with arms folded in front of him, smiling.

"Dolfin, I could, and probably should, kill you right now. Omega's left ball, I *would* enjoy it even if you hadn't shown the effrontery of pissing on me with your tiny tool when I was helpless. But your death, although a certainty, unfortunately is not for me to take." Arkell grinned as he looked at the sweating, panting monarch huffing in front of him.

Just then the door shattered and fell to the floor. Dolfin turned his head and gasped at what he saw. Filling the doorway was the bulk of Dar, and his muzzle and front legs were covered in blood and gore.

Did I miss much of the fun? he asked Arkell.

"Just in time, Dar," Arkell responded. "But it is now time to leave."

Dolfin took a deep breath and swung a mighty blow in desperation so as to cleave the massive monster's head that filled the doorway. As his arm came back over his head, his wrist was grabbed by Arkell's left hand in a very tight grip and his elbow was dislocated by an almost dainty blow from Arkell's right fist. Dolfin fell to the floor and screamed in pain. Dar walked over to the fallen tyrant and placed one huge paw on his chest, pinning him to the floor. Then carefully, almost delicately, with his right paw, he extended one long talon and slowly carved a deep furrow in his left bicep. Then he repeated the process on Dolfin's right bicep, and finally on the right thigh.

"That is enough, Dar," Arkell chided. "We want to slow him down for Lacracken, but we don't want him to bleed to death … yet."

Dolfin had passed out from the pain and terror of his ordeal. Vanjar remained huddled in the corner, nearly in shock in the wake of what he had seen. Arkell walked to the window and grabbed the framework of bars in his two hands and yanked hard. The bars came out of the wall, and he dropped them on the floor on top of two of the fallen guards.

"Time to go, guys." Arkell grinned.

"B-b-but, but how? Where? Hundreds of troops will be here any moment," Vanjar asked.

"Did you take the drugs I instructed?" Arkell asked the terrified magician.

"Y-yes," Vanjar answered.

"Then we go for a swim." He swept the magician up in his arms and stepped onto the window frame. He held Vanjar close to his body with both arms wrapped around the thin old man. "Now just relax and try to meditate for the next few moments."

Arkell then leaped from the window and gracefully floated through a slow, single backward flip in a fully extended position. He struck the water feet first and immediately scissor his legs to drive them to the surface. When he broke the surface, Vanjar sputtered once and spit out water.

"We live?" Vanjar asked.

"Oh yes, we live." Arkell grinned as he watched Dar leap from the window and land with considerably less grace and a much greater splash than he and the magician had.

I would have preferred fighting our way out the front gate, Ark, Dar grumbled. *The least you could have done was let me kill that painted fool.*

"It's not paint, furball … it's a tattoo," Arkell chided as he swam with a strong sidestroke toward the opposite shore, gently holding Vanjar's head above the water.

Chapter Eighteen

Colonel Doza and the banking chairman had concluded their meeting. Isaac moved his sled from the soon-to-be late General Ferr's office to report back to Kor-Zem and Jobikan. He was now very pleased with himself and already planning for the establishment of the new Galactic Monetary Fund organization he would squire.

Again, he had played the ultimate game at great personal risk and won. Colonel Doza had even voluntarily suggested that once the terms of the Mandate had been met and power reverted back to the Directorate, perhaps he could aid Isaac in obtaining more than just mere financial control of the Federation. Ah, that Doza was a piece of work, although an emotionless blue-skinned son of a Xighian slaver. Still waters do indeed run deep. In another month, maybe two, he would not only have the Federation purse strings in his small talented hand but also the balls of the prime minister and his lackey fop president.

After Isaac left his office, Doza slowly walked to his computer and reviewed the status of the various quadrants. As he scanned the message file, he noted that he had received a Code Omega flash from his surprise survivor. He decoded it, read it twice, and purged it from the system. Then he sat behind General Ferr's desk and listened to the digital recording of his meeting with Isaac. He transferred the transcript to his personal file, had it encrypted, and dashed off a response to the Code Omega message.

Next, he reviewed the personnel status of all those currently on station. Kor-Zem, Jobikan, Isaac, and the Archbishop were all in the conference room, as were perhaps a dozen more of the Directorate. All duty personnel were at their stations, except for those in quarters resting. Doctor Jawkinslz was still in the midsection. He noted that someone had given an order to move General Ferr to the transport bay to be loaded onto transport Zimba-008. He typed in a series of commands that would delay that flight for two hours, and then took out one of the precious general's cigars. He stared at the cigar and almost smiled.

"Thank you for the cigar, General." He grinned to himself as he clipped the end and lighted it with a small hand laser. "Perhaps I can return the favor in some small fashion."

****

Llers's second in command had just received a burst of data from the Andromeda Cartel Royal Council Headquarters and responded as required. He turned to his commander and informed him that headquarters would be sending the exact coordinates at which they were to launch simultaneous attacks on the planet below. Llers acknowledged the report and drifted back to musing about his first mating with the Queen that was still sedated and resting in the Royal Cargo Suite.

Soon, he thought, *soon it will all begin with the egg.* He would sire *millions*, an entire world dynasty of all his creation. It will more than compensate for the nearly two centuries of celibacy. *Soon, Llers, soon.*

****

Lacracken had sent word to his two other camps, and all the rebels were now marching toward a rendezvous just five miles from the city. They had mustered over four hundred hardened fighters, one hundred of whom were mounted. They were armed with lance and swords, with one company of archers and one of pike men. The plan Arkell had outlined was dangerous, but one all Lacracken's commanders had embraced. There would be no reserve for this battle other than the strange Two-That-Are-One. The entire focus of the concept of this operation was to preclude the necessity for the rebel army to engage the massive numbers of Dolfin's army. The key to a rapid and successful conclusion to this campaign was for Lacracken to personally join in battle one-on-one with Dolfin—Dolfin the Cruel, Dolfin the Terrible, Dolfin of the Dung.

In his own little private world none knew of save himself, Lacracken tasted fear. He had seen the cruelty and utter savagery of Dolfin. He *hated* the man—the man who had imprisoned his world; the man who had destroyed his village; the man who had killed and raped his friends; the man who had villainously used and abused the loving warmth of the Reverend Lady Amelia; the abomination who had damned his sweet mother to the nether world to suffer for all eternity as a lost soul. He *hated* the man with every inch and fiber of his body and the total essence of his soul. Yet he now doubted. He doubted if he, Lacracken, had the power and skill necessary to kill this vermin he was to face. This was no mountain spider to be simply crushed under a boot heal, or a swamp rat to be smashed with a rock. This was a man, an evil, contemptible man, but a man whose martial skills were only overshadowed by his lust for killing. Still, he would face the animal if it should mean his own death. He had been assured that if *he* could not kill Dolfin, Arkell and Dar *would*. And all that ultimately mattered was that Dolfin die. If the spirits allowed it, Lacracken would kill him. If not, his dying joy would be the assurance that Dolfin's death would soon follow.

The column had just come to the last of their checkpoints before the final rendezvous, with the last remaining company joining them. The flankers had been drawn in and the point element had returned. The rebel army set a hasty perimeter and paused for a brief rest stop. The leader of the point element rode up to Lacracken and gave a hard smile.

"We should meet up with Jo and his men by sunset, friend. The area is secure. I'm going to grab a bite to eat and a fresh mount, then ride back out front. I'll ride back to you in about two hours. There is sign of a storm brewing."

"A storm would be good, Zel," Lacracken responded. "It will keep down the dust and mask our noise. Go take nourishment, my friend … and be careful."

The sentries were spaced ten meters apart. All were alert and charged for battle. A small ground squirrel scurried to a tree and was immediately pinned to the ground by an arrow. Lacracken turned at the sound and smiled at the small animal en brochette.

The man who fired the arrow shrugged his shoulders and smiled nervously. "If it moves, friend, it dies." He grinned. "I figure if it ain't with us, it's against us, and anything outside our perimeter is a target."

"Stay ready, Café." Lacracken grinned as he drank from a water skin.

"May I have a mouthful of that?" Arkell asked as he stepped from the shadow of a tall tree.

Immediately, an arrow flew. Arkell caught it in one hand before Lacracken could call off his men who quickly circled him.

"Hold your fire!" Lacracken barked. "H-h-how did you get in our perimeter?" he then asked.

"Fear not, Petal's brother." Arkell smiled as he took the water skin and drank. "Your men are good. But no one is *so* good as to keep Dar and Arkell out from where they would be."

"Y-y-you have *him* with you too?" Lacracken asked and weapons rattled.

"Of course, and the magician Vanjar as well. But you had better still your men first. If they were to attempt to attack sweet Dar, or our guest, many of them would die very quickly."

Lacracken turned to his men and shouted. "Lay up your arms. This is our ally. He has another and a beast with him that will *help* us. Make *no move* toward either one, or I will skin you by my own hand."

Dar casually sauntered into the camp from a small clump of scrub. Vanjar slowly followed in his wake. Dar stood up on his hind legs, stretched his talented arms wide, and yawned. Then he sat down and gently chewed at a flea lodged under his tail. Those witnessing his appearance all backed up and dropped their hands to their sides.

Can I let them all live, Ark? Dar asked.

Yes, I think that would be appropriate, Arkell responded as he walked over to Dar and scuffed his mane. Then he turned to Lacracken and said with all seriousness, "We need to talk, friend."

Lacracken, Vanjar, and the Two-That-Are-One sat huddled close together against a tree and talked for several minutes. When they finished, Lacracken sat dumbfounded yet charged with renewed hope. He looked hard at Vanjar and asked, "You would truly do this, mage?"

"I have said so, and so I shall." Vanjar nodded.

Lacracken then turned to Arkell and asked him, "What if Dar has so injured Dolfin that he does not meet me in battle?"

"His injuries are but annoyances." Arkell grinned. "They will cause him some discomfort and slow his reflexes, but they would keep no true warrior from battle against an avowed enemy." He paused and looked hard at Lacracken. "And despite his very many faults, friend, your tyrant *is* a true warrior. Even without the use of his right hand and the handicap of the wounds my other half gifted him, he remains a dangerous and formidable enemy. That you would even for a moment question him gives proof to that fact. Show him no mercy, Lacracken, for he will surely show you none. You must fight him with all the hate and fear your heart holds."

"Arkell's plan is most sound, Lacracken," Vanjar interrupted. "Were Dolfin to be killed by Arkell or Dar, he could be made a martyr, said to be vulnerable only to demons and monsters. Someone of his lieutenants, perhaps even one crueler, could take his place. But if he be killed in open combat by the leader of the resistance, none could deny you hold to his throne."

"I *don't want* his bonking throne!" Lacracken snapped. "I want my people *free*—free to choose me or reject me and select another."

Arkell smiled and rested a hand on Lacracken's shoulder. "That is well and nobly spoken, Lacracken. But it is not *our* deal. You will have your throne whether you choose to keep it or not. You will sign our agreement with the Federation and permit our mining economy to enrich your world. *Then*, if you choose to call for free and open democratic elections, you may do so."

"What is *democratic*?" he asked.

"A fool's concept of order from chaos, which merely leads to ordered chaos." Arkell smiled. "But an experiment many test. Make your own mistakes, friend Lacracken; it is your right. But know this one fact that history teaches: the most efficient, successful form of government is ruled totally and completely by an honest, caring, enlightened despot whose focus is on the best interest of the masses."

"But before he has *any* choices," Vanjar added, "he must kill Dolfin."

****

The transport carrying General Charles-Henry Ferr and one medical officer was ready to take off. It was an old yet reliable free merchant aircraft. It had once been a troop transport during the Carbon

Jihad. When it was decommissioned, it was bought by a retired pilot who saved it from the scrap heap and turned it into his own personal (and commercial) Phoenix. They received their instructions, and after acknowledging the codes, fired their boosters. Immediately, the medium-sized craft was through the landing bay door and picked up outside by the single fighter escort that would accompany them to the first Stargate.

In the recreation room, Kor-Zem, Jobikan, and Isaac sat drinking brandy, all very pleased with themselves.

"Good-bye General Ferr." Isaac smiled as he raised his glass.

"Good riddance, you battle-scarred freak." Kor-Zem grinned.

Jobikan said nothing but silently drained his glass.

Colonel Doza, meanwhile, was busy at his keyboard reviewing data and coordinating his own Phoenix file. He had one more task to accomplish before he could join the Directorate to discuss their plans for lifting the Mandate.

$$**********$$

The transport captain was an old Carbon Jihad veteran, Swin Ory, a small but barrel-chested man with a full head of blue-black hair and full-face whiskers, who had seen much and lived to tell it. He had retired from the military after a decade of peacetime and soldiering got too boring. He had then joined the merchant fleet and would continue to fly transports until the day he failed a flight physical, which, thanks to the smuggled rejuv drugs he bought from a certain Belt pirate, would be a very long time. He had never actually served with General Ferr, but he was more than passingly aware of his accomplishments. A sin really to think that so mighty a man who had survived so much could fall victim to some little clogged-up blood vessel. Come to think of it, even back when he had been a commander with a squadron, *all* officers and men were required to take a full battery of chemical enhancements to preclude just such a casualty. Surely, general officers underwent routine medical reviews. No, something is amiss here. It could have *never* been a stroke of any kind.

But Captain Ory's thoughts were interrupted when the fighter escort paged him. "You will be approaching the Stargate in two zero miles. Say again your jump coordinates for confirmation."

Ory looked at his nav computer and read off the coordinates, then waited for confirmation and authentication.

"Correction," the escort announced, "that would set you right in the middle of battle that would probably annoy you and disrupt your cargo. I will transmit revised coordinates direct to your nav computer."

Captain Ory waited for the correction to be received and acknowledged by his computer. What was it about that pilot's voice that sounded familiar? *Aw, you're imagining things, Swim ... too many voices on too many transmissions for too many years.* After a while, they all start to sound alike. Still, there was something oddly reminiscent of a long time ago.

His nav computer blinked green and he responded to the pilot. "Acknowledged. Thanks, pal. It's been a long time since I had to dodge laser fire, and I'd just as soon keep it that way."

As they approached the Stargate, Ory turned on the intercom and alerted his passengers to prepare for light speed. Ten beats later, he gave the preparatory command over the intercom, then the command of execution. When they decelerated to sunlight speed, it took a moment for Ory to collect himself. When he looked out the window in front of him, he was shocked and more than a tad concerned to see the ass end of an Andromeda Cartel battle cruiser disappearing around the horizon of the world he found himself above.

"Omega's left ball, did I bonk up or what?"

At that moment, he was rattled again as the fighter escort came up from beneath him and hung off his starboard side.

"Everything all right in there?" the pilot asked.

"*No*, everything is *not bonking all right*," Ory responded. "Did you *see that*? And where by Dar's hairy balls *are we*? And what are *you* still doing hanging around?"

"Swin, you should be careful how you use Dar's name in vain. He's only a planet away from you as we speak," the pilot said. "As for the rest, just hang in here in a slow orbit. I'll be back in a bit after I take care of that cruiser. You remain in orbit and stay calm."

"And just who the bonk are *you*, flyboy, to be telling ME what to do and how? I have *valuable* cargo on board. And before you get any pirating ideas, I have the firepower to protect my cargo … *and* friends in the Belt."

"You have friends in *many* places, Swin," the pilot said. "You just sit tight. This won't take long. Semper fi!" the pilot shouted as the escort fighter zoomed off in pursuit of the Cartel's cruiser.

Semper fi? He hadn't heard that in decades. *Well, whoever that crazy bastard is, if he could take out an Andromeda Cartel battle cruiser full of bonking bugs, I'll just wait around. In the meantime, maybe you can determine where in the nebula you are, Swin, old man. Omega's left ball, could Dar really be on that chunk of rock below? Gods, I'd rather take on that cruiser full of bugs than have Dar pissed at me. Who the gronk is that pilot?*

Just as Ory was struggling to place old voices with faces and ancient mottos, the medical officer accompanying General Ferr called on the intercom.

"How long to docking, Captain?"

"Good question, Doc," he responded, "I haven't the foggiest." And *that* was the truth.

Chapter Nineteen

Colonel Doza joined the key members of the Directorate in the recreation room, and they proceeded to make elaborate, nefarious plans for the future.

"We have contained the aggressors in all quadrants, and anticipate a termination of hostilities within short order, gentlemen," Doza said.

"Who were they?" Jobikan asked. "Belters? The Cartel? Who?"

"I'm sorry, gentlemen, but until we execute the armistice agreement, I am not at liberty to divulge that information," Doza responded stone-faced.

"Damn it, Doza," Kor-Zem muttered. "You are *one of us* now. Surely, you can share that significant bit of information with *us*."

"I'm sorry, Mr. Prime Minister, there are indications the coordinated attack was supported with very sensitive intelligence, which could have only come from within either my command or the Directorate. Until such time as we have identified the leak, and we *shall*, it would be prudent if too much military intelligence was not shared."

"A spy?" Jobikan asked.

"Of course, a spy," Isaac snapped. "The bonking Federation is rift with spies. I have spies, you have spies ... it would be normal to assume whoever attacked us had spies."

"How long before you can terminate martial law?" Kor-Zem asked. "We need to schedule much."

"Perhaps a week ... maybe two," Doza replied. "Certainly, not longer than thirty days."

"Fine," Isaac said. "Let's plan for the worst and schedule for thirty days. Here is the proposal for the monetary fund and the pro forma. I have included each of you for a two-percent override on all profits, to be dispersed on a quarterly basis." He handed them each a small disk. Jobikan inserted his into his handheld computer and scrolled past the verbiage to scan the numbers.

"Omega's left ball," he muttered, "*So much?* I had no idea."

"And that *does not* project the revenue from the mining operation on Dolfin, *or* the hypothecations from Arbitrage that are included in Annex ARZ/00342." Isaac smiled.

"What of the military?" Doza asked. "Colonel Arkell *was* named Ferr's second in command prior to his *illness*."

"That is a bit of housekeeping *you* will have to attend to, Colonel … or should I say *General*?" Kor-Zem smiled. "When he responds to his recall order, you must set the ambush. I believe a particle beam assault positioned at the coordinates of his return at the last Stargate should prove fatal *even* to The Two."

Doza nodded. "Yes, Mr. Prime Minister, it shall be done. When can I expect my promotion to be formalized?"

"At the armistice ceremony," Jobikan said as he inclined his head. "There will be a brief ceremony terminating the Mandate and the posthumous presentation of awards to General Ferr."

"Before his *illness*, the general had already recorded commendations for General Slar and Command Sergeant Major Burn," Doza added. "Perhaps we should include those in the ceremony as well."

"Certainly." Kor-Zem grinned. "Why not? Then after you have read the commendations, President Jobikan will read the orders promoting *you* to governor general *for life*. How do you like them sweeties, Doza?"

Colonel Doza nodded his head. "Yes, I rather think I *like* that scenario. Now if you, gentlemen, will excuse me, I do have some final arrangements to make." Colonel Doza rose to his feet and a stiff attention, nodded his head to the men of the Directorate, and did a smart about-face before he marched from the room.

"Can we trust him?" Isaac asked.

"No." Kor-Zem grinned. "After the armistice, and *before* any ceremony, Colonel Doza will die."

"I like that part," Isaac said. "As long as we remember that *his* is to be the *last accident*. If anything should happen to *me*, or were you dung slugs to attempt to eliminate the poor infirmed banking chairman before my monetary fund were established, all your nasty little plans would be exposed in my summary will, which, by the way, is already recorded with my executor."

"You *fool*!" Kor-Zem snapped. "And what if you suffer some *real* accident before then?"

"That would indeed be a pity, K-Z." Isaac smiled. "And more than sufficient reason for you guys to make certain I remain healthy. If not … you'd be *bonked*."

****

Llers had entered the attack coordinates into the battle computer as he nervously opened and closed his mandibles. His hormone levels were already rising in anticipation of his soon-to-be mating. He had ordered the Queen in the Royal Cargo Suite to be brought out of dormancy. He had already decided to conduct the mating ritual during the attack, so that he might consummate his birthright in concert with the destruction of the planet below. From the sterilization of the humanoid vermin on the target planet would grow a rich new Cartel culture, populated by the offspring of the great Llers the Conqueror.

His second in command had given the orders for the attack pods to be activated, and the outer doors opened. Llers crawled along the ceiling of the consecution aft for his long-awaited trip to the Royal Cargo Suite. He would issue the final command the moment the Queen, *his* Queen, first touched his genitalia with her delicate mandibles. Oh, the glory of it all.

He had entered the suite and secured the doors. He attached the onboard communicator to his antennae and gazed in wonder at the pulsating golden glory of his massive Queen. The smell of her fertility filled the room and sent his hormones soaring to unknown heights. He commenced his preliminary posturing and danced his staccato dance in front of his future. He reached out and touched the small cavernous mouth of his Queen with his two hair-covered front legs and breathed in the aroma of impending bliss deeply. His Queen reciprocated by awkwardly touching his mandibles with the gentle soft hairs of her forelegs.

As the mating ritual continued, the second officer checked off *Ready* toggles on each of the attack pods.

****

Meanwhile, on the planet below, Lacracken's army continued their march, with Arkell and Dar at each side of the man who could kill a king.

The point element leader rode back to them and stood in his stirrups as he gazed at the strange sight of Arkell and Dar flanking his leader.

"Fear not, friend Zel!" Lacracken shouted. "These be friends and valuable allies in our cause."

Uncertain, but reassured, Zel gave his report. "You are but less than an hour's march from Jo and his contingent. I have been ordered to lead you in. Jo has sent a rider with the challenge to Dolfin as you ordered."

"Good." Lacracken nodded. "Let us join our friend Jo and end this tyranny." Lacracken turned and looked down at Arkell. "What if he doesn't come but sends instead his vast army to overwhelm us?"

"Then we shall strive to make his vast army less vast, my friend." Arkell smiled.

That *would be an entertainment far greater than any of your marathon rutting, Ark,* Dar chided his other half.

Arkell turned to a soldier behind him and said, "Bring me the magician Vanjar and your leader's sister, the woman Petal."

Not now*, Ark,* Dar grumbled. *Have your brains rushed to your short sword again?*

"It's not what you think, Dar," Arkell responded. "We approach the time for me to keep a promise."

When Vanjar and Petal came forward, Arkell dropped back behind Lacracken and spoke to them both in subdued whispers accented with gasps of surprise and anticipation.

****

Dolfin lay on his large fur-covered bed chewing on a sig leaf and swallowing the pungent narcotic juice as three of Av's assistants tended to his wounds. The room was awkwardly silent as the men cleaned and dressed the long talon wounds that had sliced through skin and muscle. His right arm, his sword arm, had been repaired, but the swelling in his elbow was considerable. And despite the drugs, it still pained him when he tried to move it against all suggestions to the contrary.

"Where is Vanjar?" Dolfin growled at no one in particular.

"Gone, my lorda," a now timid captain offered.

"Gone? Where? Is he also dead like that useless herb master?" Dolfin asked. "Was he too killed like Av and my soldiers?"

"We assume so, my lord," the captain offered, "although his body was not found in the room. Nay *only you*, my lord, survived the fury of the demon and his beast." The captain thought it wise to get that in. "Those who were not killed by the beast's charge through the city reported seeing both demon and beast leap from the Tower Keep into the River Du below." He paused and added, "It was reported by some that it appeared the demon held Vanjar to his body as they leaped into the river. None could survive such a fall, sire."

"None have ever survived my wrath," he snarled between clenched teeth. "But the Two-That-Are-One slaughtered my men like straw dolls and disarmed *me*. Gods and spirits, I'll eat his brains yet!" The attendants had finished dressing his wounds, and he swept them aside with a massive left arm.

"You should rest those wounds, my lord," one of the late Av's assistants offered. "We have sewn the wounds shut, but if you stress them, the stitches may come undone and my lord will bleed more."

"Damn your stitches, man. I am *Dolfin*, not some swatch of cloth you can patch like an old woman's dress." He stood up and awkwardly stretched, wincing twice as he tested his legs and arm wounds. "I will do what I *must do*. And if your repair work fails me, I will feed you to turtles."

A soldier entered the room and whispered a brief message to the captain, who stood by the door.

"What is it, man?" Dolfin asked. "I will stand for no secret mutterings *this* day. Speak!"

The messenger backed off in terror as he handed a message hide to the captain who diffidently step forward and addressed the rabid lord Dolfin.

"My lord, a rebel army of some three to four hundred strong stands in the wood outside the front gate." He paused and struggled to find some moisture in his mouth as he continued, "Their leader, Lacracken, challenges…" He looked nervously at the message and quietly read the remainder to Dolfin as he prepared to die at his Lord's hand. "…c-c-challenges Dolfin of the Dung … to mortal combat when the sun reaches a height of the East Wall." The captain stood with his head down and awaited the fatal blow.

"Good." Dolfin laughed. "My battle lust is such that I *need* to kill something or someone. If I can't have that overgrown demon or his flea-infested pet, I can at least cleave the skull of this vagabond burner of granaries. Fetch me my mail!"

"My lord"—one of the attendants ventured forward—"with all my respect, sire … you should *not* do battle in your condition. You could, and should, send a champion of your choosing in your stead. The stitches could open. You are not yet regained of your full strength. Your sword arm is not fit …"

Dolfin glared at the speaker of those words and stepped closer to the young man. "Damn, your stitches to the stewpot. I send no second to answer a *challenge* leveled at *me*. I can *crush* this rebel fool at *half* my strength with one arm and a hangover." He grabbed the captain's long sword from its scabbard in his left hand and swung it over his head, slashing an eight-inch wooden pillar in two with one swipe. "And *whatever* arm holds the sword is *my* sword arm, fool." He then flung the sword at the wooden door, burying it halfway its length. "Now *fetch my mail*. I ride to kill an upstart. And if his army grants me the joy, we shall have a *real* battle and rid the plains of this rebel rabble." Yet, even as he grabbed a tankard of ale from a tray next to his bed, a small trickle of blood seeped from the wound in his left arm.

Chapter Twenty

Lacracken and his forces had joined with the soldiers of Jo and were resting in the assembly area just inside the tree line, which looked on the main gate of the capital city of Dolfin. Lacracken sat in his tent with his lieutenants, commanders of the cavalry, archers, and pike men, Vanjar, Petal, and the Two-That-Are-One.

"So, *that* my friends is the plan," he concluded. "You will all be in position when I ride out onto the plain to meet with the tattooed tyrant. If I am successful in killing him, Vanjar will come out and proclaim me the new ruler of our land. If"—he paused and looked around the circle at his friends, new and old—"I am cursed by the spirits and am killed by that dung roach, then Arkell will kill Dolfin and you will *attack*. Archers first, followed by cavalry on each flank, and pike men and men-at-arms up the middle. Dar will have planted his magic fires, which will, according to Arkell, explode the gates and front walls of the city. The beast Dar will attack from the rear of Dolfin's army, driving them into our cavalry and pike men." He paused again and looked hard at his old friends. "If I *do* fail to meet the challenge of Dolfin's sword ... Jo, I want you to promise to care for Petal and speed her *and* the magician away to the safety of the hills. If we fail this day, all is lost. We shall never again have such an opportunity to rid our world of this plague that has been Dolfin. Now, go to your men and prepare them for the worst. I must rest and prepare. But before you go, know this: I, Lacracken, son of Dyes and Amelia, do hereby swear by all I hold holy and dear to exert every fiber of my body and soul to defeat Dolfin of the Dung. And whether I cleave his tattoo or fill his stewpot, it has been an honor and a privilege to lead such men as you and to share our dream." He then turned to Arkell and placed one calloused hand on his hard-muscled shoulder. "Arkell, I pray, if I fail, that you succeed where I may not. Do not let my flesh be eaten by the tyrant."

Arkell smiled at Lacracken and placed his hand on the hand resting on his shoulder. "Lacracken, you *will* succeed and split your tyrant in two. Remember to show him no mercy, for he most certainly knows not the meaning of the word. Try to kill him quickly and with *extreme prejudice*. Dar has only slowed him down for you; he has not plucked his fangs. I have prepared an herb tea for you that will give you endurance and speed. Use it well and do not dally with this foe. If you make me kill this man for you, Dar and I will surely piss on your carcass before I burn it to ashes."

Lacracken smiled and nodded his head.

****

You are again too kind, Ark, Dar replied sarcastically. *This rebel leader is frightened, Ark. Can he indeed kill old bird head?*

He can ... and will, Dar, Arkell responded. *The vey root tea will restore his faith and give him the added confidence he needs. He is a warrior of some considerable worth. Once the fighting lust has charged his blood, Dolfin will have met his match.*

A soldier's death is still too good for that corrupt dung slug. I would so have enjoyed rending his flesh, Dar replied.

Such as Dolfin does not deserve the fury of my sweet Dar. Still, I confess, although I intend to see Lacracken cleave that arrogant bastard, I too would *have taken some joy in his killing. He too well enjoyed his tormenting of your other half when I was trussed and humiliated.*

His brief joy will soon be a dead memory, Ark, Dar responded as he stretched. *Well, you see to things here, Ark. I am off to retrieve our gear and plant the charges. Take care while I am gone, and please don't dally your short sword err this battle be done.*

I promise. Arkell grinned.

Ha! The promise of a mink and a slug. Dar rose and disappeared into the shadows.

Some minutes later, Dar came to a small clump of scrub brush setting against a rocky ledge. He dug out the equipment and supplies they had sequestered there and laid them out on the dirt. He picked up the small transmitter Arkell used for communicating with General Ferr and noticed that the message light was on; three messages had been sent. He listened to the messages, at first alarmed, and then with his unique smile, which turned into a deep purr in his massive throat. He tucked the transmitter into his waist harness and deposited the explosives and detonators into a small pack. Then he leaped off to set his charges and report to Arkell before the battle began.

****

Meanwhile, Arkell sat with Vanjar and Petal in a small clearing after having had Lacracken post four armed guards around them with instructions to protect the position but not interfere in anything that occurred. Vanjar was quiet but Petal beamed with excitement and anticipation.

"So now, Petal, I honor a debt," Arkell began. "As I told you, I would help you contact and save your dear lost mother's spirit."

"Oh, if only…" she started to interrupt.

"Please"—he held up a quieting hand—"I have already taken the first step; the next is for you. After my spirit visited your brother, I 'spoke' with the lady Amelia." Vanjar and Petal both stared in amazement. "Her spirit is vital; in fact, it has been enhanced by her many travels. I have counseled her, and her essence is now tuned to your own. We will now send you on a brief journey, and you will be reunited with your mother lost."

"Oh, Ark, I can never repay you for this." She sobbed.

"Be still, child," he said, "your debt, if there be any, will be greater to this old mage err we conclude."

She looked at him and then Vanjar with a look of confusion.

"Now, you need to lie flat on your back with your hands on your breasts. Breathe deeply yet without strain. Focus on exhaling and enter Doutrin. When you can look down on us and you're resting body, soar as high as you feel you can straight up until you can see only blackness and a shining blue crescent beneath you. All the time your spirit is rising, you should call out a chant of 'Mother Amelia, your daughter, Petal, calls … Mother Amelia, your daughter, Petal, calls ….' Continue the chant until you stop in the darkness and see the shining blue crescent. Your mother is awaiting your call. She will come."

"But what do I do when I find her?" Petal asked.

"Enjoy the moment until you are joined by others. Your mother and you will be guided to her final destination." Arkell smiled.

Petal lay on her back and struggled for a brief moment to be calm. Then she entered a deep Doutrin trance and commenced to follow Arkell's instructions. As she drifted above her earthly shell, she could see Arkell with his hand on Vanjar's shoulder quietly talking. She drifted up, up, up and saw the scenery below grow small. She saw Lacracken donning his battle dress and the rebel army being deployed by Jo. She saw also the gates of the city and some commotion within the walls. Then everything grew smaller and smaller until the river Du was but a narrow pen line, which faded into the puffy whiteness of clouds. The clouds lost their substance and became patchy white shadows on a field of blue and green. She could "feel" before she saw that the utter blackness was enveloping her spirit. And all the time, she continued her chant of "Mother Amelia, your daughter, Petal, calls ..." Eventually, she felt a strange yet familiar essence engulf her, and she heard the familiar sound of her mother's voice in her being.

Petal, I have come, Amelia announced.

Meanwhile, Vanjar sat with Arkell and listened to his instructions. Then he lay next to Petal's empty supine young body; he entered his own Doutrin trance and contacted the spirit of his grandmother. She came quickly.

So, Vanjar, you have taken the counsel of the Two-That-Are-One. This is good, she said.

He has told you what I will do? Vanjar asked.

Yes, child. After he found Amelia, he came to me. Are you truly ready for this ordeal? she asked.

Yes, Grandmother, I have been badly used by Dolfin, but I count the fault mine for having allowed it. When Arkell explained his plan, it made more sense than my otherwise useless existence. I am ready. Vanjar nodded.

You make your grandmother very proud, Vanjar. I knew not such things were possible until Arkell explained it to me. It shall be a wondrous and glorious event. Come, let us off. And with that, the spirits of Vanjar and his grandmother rose high on the astral plane.

As Arkell sat guard over the two empty bodies, his mind was touched by Dar. They shared a moment's converse that left Arkell frustrated and anxious. But he could do nothing until this delicate portion of his plan was complete. He relayed instructions to Dar and agreed on a rendezvous after the battle he now hoped he would not have to join.

****

The attack probes of the Andromeda Cartel battle cruiser were ready and awaiting the final command from Llers. The second officer twitched nervously in anticipation and thinly veiled jealousy over his commander's pending chore. He was so engulfed in his own private thoughts and the task of constantly monitoring the probe launch status that he failed to notice a small blip on the nav computer rapidly approaching from the rear.

Llers was bursting with hormone intoxication as his legs and mandibles danced an erratic course over the golden body of his Queen. They were rapidly approaching the moment of joining that would result in his spewing the seed of a new generation. He was poised over her genitals and quivering with anticipation. The soft fine hairs of her legs and feathery lining of her mandibles gently caressed Llers organ of procreation. He reared up to commence his climb along her shimmering back when the entire Royal Cargo Suite was engulfed in an eruption of intense white light and awesome heat. The shock of the concussion from the proton torpedo's impact virtually imploded both giant bodies as the heat and radiation incinerated all to microscopic ash. His final conscious thought was a confused synthesis of untranslatable thoughts, which roughly approximated *ecstacy/bliss*!

****

The small fighter craft had rounded the horizon of the planet at slow speed. As soon as the pilot sighted his target, he increased speed to maximum sunlight. When he reached maximum range, he pushed the craft to another five percent beyond specs, praying he wouldn't be forced to light speed, and fired four batteries of proton torpedoes at the predesignated coordinates he had fed into the battle computer of the opened hatches. The full charge from his particle beam cannon mounted in the nose. He then executed an inverted barrel roll and eased off on the throttle. He immediately switched all remaining power to the screens in case any debris that wasn't disintegrated came flying after him. He felt one slight bump and completed his Ferris wheel ride to return to the original course to confirm the kill.

"Bonking-A!" The crusty old pilot smiled. "One less roach hotel to pollute the galaxy!" He then turned his craft around and returned to the Captain Ory's merchantman. It was once again time to repay old debts that could not be repaid.

When the Cartel battle cruiser was destroyed, Swin's monitors erupted in a cacophony of distress before they all momentarily died. Power was immediately restored by the emergency systems, and his intercom buzzed almost simultaneously.

"W-W-W-What's happening?" the medical officer with Ferr asked.

"Hold your water, man," Ory snapped. Then he smiled a broad smile of genuine relief. "Unless I'm a Directorate scribe, I believe we have either just by some insane miracle survived a far off supernova, or our truant escort has just obliterated a battle cruiser from the Andromeda Cartel."

"Battle cruiser?" the medical officer asked. "I'm not rated to be in a combat zone. I have an important patient here, and we need to get him to a hospital for treatment, *immediately*."

"Relax, man," Ory responded. "We ain't going anywhere until our fighter escort returns. Whoever that crazy son of a bitch is, he told us to wait. And any swinging dick who can wipe out an Andromeda Cartel battle cruiser and who has given me an order … I'll listen to. You just take the general's temperature or read a manual. We move when I say we move, *and not before*." He terminated the conversation by killing the intercom system. *I'm* sure *I know that fighter jockey,* he thought to himself. But even if I don't, I should give me a month's rejuv drugs. Omega's left ball, a bonking battle cruiser. What the flying bonk was *that* doing here?

****

Colonel Doza sat in General Ferr's office and completed recalling the last of the maneuver elements. He was completing his after-action report, which he would deliver to the Directorate at dinner that evening. The banking chairman had already submitted his facilities requirements for his monetary fund organization and asked that a full battle group be assigned as a dedicated resource for the transition period. Doza entered all the information he had collected in the special file and encrypted it for storage.

Kor-Zem and Jobikan each approached him alone, with *revisions* to the post-armistice scenario. He smiled thinly to himself as he worked. During the isolation, he had had the Galactic Intelligence Consortium develop more detailed intel reports on each man of the Directorate (an action expressly prohibited during normal peacetime but permissible under martial law). The reading of those reports was more than a little frightening as well as amusing. They revealed the usual sexual perversions one might expect to find in powerful men, young boys and girls, interracial and even interspecies experimentation, and the like. The financial intricacies of several were so complicated and shielded to prevent even the most comprehensive investigation. Two items, which were almost surprises, were Kor-Zem's links to the Belt pirates and the almost absurd revelation that Jobikan was *not* as vacuous and two-dimensional as he appeared. Despite his benign and attractive appearance, the president was as ruthless, depraved, and manipulative as either of his coconspirators. Doza digitized all that data also and encrypted it for his special file.

He was nearing the end of his after-action report, but he stopped before finishing and rose to pour himself a drink from General Ferr's exotic stock. As he rose, his left hand fell on the medals he was to present posthumously to General Ferr, that puffed embarrassment Slar, and Command Sergeant Major Burn. He separated two from the stack and set them in the middle of the desk. The medal for General Slar he edged off the side of the desk and into the disposal chute, which would incinerate it to sterile white ash before integrating it with the station's waste treatment plant.

He then walked over to the bar and looked for the most expensive, exotic intoxicant he could find. He looked at a two-hundred-year-old bottle of Stoellean Cordial, but passed on it. Nothing from Stoellus would ever pass his scarred lips. He browsed through the bar compartment like a child in a toy store until he found an item that struck his fancy. It was an old titanium sealed box, which he opened to reveal a bottle over one thousand years old from old Earth Prime. It had an actual paper label over a glass bottle. The liquor was dark cinnamon in color, and the label was written in an old text he could not decipher. It showed a picture of an ugly, strange-feathered fowl … not fur, as was normal, but feathers. He chose to open the bottle, partly because it was closed with a real cork. He had never opened a bottle sealed with a cork. Also, the one bit of script he could decipher were the numbers "101"—the number of his old squadron—centered at the bottom of the bottle's label. It was Colonel Doza's first (though not last) shot of Wild Turkey 101. The fiery bourbon burned its way down his throat and settled in a warming glow in the pit of his stomach.

"Wow," he sighed. "I rather like that. I do believe I shall take this as partial payment for my deeds."

Chapter Twenty-One

Dolfin was seated on his huge black steed with razor-sharp blades mounted on its horns. He wore a heavy leather tunic covered in light chain-link mail. His head was adorned with a metal helmet shaped like the bird tattoo he wore, with wings sprouting from the sides. He had taken a large quantity of sig juice to dull his annoying pains. He had a medium-sized mace tied to his injured right hand. His right elbow didn't work, but his shoulder could still rotate the mace up for a feint or to block a blow. Strapped to the right side of his mount was his long sword, ready to be drawn with his left hand when he charged the rebel louse. He felt good as he rode slowly out the front gates and onto the plain where he intended to leave the hacked body of Lacracken, the upstart.

Dolfin rode out of his city with two companies of cavalry at his side. Four companies of men-at-arms were preceded by two companies of pike men. The mass of armed might spread out as they emptied the city and stretched out beyond the ends of the city's walls.

"If this mountain grub doesn't soil his trousers in fear at this spectacle, I will kill him quickly." Dolfin laughed to one of his captains.

Lacracken sat on his tan steed with black tail and looked at the approach of his sworn enemy. A tinge of fear swept through his body in a chill as he gazed at the ominous figure of the mounted Dolfin confidently approaching at the head of his vast line of soldiers. Then he recalled all the evil deeds this man had done. The women, children, and old people he had raped, tortured, or killed. The oppressive taxes he demanded and the fate to which he had damned Lady Amelia, his mother. This hardened him. He glanced once over his shoulder seeking out Arkell but could not see him. Rather, he turned to his old friend Jo and smiled.

"Death awaits." He smiled.

Jo was frightened as he quickly responded, "Don't even *think* that, friend. That pig is not half the man you are."

"Death awaits *the dung tyrant,* Jo, not this hard rebel." Lacracken grinned. "For the good of the many, I will carve me the tattooed slug," he said to Jo. And then he wheeled his mount and galloped off to the center of the plain. During the brief ride, he fired his battle lust and only for a moment thought that he might yet become a martyr. Then he thought of Arkell having the joy of killing Dolfin and of the Two-That-Are-One pissing on his carcass. "Not in this lifetime, Arkell!" he yelled as he halted his mount on the plain between the two glaring armies where a single small signal fire burned as a marker at which the two adversaries would meet.

Dolfin stopped some twenty paces in front of Lacracken and removed his helmet as he stood in his stirrups to look at his enemy.

"So, you bastard son of a mountain louse, you would challenge the Great Lord Dolfin, conqueror and ruler of our world?"

"I would exterminate a foul disease from the face of our world Dolfin of the Dung," Lacracken responded.

"Strong words from one who will feed my lowest slaves this night."

"Words will be proven with deeds, though the dung of your court lackeys blocks your hairy ears, old man."

Dolfin bristled. His blood pressure pounded a marshal beat in his veins. His recent wounds twanged as he took a deep breath and yelled, "I had thought to kill you quickly slime, but your proud words offend me. I had hoped to finish my fight with the demon and his beast before they fled my fury, but I will content myself for now with killing you and your irksome rebel cause," while he put his helmet back on his head and loosed his sword from its scabbard.

"Know this then, dung slug. If you can kill me, which is unlikely for one so old, infirmed, and ugly, the Two-That-Are-One awaits with my army and their vow to rip you to shreds should I fail to do so."

Dolfin looked hard at Lacracken and felt a slight twinge of fear. This fear thing was a new emotion to him, and it annoyed him much. "The desperate lies of a dead man will not save him from the stewpot, fool. Prepare to die slowly before the sword of your true and only lord."

Just then Arkell walked out and stood in front of Lacracken's army. He smiled as he waved his hand at Dolfin, and then shook a cajoling finger.

Dolfin dug his spurs into the flanks of his mount, *screamed* an obscene battle cry, and dropped his reins. He held his long sword in his left hand and the mace strapped to his right arm over his head. His mount was well trained in battle and needed no coaxing from bridle to join the heart of the battle. As the two mounted warriors approached each other, Dolfin's mount dropped his massive horned head and drove a bladed horn into the chest of Lacracken's blonde mount between the pulsating front legs, piercing heart and lung. Dolfin swung a mighty blow with his left arm that was awkwardly blocked by Lacracken's sword from his right hand. As Lacracken and his mount fell into the dust, the rebel leader swung his other arm with the short double-edged blade and cut off the right rear leg of Dolfin's mount, which stumbled and limped in a braying circle.

Lacracken was on his feet and ready as Dolfin dismounted and stabbed his own mount through the heart in frustration. He limped forward toward Lacracken as his right leg stiffened up on him, and he felt a warm wet stickiness soaking his trouser leg from where the stitches had let go.

The two men circled each other cautiously for a moment before Dolfin screamed an animallike yell and charged. Despite his wounds and considerable bulk, he moved with surprising speed and grace. His long sword swung an intricate pattern of figure eights in the air as he inched forward in a steady left-side forward shuffle. When he swung the mace at an opening in Lacracken defense, it was met by a feint and mighty backhand swipe, which cut the mace in two and sent an electric shock from Dolfin's injured elbow to his shoulder. He responded instinctively from years of battle experience with a backhanded riposte, which sliced through Lacracken's mail and bit into his right side above the hip, drawing blood.

Lacracken never felt the pain as he reversed his swing and chopped off the right wing from the metal bird helmet on the tyrant. He was disappointed he didn't cleave Dolfin's skull as he intended, but his blade, after slicing through the metal wing, did connect with Dolfin's right shoulder, carving a slice of meat and bone and causing the enemy's already injured right arm to hang useless.

Dolfin also ignored the new pain and increased the speed of his sword's frenetic dance. He switched with reckless abandon from the blinding figure eights to short thrusts and full roundhouse swings. One attempt by Lacracken to parry one of those massive swings chopped six inches off the tip of his sword. He then thrust his sword at Dolfin's extended left leg, but without a point, it just bumped the tyrant's thigh. Although it did not pierce the flesh, it did lacerate the wound Dar had inflicted there and caused more blood to color Dolfin's trousers. When Lacracken tried to capitalize on the sight of blood, he slashed at an apparent opening intent on cutting off Dolfin's left leg behind the knee. But Dolfin reversed his stroke and chopped off Lacracken left hand complete with short sword. The hand of the rebel leader fell into the dust still grasping the sword, which it would not release.

Lacracken backed up in shock. He looked at the huffing enemy before him and the blood spurting from the stump of his wrist. Then he swung his right foot into the dirt and sent a shower of dirt and gravel into the face of the gloating Dolfin, as he then dove in a somersault and landed next to the signal fire. He glanced back at the figure of the limping Dolfin rubbing his eyes with the back of his left hand and advancing at a limp. Lacracken smiled and thrust his left arm into the fire and pushed his wounded stump against one of the white hot rocks. He held it there for three beats and *screamed*. Then he stood up and turned to face Dolfin with a renewed and added resolve to carve him into pieces.

Both men had lost blood. But Dolfin had lost more as all the stitches from his wounds gifted from Dar either had given way or had been ripped away. Dolfin was bleeding from his shoulder and both thighs. Both arms were wet and sticky with the blood that flowed from ripped biceps. As the loss of blood fatigued him, he realized he needed to finish this fight soon or die.

Lacracken appeared to have lost any and all reason when he cauterized his wounded left arm. He was now functioning on adrenaline, hate, and full battle lust. He charged Dolfin with an apparent reckless abandon. Dolfin smiled as he saw the folly of this headlong charge. He braced himself for the attack and prepared to time his final blow that would decapitate this rebel pig. As Lacracken lunged from ten feet, Dolfin put his full back into a massive swing, which would behead this enemy, but Lacracken suddenly stopped dead in his tracks and let the swing of Dolfin's sword breeze beneath his nose by mere inches as he sidestepped and chopped down on the passing arm. He severed Dolfin's left arm just below the elbow and immediately reversed his blade to chop through the tyrant's left calf above the ankle. Dolfin screamed like an animal and fell to the ground. He was writhing in pain and swearing a stream of complex obscenities.

Lacracken walked over to the severed arm, and, dropping his own sword, he removed the sword from the grasp of the tyrant's hand. He then walked back to the frothing fallen enemy and spoke in a calm quiet voice.

"You will not die with a sword in your hand Dolfin of the Dung," he said. "And you shall not die by any other sword apart from your own." Then Lacracken hacked off the right arm of Dolfin at the elbow. Dolfin *screamed*. He chopped off the right leg at the knee. Dolfin *screamed* even more. He sliced off the mail and tunic of the babbling tyrant and dropped the sword. What remained of Dolfin was stripped naked and bloody, the dirt turning red as it struggled to absorb all the blood. Lacracken reached into his boot and took out a small very old knife with a notched dull edge. "Don't die on me yet, slug. This is the knife of my mother, the lady Amelia, whom you raped and killed while her spirit was away from her body. You killed our family, raped our women, bespoiled our fields, and cursed my mother to a limbo from which she can never find peace."

He reached down between Dolfin's legs and grabbed his penis and scrotum in his hand as he held the knife in his teeth. He tugged once, freeing Dolfin's genitals to the cool air. Then he released his grip and placed the knife under the sagging hairy scrotum and placed his boot on top of the shrunken penis. "You'll rape no more in this world or the next Dolfin." And he pulled the knife up against his boot bottom and severed the tyrant's genitals, which fell into the bloody dirt as Dolfin, once absolute ruler of an entire world, drew his last garbled gasp.

When he looked up, he found Arkell and Vanjar standing on each side of him and the two armies slowly advancing toward their location.

****

Colonel Doza sat at his computer screen and reviewed all the data displayed from various quadrants as he scrolled through the most recent SITREPS, choosing which data he would include in his consolidated status report. When he had completed the task in front of him, he copied what he wanted onto a single digital disk and picked up his small handheld computer, straightened his tunic, and buzzed the conference room where the members of the Directorate were waiting for him.

"Gentlemen, Colonel Doza here. I will be there in just a few moments to provide you with my final report." He terminated the call and collected the material he would bring.

Kor-Zem and Isaac smiled wicked smiles. Even the recently introspective Jobikan ventured a thin smile. The Archbishop looked pensive, and the governor was immensely relieved. The other members of the full Directorate mirrored various looks of apprehension, relief, and apparent satisfaction about a return to a more comfortable status quo.

Five minutes later Colonel Doza walked into a conference room charged with anticipation and apprehension. He ignored the pleading looks he received and walked directly to the computer console into which he inserted the data disk. He began his briefing.

"Gentlemen, we have concluded hostilities with the aggressor force, which I can now identify to you as having been from the Andromeda Cartel and a mercenary force comprised of Belt pirates from the asteroid jungle off Sirius." He sat down and removed a small stylus from his tunic with which he proceeded to conduct his briefing. "Please be seated and hold all questions until I have concluded my briefing." He then launched into an hour-long delineation of casualties, specific actions, cause and effects, and other boring statistical analysis presented in a detailed SWOT (strengths, weaknesses, opportunities, and threats) analysis.

All during the briefing, Isaac appeared to be only half paying attention as he futzed with his own plans for the formation and implementation of his monetary fund. Kor-Zem scribbled coded plans for the "fatal accident" of Doza and the contingency plans he considered necessary for the elimination of Arkell and Dar. Only Jobikan appeared to be listening intensely to every word Doza spoke.

At the conclusion of his briefing, Colonel Doza paused, closed his handheld computer, and looked around the table. "Now, what are your questions, gentlemen?" This was an old Charles-Henry Ferr phrase. The general had always told his officers that when providing information to subordinates, always ask "WHAT your questions are" and never "ARE there any questions." As General Ferr noted, by asking for questions, you usually got them. If you asked them if they had any, there was always the implied threat that the listener didn't comprehend what was presented and therefore a question, any question, might impugn the status of the briefer. Or worse still, the listener didn't understand what was presented because of some basic lack of intelligence. The usual result was for the listener to remain silent whether or not they did have questions. And every leader had the inherent responsibility to provide answers to *all* questions asked and unasked. It was always better to get them asked. It was an old concept and a relatively small point, but it reflected the nature of General Ferr and the quality of his leadership that he had always strove to make his subordinates both competent and comfortable.

Erupting from around the table was a cacophony of questions, which Doza calmly and professionally answered one at a time. About thirty minutes through the question and answer section of the briefing, Kor-Zem looked up from his notes and asked quietly, "When can we anticipate a termination of martial law and the revocation of the provisions of the Mandate?"

Doza looked at him with a blank face and responded quietly, "We still have three or four major 'housekeeping' chores to complete." This phrase drew a smile from the prime minister. "I suspect within thirty-six hours, I will be prepared to formally return control back to the Directorate. The military *will* remain technically in charge for the balance of the thirty days prescribed by the Mandate, but effective control would return to you, gentlemen, during the balance of the required thirty-day term. However, it would be a mere technicality, which, although it would restrict your plenary powers, would not preclude you from conducting business as usual."

The conspirators of the Directorate all smiled.

"There *is* one annoying anomaly that we need to clarify in the meantime," Doza said.

"And what is that, Colonel?" Jobikan asked well-naturedly.

"The merchant ship that was transporting General Ferr never reached its destination," he said.

Kor-Zem and Isaac immediately snapped to attention from their work. Jobikan looked up with a thinly disguised expression of terror. This was not the message they had expected. They were supposed to hear that the merchantman was destroyed by ambush after passing through the Stargate, and that General Ferr had been confirmed as a fatality of the action. They exchanged glances and looked hard at Doza, who continued with his inimitable calmness.

"There is a possibility it was destroyed by a battle cruiser from the Andromeda Cartel. We are awaiting further intelligence. Also, there has been no word from Colonel Arkell and Dar. We know not the status on the prospect planet Dolfin."

****

Arkell, Petal, Vanjar, and Jo were calmly walking onto the battlefield. Dolfin had fallen and Lacracken was in the process of hacking him to pieces when Dar communicated with his other half.

Ark, it is time we finished here, Dar called.

We are about done, Dar, Arkell responded. *There are just one or two loose ends that need tying, and we can be off.*

Well, you had better tie those ends fast, *because we have had several messages ... and shit is happening elsewhere that requires The Two.*

Arkell was suddenly concerned. He lengthened his stride toward Lacracken and the fallen Dolfin as he asked Dar, *Tell me all, furball.*

Repeat each message word for word, and do so as you move toward us. I want you with me for this final scene.

Dar proceeded to tell Arkell everything that had been communicated in the messages they had received. As he repeated the messages, he tucked the communicator into his harness and loped off after Arkell and the company.

When Arkell and company arrived at the scene of the dead Dolfin and the one-handed rebel leader, they could see the army of Dolfin walking their mounts forward in a slow, straight skirmish line. The line parted in the middle in a slightly confused hustle as Dar came galloping up the center of the plain, passing Dolfin's infantry, pike men, and cavalry. He arrived in a thud as his final leap landed him just in front of the panting, bloodied, and still glazed Lacracken. Arkell, Vanjar, Petal, and Jo stood on the other side of the grizzly pair of recent combatants.

Everyone was silent as Captain Bot of the late Dolfin's cavalry stopped some twenty yards in front of the group and removed his helmet.

Dar looked over his shoulder at the mounted warriors and then at Arkell. *May I, Ark?*

"Go ahead, Dar." Arkell smiled.

Dar walked over to Lacracken and gently moved him away with a nudge of his snout from the welter of the gore, which had been Dolfin. He then lifted one huge hind leg and pissed gallons on the bloody carcass of Dolfin the Dead.

Vanjar walked forward toward Dolfin's confused and frozen army. He threw off his dirty green robe and stood before all in a full-length white caftan, with billowy full sleeves draping to his waist when he spread his arms wide, and spoke.

"I am Vanjar, magician and counsel to the late Dolfin, once your lord. Hear me." Captain Bot and his entire army were startled and mesmerized by the sound of the magician's voice. It was not merely loud and clear, but it *commanded* them to listen. It was as if they were listening to the words of the Gods.

"The cruelty and tyranny of Dolfin is ended," he continued. "Dolfin has been slain in single combat by Lacracken, leader of the revolution and divinely ordained commander of the new order. You all know me, and you know I hold converse with the spirits. The spirits of your ancestors have counseled me on this. Captain Bot, even grandfather's father, Phot, has confirmed what I now speak. Lacracken shall rule our world henceforth. So it shall be written, and so it shall be done. He has received the blessing of the Gods, and the Two-That-Are-One, who now stands at his side. Fighting among men ends this day. Lacracken has sacrificed a hand that it may be so. If there be any among you who challenge the words of the Gods and your new lord, Lacracken the Pure, let him step forward now that he may meet the fury of the demon Arkell and his benevolent beast, Dar. For so have the spirits commanded."

Just then there was a blinding light in the sky as the entire plain flashed white. The earth shook once as if a giant had placed one annoyed boot on some distant mountaintop.

All was silent save the breathing of mounts and the whisper of the wind. Arkell and Dar exchanged private thoughts and feelings as Captain Bot stood up in his stirrups, looked up into the sky, and called to Vanjar.

"We accept this new order, mage. May we now take the body of Dolfin to prepare his hide and add his meat to the banquet feast?"

"No!" Lacracken shouted as he limped forward. "From this moment forward, there shall be no eating of human flesh by man of this world. The remains of this vile disease shall not pollute our people. His body shall be impaled on his lance and left here on the open plain for the carrion birds and scavengers to consume should they have the stomach for it. In thirty cycles, whatever is left of Dolfin shall be ground up and burned. The ashes shall be added to the dust of any and all statues of his image and spread in the sewers with our garbage and human waste. The days of Dolfin are ended. The new order shall command the greater good for the greater number. Henceforth, the function of rule shall be to provide for the comfort and well-being of our people, not the private vanities of tattooed ruthless rulers."

There was a gentle uneasiness that rumbled through the ranks of Dolfin's army, which slowly built in intensity and finally erupted in loud cheers of "Ho! Hail the new order and long live Lacracken."

Arkell turned to Vanjar and placed one large hand on his shoulder. "Well done, mage. Now my other half and I are needed elsewhere."

"You cannot go yet," Vanjar said. "We need you *now*, and soon there will be a banquet announcing the precepts of the *New Order*. Your presence is needed for support and to receive honors."

"We need no honors other than Lacracken's agreement to keep his word about the Federation treaty and mining contract." Arkell smiled. "You folks take two rotations to consolidate all and settle in the change of command and administration. Dar and I are needed urgently elsewhere. We will return in that time and join you at a feast honoring the new beginning of this world." Arkell paused and looked at Vanjar and then Lacracken. "You may want to consider renaming your world also."

"The name Dolfin shall be purged from everything and anything on the entire world," Lacracken announced.

"Then what shall you call your new world? Lacracken?" Arkell smiled.

"No. Certainly *not* for this one-handed, beat-up rebel." Lacracken grinned. "Our brave new world must have a name worthy of our great new cause and the promise it offers. I will give it some thought and take counsel with Vanjar, Petal, and our mother's spirit. We will announce it to the world and to the Two-That-Are-One when they return to our bosom two rotations hence."

Ark, it is already past time. We need to be off, Dar called.

"Gods willing, we shall return soon," Arkell said. "In the meantime, get what little rest you can." He grabbed Lacracken's good arm with his big right hand, placed his left hand on the leader's shoulder, and gave it a gentle shake. Then he turned to Vanjar and gently lifted his right hand and kissed it tenderly. Vanjar placed a thin vein-covered hand on Arkell's hard blonde head and kissed his forehead. Strange glances passed across many faces who witnessed this strange homage. Petal walked up and grabbed Arkell by both ears and kissed him hard on the mouth. When she let go, he stood up and smiled. Then she walked over to the huge Dar, who was lying down like a watching sphinx with his massive fierce head between his two awesome front paws. She gently grasped his big hairy jowls in both her dainty hands. Dar's big yellow eyes looked into the soft, gentle face of Petal and actually smiled. Petal leaned down and also kissed Dar on the mouth as he pursed his flexible lips to receive the gift.

Ark, this one is real *special.* And he gently nuzzled her thigh with his snout. Then he stood up on his hind legs to his full nine-foot-plus height and spread his arms wide, exposing his talons and fangs, and *roared* loud. *Ark, we be outta here!* And the *Odd Couple* sprinted into the woods and were gone.

Chapter Twenty-Two

Captain Ory's computers picked up the returning fighter pilot's craft as it rounded the curvature of the world below. "*Who* by Omega's left ball *are you*, man?" Swin asked the advancing fighter.

"An old friend who remains at your service and yet requires your service," the fighter responded.

"What happened to the bugs?" Ory asked.

"Exterminated and vaporized, Swin."

"Okay, sport," Ory responded, "you obviously know me. Who the bonk are *you*?"

"Open your cargo bay and we can share a drink as we renew our acquaintance as we prepare to write history."

"I carry secured cargo," he said as he thought on the potential dangers of denying this pilot courtesy. Ory had firepower to engage an attacker, but this man was obviously more than capable. If he could destroy a full Cartel battle cruiser, he could certainly take out a fat old merchantman. Friend or foe, he could be better neutralized on board than dodging around outside. Besides, General Ferr was a virtual vegetable now anyway. "I'm opening the cargo bay on the port side. You are cleared to land." *If nothing else, I'll finally find out* who *this man (if he* is *a man) is.*

The fighter dipped below the swollen belly of Ory's transport and rose up on the port side. The landing was quick and textbook perfect. Swin was standing at the loading dock with a hand laser in his right hand and his comlink to the ship's main computer turned on.

The fighter shut down its engines and the side entry hatch opened. The steps dropped down out of the side of the craft and the pilot emerged with a thin smile.

Ory's hand dropped to his side and his mouth fell open. "Omega's left ball!" he exclaimed. "Lee Burn, you Stoellean-sucking Urt bonker … they said you were dead."

Command Sergeant Major Burn walked down the steps toward Ory and smiled. "It would appear that once again, the great powers of the Xighian dung beetle Directorate have suggested their dreams as reality."

"Crex, man, I haven't seen you in a decade." Ory smiled as he holstered his laser and slapped Burn on the shoulder.

"I was going to look you up on station when the alert sounded," Burn replied. "Is the general all right?"

"What's all right?" Ory shrugged. "He is still alive, but his stroke, or whatever really happened, has turned him into Xighian swamp moss. I was transporting him to an R and R colony where he could be retired to comfort and further medical research."

"You were delivering him to his (and *your*) death, comrade Swin," Burn said.

"What?"

"Another gift from the Directorate. I'll fill you in as we walk. Take me to him now. Is there just one med officer?" Burn asked.

"I see you are as usual well briefed in matters that are supposed to be classified."

"Count yourself fortunate that this old trooper is nothing if not competent. The med officer does not know his role in this. He too was scheduled to die. Had you taken those original coordinates from the Stargate, you would have entered into a particle beam ambush that would have destroyed all evidence of the Directorate's treason, along with this fine bucket of scrap you command."

Ory took a moment to consider what was and what might have been. "Come with me. We'll get that drink *after* I show you Ferr." The two men walked off to the secured cargo area that held General Charles-Henry Ferr and his medical escort.

****

Colonel Doza had returned to his office, and Kor-Zem was deep in heated conversation with Isaac and Jobikan.

"Matters are moving nicely." Isaac smiled as he inspected his long fingernails.

"They *do not* move nicely, you crippled old fool," Kor-Zem snapped. "Doza will lift martial law and permit us to work, as clerks, for the duration of the Mandate's term, but *he* retains absolute control."

"K-Z, it cannot be helped," Jobikan said. "We knew that all along. We can do *nothing* about eliminating the Mandate until after the term has expired and we can call a full Directorate hearing. At least he is allowing us to proceed in the interim, *which,* you know fully well, he need not even do."

"I tell you two," Kor-Zem said through clenched teeth, "I trust that cadaverous lump of blue rock no more than his predecessor."

"Which one, Mr. Prime Minister, Slar or Ferr?" Isaac smiled.

"Ferr, you fool," Kor-Zem fumed. "There is something about that man I simply do not trust. There is more to that man that meets the eye."

"You don't trust *anyone*," Jobikan responded. "You have made that abundantly clear on several occasions."

"Oh yeah? Well, what about Ferr? The plan was simple. That cargo ship had only to fly up to Stargate and pop into our ambush. Doesn't it strike you two as odd that there was no mention of such an ambush? No mention of particle beams? No cruiser-sized craft could have been in the vicinity of the Stargate. Even in the worst of times during the Carbon Jihad, major battles were confined to deep space," Kor-Zem said.

"Doza mentioned Belters," Isaac said. "They could have penetrated the perimeter disguised as merchantmen. Their smugglers do it all the time. *I've* had it done myself when necessary."

"During a full alert? Under martial law? Not in a millennium." Kor-Zem shook his big head.

"K-Z," Jobikan interrupted, "what difference does it make if Ferr was destroyed by our ambush, a Cartel asset, or a Belt pirate? The mere fact he has been vaporized should thrill you."

"Because, if he wasn't killed by *our* plan, there can be no proof his body has been destroyed. If that cargo ship was captured (by Omega's left ball, may it not be so), he will recover from the drugs. If he is tested, traces of our chemical tampering can be made known. Would either of you idiots want *that* known to friends *or* enemies? And what if (Gods prevent it) Ferr somehow recovers and survives? Need I detail what we could expect from that pieced-together freak and his Odd Couple *then*?" Kor-Zem was angry and frightened. The shocked looks of Isaac and Jobikan mirrored his concerns.

"Gods," Jobikan sighed, "I was the one who poisoned him. He *knew* the moment I touched him. I *saw* the death in his eyes. K-Z, he'll *kill* me."

"He'd do more than just kill you, Pat, my lad, *you,* Isaac, and *me,*" Kor-Zem said. "It is *imperative* that we learn what happened. Doza has to be made aware of the threat."

"Impossible!" Isaac shouted. "Are you *mad*, man? We can't take that man into our full confidence. If you expose us to that kind of leverage, *he* could do what you fear Ferr will."

"He could *never* do what I fear Ferr will," Kor-Zem muttered. "Besides we have no choice. He is a dead man anyway. As soon as the Mandate is revoked, Doza dies."

"What?" Jobikan asked. "Why? If he is an ally, why not reward him and use him as the valuable tool he can be?"

"Because, you mutated fop, we have conspired with him already. He is a *soldier*, albeit a disgruntled one. He has received the conditioning drugs. He could never consciously or subconsciously act directly against his commander. We can only trust the good colonel-who-would-be-general when his body is vaporized and discharged with the rest of the station garbage." Kor-Zem stood up and waddled in small erratic circles.

****

Ory and Burn entered the medical holding area and were confronted by the med officer.

"I *demand* to know what is going on, Captain," he snapped at Ory. "Who is *this*? Don't you know this is a restricted area? Remove that man at once."

Ory smiled and stroked his long beard. "Doctor, this man is Command Sergeant Major Burn. Perhaps you have heard of him. If not, then perhaps *you* would like to try to eject him."

The doctor stood stone still. Of course, he had heard of Burn. But what was he doing here? The last word he heard was that Burn had been killed along with General Slar. Something was afoot here for sure.

"Doctor"—Burn stepped forward with a rock-hard look and a tangible confidence—"you have been sorely used in a most evil plot to kill General Ferr. He has been poisoned, and the tranquilizers you have been pumping into his blood have been aiding a treason."

"No ... no ... no ... my orders came direct from Doctor Jawkinslz," he muttered.

"Who is in league with the prime minister, president, and banking asshole?" Burn interrupted. "Show me what your orders are and what you have been pumping into the general."

The doctor moved in a daze but retrieved a handheld computer and showed Burn what he had been giving Ferr. A conspiracy of Jobikan, Kor-Zem, and Isaac, aided by Doctor Jawkinslz? He wasn't even rated for a combat zone. This was all *way* over his head.

Burn reviewed the notes given him by the doctor and nodded once. He looked hard at the confused doctor.

"Give the general 500 cc's of AS-386744 *now*," Burn said.

"Y-y-yes-s-s of course," he responded. "But if Doctor Jawkinslz diagnosis is correct, it will do no good," he said as he administered the injection by air gun.

"The doctor's diagnosis is *not* correct, as you shall soon see, man," Burn said as the three men waited and watched the supine body of General Ferr. In less than thirty beats, the body breathed deeply. His body shook twice and he opened his one good eye and smiled.

"Hell-o, Lee, how long have I been out?" General Ferr asked.

"Too long, sir, but not too long that we can't put things to right," Burn responded.

"Omega's left ball, is that Swin Ory standing behind you?" He showed a half grin.

"Y-y-yes, SIR, General Ferr," Ory stammered suddenly, very proud and feeling twenty years younger than even his rejuv drugs made him. *Gods, Charles-Henry knew me, and I never even met the man.* At your service, General. I'm surprised and flattered you know me."

Ferr struggled briefly into a sitting position. "Swin, I may be growing older faster than those who can get access to banned drugs, but I don't forget *any* of the men who fought the Carbon Jihad ... living or dead."

Ory looked at his feet, embarrassed to have been spotted as a drugger.

"Don't look so hangdog, Swin. The ban is a foolish law that I think will soon be revoked." He swung his legs onto the deck and steadied himself. "Sergeant Major, you can brief me as we go along, but first, I need something solid in my gut. Who is this med officer?" he asked with a dangerous stare.

"Another simple pawn in the game of the nefarious Directorate, General."

Ferr nodded once and smiled as he looked at the nervous doctor. "Then you can live, sir. Although, I fear your doctor Jawkinslz may not enjoy that same privilege." He turned to Burn and asked, *The Two*?

"On the way, General. They should be here by the time you are fed and briefed," Burn responded. "Much has happened."

"And much shall happen." Ferr flashed his lopsided grin.

Chapter Twenty-Three

Arkell and Dar were sprinting from the battle plain to the place they had hidden their scout craft. Arkell was actually in the lead as he pumped his arms like twin pistons and raged.

"Dar, I *swear by Omega's left ball* that if those pontificating assholes have harmed the general, you and I shall wage jihad against the bonking Federation itself."

Do not look to me to temper your anger, Ark. I can taste the blood of the prime bonking minister in my mouth, Dar responded.

They remained silent the remainder of their journey, allowing their increased heartbeats to percolate the fury they were building. If the sight of a pissed-off Dar was frightful, the sight of an enraged Two-That-Are-One was terror of epic proportions.

They arrived at their scout craft and disturbed three large wild pigs, which had been rooting around the base of the craft. The pigs looked up and snorted a brief challenge. Dar swung at one with his talons exposed and cut him in two messy halves. Ark snapped his right hand out like a striking snake and grabbed another by the snout before flinging the four-hundred-pound beast twenty yards into a rock pile where it died frightened and confused. The third pig ran off at a speed it was not supposed to be capable of.

"You preflight this scow, Dar," Arkell barked. "I'll contact Burn."

****

"The general is all right, Colonel. He's right here." Burn turned the communicator over to Ferr.

"How was the vacation, Ark?" Ferr asked as he chewed on piece of meat.

"Interesting, sir," Arkell responded, calming slightly at the sound of his mentor/commander's voice. "Are you really all right, sir?"

"None the worse for wear, although I must confess to being more than moderately pissed."

"Well, you've got the treaty and mining rights everyone wanted," Arkell said before he asked, "What the bonk has been going on anyway?"

"Shit happens, friend," Ferr said. "The Mandate has been imposed. Slar (may his memory fade) is dead. The Directorate has plotted a very nasty treason. They have conspired further still with Colonel Doza to ensconce him in my stead. I have played a little finesse and been poisoned by, of all people, President Jobikan. Oh yes, I have been rescued, thanks to Sergeant Major Burn and Swin Ory."

"*That's* good news. I thought Ory was dead. We look forward to seeing you, sir, *and* Sergeant Major Burn," Arkell said. "Dar always liked Lee."

"So did his fleas as I hear tell. We'll meet you in the loading dock in five. Ferr out."

"Well, Dar, you heard. Charles-Henry is safe."

Which is more than can be said for that gaggle of fools in the Directorate.

"Yes, there are consequences to everything we do and don't do. All debts must eventually be paid."

Even banker's debts.

"Especially banker's debts," Arkell said as he scanned the control console. "Can't this scow move any faster?"

****

Arkell and Dar landed in the starboard cargo bay and immediately leaped to the deck. Standing there were General Ferr, Sergeant Major Burn, Swin Ory, and the confused med officer. When The Two landed on the deck, Ory took a step backwards and the med officer took three and hid behind Ory.

Arkell snapped a sharp salute to General Ferr, who returned it. He looked over at Burn, who saluted Arkell, who in turn returned it.

"General Ferr, sir, the Two-That-Are-One report as ordered. Speak the words that our fury may be unleashed. We can taste the commingled blood of the traitorous Directorate in our mouths."

"Welcome, friends." Ferr grinned. "You two take a deep breath and try to calm down. I'll brief you fully on the plan in route. The sergeant major will join us for the briefing and then has to fly ahead." Ferr walked up to his Odd Couple and grabbed Arkell's hand and shook it once. He maintained his grip as he reached over and scratched Dar behind an ear. When he released the grip, Burn walked up and shook Arkell's hand, and then looked at Dar and smiled the only real full smile any had ever seen of him. He held his right hand out in front of the massive snout of Dar and whispered in a voice that could be only heard by Dar and Arkell.

"Good to see you, cousin," he whispered.

Dar reached out with a long coarse tongue and licked the calloused hand of Burn.

I remember this one from Stoellus. He saved your hairless hide when I was unavailable. I liked him.

"Come," Ferr said, "we have plans to make … and a Federation to save."

****

Lacracken lay on the freshly made bed of the late Dolfin. Men of the healing guild had dressed his wounds and given him herbs to help him rest. Not that he needed any help to rest. The post-battle depression and trauma of having lost a hand fought against his diminishing will to pull him into the peaceful tranquility of sleep. He had rattled off orders and decrees like a child's wish list. Now that he was alone with only his sister and two medical attendants, he longed to yield to the call of sleep.

"Healers, leave me alone with my sister," Lacracken said. "You may attend to changing my bandages in the morn. For now I need a few moments in private with my sister before I sleep."

"Yes, sire," they both said as they bowed and left the room.

"So, brother"—Petal smiled as she gently touched his bandaged stump where once there had been a hand—"you have killed the bad man and now are king."

"No king, Petal"—he struggled to grin—"but a custodian of the well-being of our people."

"And what will you do *now* that there is no need for further revolution custodian/king/brother?" she asked.

"There is much to do. After I meet with the finance ministers in the morning, I will be reducing taxes, appointing regional governors, establishing winter food stores, selecting a group of advisers for dealing with Arkell's *Federation* and establish simple rules for the good of the many."

"You sound like a ruler already." She smiled.

"Have my orders been followed yet?" he asked as his eyes fought to close.

"Yes, and the fire burns still. Every scalp, human skin, bone, and grizzly trophy has been, or is being, burned in a common fire in the center of the city. There has been no hesitation to comply with your orders. When it cools in the morning, all the ashes will be collected and buried on the highest hill of the mountains." She touched his shoulder to waken him briefly. "Lac, we need to think of names soon. We can't continue to have the people call this city, our world, the oceans, and the highest mountain Dolfin still."

"I have scribbled a list already while the healers tended to my wounds. I had to send out for parchment since I refuse to write on human skin. It is on the table by the fire. Bring it to me please."

Petal retrieved the scrap of yellow stained paper with the list written in her brother's hand. She smiled as she looked and carried it to him. She gladly handed it to him with a tear.

"The mount shall be called Mount *Amelia*, for our mother lost and found. The ocean, for its fury and bounty, shall henceforth be called *Dar*. This city is now and forever *Arkell*. The rest you can read and I will announce from the balcony at noon tomorrow. I am having messages written announcing all, along with my intention to guide our people as custodian for one year. On this day next year, we shall poll the people and determine what form of government they choose and how we should select our ruler." The paper fell from his hand onto his chest, and he was suddenly and completely fast asleep.

His sister leaned down and kissed his forehead as she whispered, "I am very proud of you, my reluctant custodian/king/brother."

Chapter Twenty-Four

Colonel Doza sat at his (Ferr's) desk and nursed a half-empty glass as he stared fascinated by the label of the glass bottle next to it. Wild Turkey 101 was potent stuff. It had a bite to it, but the colonel liked it. It set a warm fire in his stomach and gave him a gentle lightheaded buzz. He had been rationing the liquid since first discovering it—one two-ounce drink at noon and another before Vespers. Gods, that feathered fowl was an ugly bird. It was a shame that once this was gone, it was gone. It may well have been the sole survivor of a violent Earth Prime history. He glanced at his computer monitor and then at the comlink. He depressed the key for the conference room and called the Directorate.

"Gentlemen, Doza here," he said.

"Yes, we are here," Kor-Zem answered quickly. He struggled to keep his voice calm and volunteer no uncertainty.

"I am concluding the last of my after-action reports," Doza responded. "If you will have the full Directorate present in the morning after we breakfast, I will officially relinquish administrative command to you."

About time, thought Kor-Zem. He took a calming breath and matter-of-factly asked, "Any further word on the ship carrying General Ferr?"

"None. We are scanning the entire quadrant for debris or ID markers. I am also dispatching a scout craft to the prospect planet Dolfin to determine the status of Colonel Arkell and Dar."

The members of the Directorate looked at one another, and Jobikan leaned forward and responded, "Please keep us advised, Colonel."

"Yes, Mr. President, I shall. Enjoy your last day of vacation, gentlemen. Tomorrow morning, it's back into the breach," Doza said. "I am prepared and anxious to retire from civil service and return to the military full time. I leave finance, commerce, and governing to those better suited for its subtleties." He took a final swallow of his drink. "Please meet me in the amphitheater at 0900 hours station standard, and I will provide you with a final situation and status report. Doza out."

Isaac looked at Jobikan and Kor-Zem and asked, "What do you think?"

"I still don't like it," Kor-Zem said. "But it appears we are progressing. Once we have control, regardless of the restraints of *form*, we can establish the necessary safeguards to protect us from any unforeseen contingencies. As far as his retiring his skinny blue ass from public service, I can guarantee *that* ... along with a *full* retirement from life."

"Perhaps the Cartel or Belters did the job for us?" Jobikan half asked, half stated. "What real difference does it make *how* Ferr died as long as he is gone?"

"I agree," Isaac said. "The method of that martial freak's death is less significant than the fact he is removed from the board *permanently*."

"I don't like loose ends any more than I like coincidences," Kor-Zem interrupted. "Agreed that the method is less important than the result, but until we have confirmation of his destruction, I for one will remain concerned."

"Frankly, I am less concerned about who eliminated Charles-Henry and how than the status and location of the Odd Couple," Jobikan added.

"After breakfast tomorrow morn, it will make little difference." Kor-Zem grinned. "Even The Two cannot challenge the full armed might of the entire bonking Federation."

"I recall a certain Stoellean general suggesting something similar several years past," Jobikan muttered.

"Pat, your theater background makes you annoyingly susceptible to hyperbole," Kor-Zem chided. "A man and his genetic nightmare of a pet cannot stand against the armed might of the Federation. Get real, man," Kor-Zem shook his head.

"I am a businessman, not a soldier," Isaac said. "But your annoyingly handsome president should not be ignored regarding the dangers of underestimating the threat of the Two-That-Are-One."

"I neither underestimate them nor overestimate them," Kor-Zem responded. "Remember, much of the psychological advantage they have enjoyed has been created by the Psyops Division and our late propaganda minister." The prime minister poured himself a stimulant with his evil smile. "By Omega's left ball, men, give me the morning, and I'll give you the galaxy."

"As long as I get my monetary fund, you can have all the time you need." Isaac grinned.

"My hope is that all the time we need is this last day as hobbled nonentities," Jobikan mused.

****

The day passed slowly for the Directorate conspirators. Kor-Zem tried to bury himself in work and his plans for the elimination of Doza. Isaac was immersed in playing with his plans for controlling the galactic economy and the potential of synergistic wealth. Jobikan got his haircut and brooded over recent nightmares of dark passages and blind corners filled with vengeful Ferrs, Arkells, and salivating Dars. He had vomited twice already: once after the noon meal and once again after the small supper that was served at 1500 hours. Before the cocktail hour, he had taken a very illegal depressant in the hopes of sleeping away the remaining time. That night his nightmares returned.

****

The large amphitheater was designed to accommodate live stage performances and visiting lecturers. There were over nine hundred seats in front of the stage in a large ascending bowl. Above the stage were three large vidscreen over forty feet in size. Cameras were set in the grid work of the ceiling amongst the various lights to capture everything onstage. There was a control booth high above the back of the theater where a director could control the robotics, which manipulated the cameras, a master switcher, and all the lighting and special effects controls.

Colonel Doza was already standing behind the podium when the members of the full Directorate walked down the steep aisle to the front of the theater. Isaac floated down the ramp on his antigravity sled with his laptop computer scrolling numbers.

The Directorate filled the front two rows of the audience, and Kor-Zem waved a hand to Colonel Doza as he said, "You may proceed with your final briefing, Colonel. We trust this won't take long."

"No, Mr. Prime Minister," Doza shook his head. "We will conclude shortly."

"Please proceed, Colonel," Jobikan called as he sat down, crossed his legs, and brushed an invisible piece of lint from his sharply creased knee.

Doza depressed a switch on the podium and the vidscreens above him came to life with his image displayed on the center screen and various charts and graphs appearing on the two flanking screens.

"Good morning, gentlemen," he began, "I am sure you are anxious for me to complete this last formality so that you may all return to work." He paused and awkwardly and unnaturally smiled. "However, I am afraid you are to be disappointed."

"WHAT!" Kor-Zem shouted.

"What do you mean?" Jobikan asked.

"Don't push our good natures, you adenoidal sump," Isaac growled.

"Gentlemen, in the wake of the most recent information and circumstances, it is no longer feasible for you to assume control of the Federation," Doza calmly said.

"Now see here, you blue-skinned cadaverous hemorrhoid. We had a *deal*," Kor-Zem snapped.

"No, Mr. Prime Minister, *you* proposed a deal. I have merely been a collator of data and a soldier. On the grand chessboard of this game, you may have played me as a pawn, but I have in fact been functioning as a knight. And as you gentlemen most certainly realize, a knight may move in two directions at once."

"What is your game, Doza?" Kor-Zem growled.

"My *game*, Mr. Prime Minister, has always been the same. The one I had sworn a solemn oath to a lifetime past—'To bear true faith and allegiance. To serve and protect ... to faithfully and unconditionally dedicate my skills, knowledge, and experience to the sustenance and perpetuation of the ideals and philosophy of the Federation of Sentient Planets.'" He leaned into the podium and ventured a strange half grin. "You had believed you did a comprehensive and in-depth analysis of my service record, efficiency reports, and psychological profile. However, you failed to seek out ancillary elements of my background and tangential information, which could impact on my anticipated performance."

"Get to the point, man," Isaac snapped.

"You collected accurate data on me, but you failed to interpret it accurately."

"What do you mean?" Jobikan whined.

"It is true I would not have received a command. It is true I have an uncommonly high ambition profile. However, my ambition has been directed *and* cultivated to position me to be the best *staff* officer in the Federation. I could never assume to achieve the charismatic leadership talent of General Ferr or the combat skills of a Colonel Arkell. But *they*, gentlemen, could never crystalize *their* abilities in the area of administration, analysis, and planning as their servant Colonel Doza." He paused and looked hard at the men seated below him. "You *assumed* that because power, greed, and control were the narcotic that sustained *you*, it was likewise the bait to dangle in front of *me*. You were wrong. I have never wanted General Ferr's job and most certainly would never actually conspire against either the form or substance of one so righteous and good as the governor general ... and you know, as we enter the final endgame, you learn it."

"Nice speech, Colonel," Kor-Zem said as he reached into his boot for a small pen laser with which to fry Doza's brain. "What do you intend to do *now*?" He inched the laser into his lap and covered it with his computer pad.

The nonmembers of the conspiracy who were the directors exchanged worried glances of confusion and disbelief.

"In answer to that, I would like to show you *and* the *entire Federation* the following record (which has been patched into the Galactic Vid Network and is being broadcast galactic wide)." He then depressed a switch on the podium and the three screens overhead came to life. It showed conversations between Kor-Zem and Jobikan conspiring to drug General Ferr. It showed conversations between Kor-Zem, Isaac, and Jobikan. It showed Isaac making his proposal to Doza. It showed more whispered conversations between the conspirators. It showed the details of the Isaac plan for the monopoly on galactic finance. It showed the message General Ferr had sent to Slar detailing his plan. And it concluded with the three screens showing close-up shots of (from left to right) Arkell, Ferr, and Dar, with Ferr saying, "We're ba-a-a-a-ck!"

"Bonk," Kor-Zem snarled as he lifted his pen laser to kill Doza and had his hand shot off by a laser fired from the wings of the stage. He *screamed* and Isaac and Jobikan looked nervously around the auditorium.

Arkell slowly walked out from behind a curtain to the right of Colonel Doza. Dar followed him, walking on his hind legs with his talons popping in and out of his paws. They walked to the podium and flanked Colonel Doza, who quietly announced, "Ladies and Gentlemen of the Federation, it gives me great personal and professional pleasure to present Governor General Charles-Henry Ferr, who will conclude this briefing."

Ferr walked out from behind a curtain to the left of Doza. He was in full dress uniform and was an impressive and frightful sight. One step to his left and two steps behind marched an erect Command Sergeant Major Burn with a look of unbridled disgust on his stone-cold face. All the time this entire scene was being transmitted to the entire Federation over the Galactic Vid Network.

Isaac snapped. He pointed his sled at Ferr and pushed the throttle to maximum as he held out his poisoned talons in front of him, making himself a projectile of death. His sled rose like a fighter screaming into a dogfight until it was less than ten feet in front of the majestically still Ferr when Dar *roared* and swung one massive sidearm clawed paw. The blow ripped through the bottom and the side of the banking chairman's antigravity polymer sled and the crippled body it held. The force of the blow sent the sled rocketing like a cue ball against a pastel pillar at the proscenium of the stage, and it cracked like an eggshell, with its gory contents oozing out onto the stage, creating a large dark puddle.

Charles-Henry Ferr walked to the podium and Colonel Doza turned to him, saluted crisply, and stepped back behind Arkell.

Kor-Zem was holding the cauterized stump of his right hand and snarling incoherently as he glared at Ferr. Jobikan, who had soiled his trousers, stared blankly at the uniformed figure of his nightmares and tried desperately not to consider the options of his death that now faced him. The Archbishop and other members of the Directorate were confused and uncomfortable.

"Ladies and Gentlemen of the Federation of Sentient Planets," Ferr began, "Not since the Carbon Jihad have the forces of our Federation been so challenged as in recent days." He paused and looked down at the men seated below him. He showed a strange half smile, which, as always, ended in a sea of scar tissue. "So good to see you again, Mr. President." He glared at Jobikan before returning his attention to the camera in front of him. "Certain members of the Directorate have conspired and attempted to implement acts of treason against the Federation. You have just seen some of the evidence against them. There is more. We have in our possession transcripts and recordings of conversations involving Prime Minister Kor-Zem, President Jobikan, and the recently late banking chairman Isaac, which demonstrate with devastating clarity the breath and scope of their treasonous intentions and acts. Regrettably, I am forced to turn Kor-Zem over to the minister of the attorney general. However, President Jobikan committed a felonious act against the authorized commander of the Federation *during* a time of declared Galactic Emergency. Therefore, HE will be tried and sentenced under the Federation's Code of Military Justice. The trial will be held in closed session, but his execution (should a sentence result in such) will be transmitted on the Galactic Vid Network. The details of the Evil Troika will be made public immediately through the office of Galactic Information. The future of the Mandate shall be voted on by the entire Directorate *subsequent* to their resumption of power. It is our hope that the remaining members of the Directorate will see the value in maintaining the Mandate as indissoluble and grant it perpetual life." He paused and looked at the stern yet awed faces of the Directorate, and then glanced at the coagulating gore of the former banking chairman.

"Colonel Arkell has just recently reported success in securing a treaty arrangement with the mining prospect planet, formerly called Dolfin. He will report the new name of this potentially valuable asset to us when he returns from the formal treaty signing. In the meantime, I have promoted him to the permanent rank of brigadier and given him lifelong command of the Special Operations Group of the Federation. Colonel Doza, for his exemplary performance and faithful dedication to his oath, is hereby promoted to the rank of major general and shall assume command of the Department of Inspector General. Finally, I have granted a field commission in the rank of full colonel to Command Sergeant Major Burn…."

"Sir?" Burn started to interrupt but was cut off with a halting hand of Ferr.

"Colonel Burn will assume command of the Training Command and the stewardship of the training of our cadets as future commissioned and noncommissioned officers. That is all. We now resume with normal programming." He stepped back from the podium and the lights dropped low.

Jobikan was in a near faint. He further soiled his custom suit and sat in a foul mess of his own urine and feces. Four armed guards appeared as if from nowhere and grabbed Kor-Zem and Jobikan by their respective arms. They were dragged away, with Jobikan whimpering and Kor-Zem already plotting an escape and retribution, neither of which would ever come.

Arkell walked up to General Charles-Henry Ferr and glared at him. "With *all due respect, sir,* if the general thinks he can sentence me to the plasteel shackle of a *desk*, the general is mistaken, *sir*."

"At ease, Ark." Ferr smiled. "You never could and never will be damned to any *chair-borne* assignment. However, although I'm sure you never bothered to notice, your time in grade as a full colonel is about complete. I have no intention of permitting you and your hairy partner to retire, and the rank of general is like a judgeship these days. You hold *that* rank for *life*. Your function will not change, just your pay grade. And you get to pick your own chief of staff who will probably run the operation anyway."

"General"—Burn walked up stiffly—"begging the general's pardon, sir … but by Omega's left ball, that was a lousy Xighian bonking thing to do, SIR." He stood at attention and braced himself for an argument. "I've already turned down offers to hold a commission. I *like* being a top NCO. I'm *good* at it. Oh, I've enjoyed teaching Tactics and Leadership, but I'll be buggered by a Gayamedan swamp lizard if I can be a bonking headmaster to a bunch of adolescent would-be heroes."

"Sorry, Lee, the orders have already been recorded. I can't take back the rank." He paused and with a half smile looked at Arkell and Dar, and then back to Burn. "*However*, if you don't want the Training Command, you *could* talk to General Arkell about the number two slot in Special Operations Group."

Arkell nodded and comprehension flooded across Burn's granite face. "Bonking-a-Bob, SIR. If The Two will have me, *that's* a job I *can* do."

"Good. Then it's settled," Ferr said as he turned to Colonel (now General) Doza. "If the general hasn't depleted my bar, how about we all retire to my offices and have a drink. We may not have another chance for quite a while."

Doza looked at his feet and then up at Ferr with a hard yet apprehensive look. "General, your bar is intact … except for one bottle, sir."

"Good enough. Then there's still plenty."

"Begging your pardon, sir, but the one bottle I consumed was … I believe quite rare. I selected it BEFORE I learned you had survived, sir."

"There was nothing there that couldn't be replaced. You were welcome to it." He grinned and then looked over his shoulder. "As long as it wasn't my thousand-year-old bourbon."

"That was it, sir. Wild Turkey 101." Doza gulped.

Ferr froze and turned very slowly to look at his new general. "General Doza, that bottle was *the* rarest in my entire collection of exotics. Do you realize that *that* was one of the *only two* bottles that have survived the centuries.…"

"Sir, I am sincerely sorry. If the general wishes, I will resign my commission immediately," Doza said from a rigid position of attention.

Ferr stared at him hard for a moment, and then softened as he stepped closer and said, "As I said, it was *one* of only *two*. It so happens the other bottle is in the office of Prime Minister Kor-Zem. And somehow, I don't think he will miss it if we confiscate it for matters of Federation security."

They all laughed heartedly and Dar nuzzled Burn's back, allowing several dozen fleas to make the jump from Dar to Burn. They marched off the stage toward General Ferr's office as Colonel Burn occasionally scratched at his gifts from Dar.

Epilogue

General Ferr walked into his office followed by Arkell, Dar, Doza, and Burn. He stood in the middle of the large room for a moment and just looked at it in silence. Then he walked over to his desk and picked up the small transmitter to open his bar.

"Well, gentlemen, let's see what General Doza left us." He flashed his half smile as he looked over the shelves of exotic liquors.

Arkell was standing behind him looking over his head at the refreshments. "Gods, what a collection! Do you actually ever drink this stuff, General? Or do you just keep it to look at." He picked up a Xighian crystal decanter of yellow cordial and smiled at the small slug floating inside.

"I hate collectors who don't use what they collect," Ferr responded. "Like unfired weapons, collecting dust is as senseless as and useless as Dar in a cage."

Dar growled menacingly at the metaphor.

"Just a figure of speech, furball," Arkell chided. "So you actually drink these treasures?"

"At least one a year … more if there's a special occasion." He looked at his comrades and grinned. "And *this* is a special occasion, as well as a promotion party I guess."

"Then how about we stop staring at it and the general selects what he intends to share with us?" Arkell asked.

Ferr nodded. "Since we *know* General Doza has such excellent taste, why don't you select, my blue friend."

"No, sir." Doza shook his head. "I defer to men of greater experience than myself. You select, Colonel Burn."

Burn looked at Doza and then at Ferr, who nodded his agreement. "Well, I *still* don't feel like an officer, but I *do* know what nomenclature of intoxicants to pour into my engine." He reached up and selected a dark blue-black bottle with no label but a distinctive pear shape and embossed rune in the center. "Formozekchlz Brandy. Gods, I haven't tasted that since before Krz. Would that be all right, General Ferr?"

"An excellent choice, Colonel," Ferr acknowledged. "Some may call it zek semen, but it is potent and smooth."

"And leaves a wonderful musky aftertaste with virtually no hangover," Arkell added.

Dar curled up in a corner behind Ferr's desk and next to the computer wall as he rested his chin on his paws. *I'm going to take a nap while you hairless Federation officers all poison your bodies and strive to kill brain cells.*

Arkell grinned and threw an old obscene hand gesture at his other half.

Same to you, Dar responded with a yawn.

When everyone was seated and with a drink, Ferr turned to Doza and asked, "Why don't you fill in the blanks, Major General Doza?"

Doza nodded and remembered past cautions about never thanking a superior for a promotion or for doing his job. "Well, before I heard from Sergeant Major … I mean Colonel Burn, I had reviewed all the secured data in the general's personal file under my summary duties. I confess I was surprised to find our little war was just a TEWT, but also more than a tad relieved. Before that I was totally confused. I mean the scope and apparent coordination of the reported simultaneous attacks was so unique. No known adversary, past or present, could coordinate such a well-timed and executed attack." He sipped his drink and continued.

"Shortly after the reported death of General Slar, I received an Omega message from Colonel Burn. I briefed him on the plans for moving General Ferr and coordinated the delay and subsequent assignment of an escort fighter." He paused again to sip at his drink that Burn picked up.

"I stole a fighter and had the colonel arrange to get my craft assigned as escort. Then he heard about the Andromeda Cartel battle cruiser and the late horny bug Llers's plan for genocide and dynasty making, so we decided I should grab the general and get to Dolfin before The Two could be surprised."

"Thanks, Lee." Arkell smiled. "We appreciate that."

"No big deal, sir," Burn responded.

"Oh, it most certainly WAS a big deal," Ferr said, "as was General Doza having the foresight to record all the ramblings of our former Directorate conspirators." He finished his drink and poured another round for everyone.

Arkell cast a hard look at Doza and said, "No disrespect intended, but we *are* lucky Doza wasn't tempted by the offers of the Evil Troika. Forgive me, General Doza, but you are Dynos."

"General Arkell," Doza replied quietly, "I realize that we blue-skinned devils of Dynos have been and can be attributed with treachery and that our immunity to the loyalty conditioning drugs may make some of us suspect, but there remains much about Plig Doza that my service records and profiles do not reveal."

Ferr leaned forward and firmly said to Arkell, "Ark, I trust Plig as I do you and Dar."

This caused Dar to open one eye and raise a bushy eyebrow.

"The principle oversight the Directorate fools failed to find in General Doza's records relate very directly to that trust."

Burn downed his drink and poured himself another and said, "Hey, gentlemen, I'm new to this officer shit. Can someone please speak plainly for the junior man present?"

"My race, Colonel Burn, General Arkell, despite our dark past, is bound by certain unalterable standards," Doza said. "If you should slight a yeoman, it is *never* forgotten. Any injury suffered—physical, professional, or spiritual—becomes a legacy to be passed down from father to son until an appropriate revenge is achieved."

"Yeah," Arkell nodded. "I've heard of Dynos vendetta's lasting over a century. So what?"

"The colorway to that is, should someone do a great service or kindness to a yeoman, the repaying of that debt also becomes inherited." Doza smiled.

"So are you saying you *owed one* to General Ferr?" Burn asked.

"A gross understatement inimitably inadequate to express my (and my progeny's) debt to General Charles-Henry Ferr," Doza said. "Not only did the general's grandfather save the entire village of my ancestors from a Stoellean genocide ... *this* man here had the unknown audacity to rescue my brother, his wife, and ten children from Xighian rapists before I could even retire the first debt."

"I see," Burn muttered as he poured himself another drink.

"I have a genetic, as well as a deep moral, debt to General Ferr, which I can only pray my children or my children's children's children can someday repay," Doza sighed. "Loyalty conditioning drugs could do no more, and indeed far less, than my own birthright."

"Enough heavy talk," Ferr snapped. "Ark, you and your snoring companion will leave in the morning for Dolfin to consummate the mining rights treaty. You will take Director Ds Dario and Minister Folk with you, as well as a survey and marshalling team. They will remain and prepare for the arrival of the first phase of mining operations. You can leave any time after the treaty signing. See if Swin Ory is available to fly transport. Tell him we'll even pay his commercial rates. You can dictate your report on the trip there and back. Give me all the graphic details. I will edit it for the Directorate's consumption."

"General?" Doza asked.

"Yes, Plig?" Ferr responded.

"I still have about six ounces of 101 left, sir. By your leave, I would like to share it with this group."

"Excellent idea, General," Ferr responded. "I've often wondered what thousand-year-old bourbon tasted like."

"Like Nirvana, sir," Doza responded with a smile. "Like Nirvana." He passed the bottle around to Ferr, Arkell, and Burn.

****

Captain Ory turned from his seat at the command console and called to Arkell. "Yo, General, I'm about to enter orbit around this chunk of rock. Where would you like me to put it down?"

"Use the coordinates I gave you this morning, but before touchdown, skim the ground toward the city until we're about a hundred meters off. There's a wide barren boarder between the city walls and the woods," Arkell responded.

You can tell him to target in on the diskless decaying corpse of old bird head, Dar purred.

"Yeah." Arkell grinned. "Swin, I've just been reminded you can target in on what's left of a corpse on a lance outside the city."

"Nice, peaceful folks you're going to meet." Ory smiled sarcastically.

"They are *now*," Arkell said curtly.

Ory put his transport down about a hundred meters from the front wall and some forty meters from the single lance and its grizzly trophy. A dozen vultures flapped noisily away, obviously annoyed at the arrival of this strange big new bird.

When Arkell, Dar, and company exited the aircraft, a delegation was already emerging from the front gates in obvious awe and wonder at what they saw. The general mood of fear and apprehension soon dissipated when they saw the two large forms of Arkell and Dar. The crowd started running toward them, shouting, "Arkdar! Arkdar! Arkdar!"

Before the crowd reached the Federation delegation, a single mounted rider galloped past them and held up a handless arm in welcome.

The entire Federation contingent walked into the city escorted by Lacracken, leading his mount and hordes of shouting well-wishers in their wake.

"What's with this *Arkdar* Lacracken?" Arkell asked. "Can't your people keep our names straight, or are they confused?"

"I'll let Petal explain. First, let's have some wine and get your visiting dignitaries settled. Then we can sign your papers and share some time together. I have much to tell you and much to ask."

"Where is Vanjar?"

"The Holy One is with my sister," Lacracken responded. "They prepare your welcome."

"How goes the transition? Any major problems?" Arkell asked as they walked up the palace steps.

"Strangely, no. Apparently, Dolfin so abused even his closest supporters that they gladly accepted the new order. Those who collected scalps and ears are now harvesting gors and boars. The price of leather and fur may drop, but its availability will greatly increase."

"Dar! Arkell!" Petal shouted from the doorway as she ran down the steps toward them.

I told you she was special. Notice whose name she called first.

Arkell frowned and slapped Dar's rump with his open hand. Petal threw herself into Arkell's arms and kissed him eagerly, fencing with his tongue and pressing her body to his.

"Notice who she kisses first, furball," Arkell replied to Dar.

She slid down Ark's hard body and dashed over to Dar; she stroked his massive head as she gently kissed his big wet nose.

"Oh, it's *so* good to see you," she gushed. "*Both* of you, before you can sign your silly treaties or share my bath, the Holy One wishes to speak with you and give thanks."

"Then let's not keep them waiting," Arkell said as he swept Petal up in his arms and walked up the steps into the palace with Dar in his wake. When he got to the door, he turned and shouted over his shoulder to Lacracken, Ds Dario, and Folk. "Lac, introduce yourself to Ds Dario and Folk and arrange to get this formal shit over with quickly. We will meet you in the great hall shortly."

As Arkell walked down the long stone hallway to Vanjar's suite, he smiled at Petal in his arms and asked, "So, my little piece of flower, now that Dolfin is an unlamented memory, what do you folks call places these days?"

Petal beamed and nuzzled his neck with her soft warm lips. "The tyrant's name has been cast from our language. The list of names has been posted and sent to all outlining regions. The great mountain has been renamed Mount Amelia."

"Most appropriate." He smiled. "I like that."

"The mighty ocean, because of its rage and strength, yet also because of its gifts and bounty, has been renamed for your sweet other half, Dar."

Ah-h-hr, I rather like that. Don't tell her I get stomach sick at sea, Dar purred. *Ask her what they named for my tiny hairless gibbon/mink/slug.*

"Dar thank you for the great honor, which he acknowledges he in no way deserves. I suppose the sewers are henceforth called Arkell." He smiled as they rounded the corner to arrive at Vanjar's suite.

"In part, I guess you could say so." She grinned as he put her down by the door to the magician's suite. "This capital city has been renamed *Arkell*, for our champion and savior."

Not bad, Ark. But an ocean is still mightier than a city.

"We are flattered," Arkell said sincerely. "But what name do we put on the treaties we sign? Is the planet Dolfin now the planet Lacracken?"

"Gods no." Petal grinned. "My suddenly humble one-handed brother would allow nothing to be named for himself. But we discussed in detail many options for the renaming of your new Federation protectorate."

"Well? What did you decide?" he asked.

"When you fill in the blanks on our treaty and publish your maps, this world shall henceforth and for all time be called *Arkdar*."

Ark was genuinely surprised. Even Dar sat down and stared blankly at Petal.

"We all agreed—Lac, Vanjar, my mother, and myself—that without the promise, support, and new alliance you bring, our new order would have never been. We struggled with options, but they were all too ungainly: ArkellDar, Darkell, The Two, Two-That-Are-One. None of them fit or seemed comfortable."

"It is too great an honor, girl," Arkell whispered. "*No* world should be named for mere mortal, and certainly not for any alien soldiers. We cannot allow this."

"Ark, my brave, strong lover, you cannot deny it. It is the recommendation of the spirits and the wish of Lady Amelia, who said our new world is the fruit of the Two-That-Are-One, and the Two-That-Are-One she spoke of are Ark and Dar—hence, *Arkdar*." She stroked his chest and smiled. "Accept it, demon lord, for it is so. And even you and Dar cannot prevent it from being so."

Before Arkell or Dar could react further or respond, Petal opened the door to Vanjar's suite and gently nudged them both through the doorway.

Vanjar was seated on a large cushion dressed in a full white caftan. His long white hair and braided white beard shone like silver white snow on the high Mount Amelia. He looked healthier than Arkell had ever seen him and much more content and at peace.

"Ah ... welcome to the Two-That-Are-One"—Vanjar smiled—"saviors of my world and the reverend Lady Amelia."

"Hail, Holy One," Arkell said with a short formal yet sincere bow. "How goes the adjustment?"

Vanjar walked down two steps and hugged Arkell once. Then he walked over to Dar and placed one thin confident hand on his muzzle. "I had feared a loss, but I had no idea how much I would gain. I half think I know now what you and Dar share."

"I understand"—Arkell smiled—"you wanted to see us."

"First, a grossly insufficient thank you for what you have done for my son and daughter. Second, my humble appreciation for the joy and bounty you have offered our world." Vanjar smiled.

Arkell nodded his head in acceptance.

"And last, for being the catalyst in creating another *Two-That-Are-One* by permitting a pitiful, thin, and misused old man's body to serve as a host for the essence of the reverend Lady Amelia."

Arkell took Vanjar's hand and kissed it respectfully. "It is a task that has not been done often, and when attempted, has frequently failed. But when I tasted that Vanjar's affection for Petal reached beyond the mere sexual aspect of their relationship ... well, the key ingredients were all here: Vanjar loves Petal, Amelia loves Petal, Vanjar was lost in this world, and Amelia was lost in the nether world. Both were skilled and trained in Doutrin, and both wanted to contribute to the new order. As a third-degree master of Doutrin, I had both the means and obligation to attempt such a joining."

"And for that we are eternally grateful," Vanjar/Amelia smiled.

"It has ended my sexual life." Vanjar smiled. "But then I am old and had no desire for any but Petal. And I couldn't in either good conscience or with any morality ever have sex with my own daughter." Amelia smiled.

"How does Petal respond to the new situation?" Arkell asked.

"She is ecstatic," Vanjar/Amelia responded. "The world is at peace. She is at peace. She is with her brother, her mother, and her new *father*. Her life is good and she contributes much."

"It has been good to talk to and see you, but I need to get this treaty stuff over with so we can all truly celebrate together." Arkell smiled. "If Your Holiness will excuse us, we will see you again shortly."

Vanjar/Amelia nodded and gently touched Arkell's chest. He felt a warm rush of love and peace surge into his soul, and he smiled politely in thanks before he bowed and left the room.

As Arkell and Dar walked out into the hall where Petal waited, they could hear the shouts of the people through the windows: "Arkdar! Arkdar! Arkdar!"

THE END